FROM DUSK

A. B. Owings

Twilight Tomes

Presents

FROM DUSK

A Dark Stalker Romance

A. B. Owings

Twilight Tomes

Twisted Hearts & Haunted Souls

Trigger Menu

Appetizers:

Explicit language
History of trauma
Gruesome deaths
Heathenry

Salads:

Drug Overdose
Murder
Drug use & addiction
Stalking

Main Courses:

Horrific situations
Dubious Consent
Blood Play
Kidnapping

Sides:

Suicidal thoughts & actions
Consensual-non-Consent
Knife Play
Unprotected sex

Desserts:

Mental Illness
Unnecessary violence
Guided Play
Cannibalism (implied)

Beverages:

Car Accident
Necessary violence
Improper use of a fire
extinguisher
Bondage

Playlist

Prologue: High Water-Sleep Token
Chapter 1: Drown In You-Daughtry
Chapter 2: Rain-Sleep Token
Chapter 3: Heavy-Linkin Park (ft Kiiara)
Chapter 4: Savior-Perfect Dark
Chapter 5: Can't Help Falling In Love-Tommee Profitt
Chapter 6: Day By Day-Picturesque
Chapter 7: Give-Sleep Token
Chapter 8: Stuck In My Head-Sleep Theory
Chapter 9: Jaded-Blind Love
Chapter 10: Wicked Game- Colm McGuinness
Chapter 11: Sweet Dreams-Marilyn Manson
Chapter 12: Ascensionism-Sleep Token
Chapter 13: Vacant-Awaken I Am
Chapter 14: Just Pretend-Bad Omens
Chapter 15: Take Me Back To Eden-Sleep Token
Chapter 16: Who Are You-Srvinca
Chapter 17: Forbidden Fruit (Slowed Down)-Tommee Profit
Chapter 18: The Apparition-Sleep Token
Chapter 19: Blood Sport (From The Room Below)-Sleep Token
Chapter 20: Dying To Love-Bad Omens
Chapter 21: Never Know-Bad Omens
Chapter 22: Will I Make It Out Alive-Tommee Profit
Chapter 23: The Death Of Peace Of Mind-Bad Omen
Chapter 24: Dreastate-Dayseeker
Chapter 25: Shame On Me-Cath Your Breath
Chapter 26: Roses-Awaken I Am
Epilogue: The Black-Imminence
Haunting-Braeker

Scan For Playlist

Dedication

To those we have loved and lost, may your

holidays still be
merry and bright.

Also

To my real-life book boyfriend, my
wonderful husband, that is every dark
romance girly's wet dream.
Thank you for helping get me through the
tough times.

C. D. Owings

TABLE OF CONTENTS

◇ ◇ ◇

TABLE OF CONTENTS

◇ ◇ ◇

Dear reader, do not turn this page, do not keep reading and whatever you do, do not spread these pages wide and dive deep into its folds as you explore fantasies unknown.

Hm.

Naughty Little reader, for that you will be punished.

Stop here and I may forgive you. Keep reading and don't say I didn't warn you.

Sign here in acknowledgement of your disobedience.

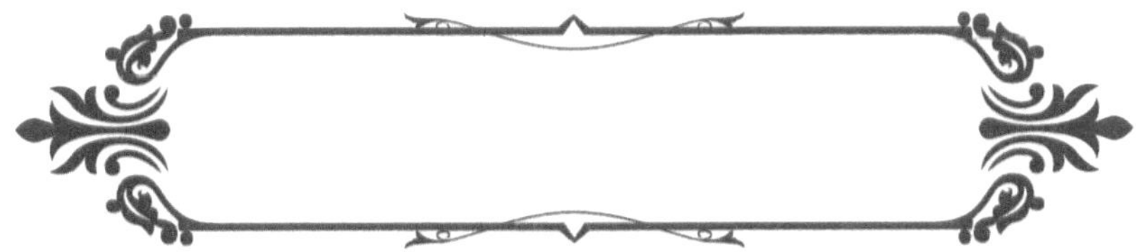

SYNOPSIS

◇ ◇ ◇

**Your mental health matters. This book contains
dark imagery and explicit scenes. Viewer
discretion is advised.**

"From Dusk" by A. B. Owings is a twisted dark
romance steeped in obsession, trauma, and the
unbreakable bond between twin sisters caught in the
shadows of the Selby Estate. After a harrowing
accident, Evelyn vanishes to a secluded, out-of-state
rehab center, haunted by the weight of her addiction
and the secrets she refuses to share. When the silence
stretches too long, her twin sister, Emory, begins to
suspect something far more sinister is at play. A
cryptic letter. A disturbing phone call. A stranger who
knows too much.

Emory's search is what leads her to Selby Manor--a
decaying estate with a legacy of madness and secrets
buried in its walls. However, the true danger is Oliver.
Obsessive. Territorial. Beautifully unhinged. He has
been Emory's shadow for years... watching from the
edges of her life and now... he's ready to step in,
whether she wants him to or not.

Evelyn--on the other hand--spirals deeper into her
darkness, finding herself drawn to someone just as
damaged. The sisters are forced to confront the men
who claim to love them--and the parts of themselves
they've tried to hide. In a world where desire becomes
possession and love turns dangerous. Emory and
Evelyn must face a truth that could shatter them both.

"From Dusk" is a slow burn where *he is not human, she is not safe ... but
sometimeslovedoesn't need permission.*

"*Even in the darkest depths, hope can be the hand that pulls us to the surface.*"

PROLOGUE

Emory

Dark, cold, weightless... lost in a stygian ethereal realm. I feel my arms floating, a tugboat trudging into an equanimous sea. My chest is burning as metaphorical flames are caning my lungs, and numbing silence entrances me. Strands of my sandy blonde hair dance with the flow of the water. Like a blanket, it surrounds me, begging me to surrender to its cold embrace.

I pull at my seatbelt one last time, my vigor dampened by prior efforts. Hoping it gives, praying I will be able to swim to safety... to no avail. I look around one last time before my chest begins to heave. It tightens as the air escapes, and water fills my respiratory system. My eyes get heavy as all the energy drains like a pinhole in a balloon.

Suddenly, I feel pressure around my waist, prying me from what was meant to be my watery grave. I hear the sloshing of the water partitioning, yielding beneath my savior's shoes. The snow sinks as it welcomes the weight of my body. Sirens, like banshees, blare. Evelyn's tear-stricken screams gradually amplify as she draws nearer, calling my name, howling like a lone wolf baying at the moon.

Another voice drowns hers out... softer... closer. "Emory," it whispers my name—dripping with concern and laced with a hint of anger, cloaking his fear in a false sense of calm. "Emory," the velvety notes float on the soft winter breeze. For a moment, everything else is quiet. A safe feeling washes over me.

He speaks again, "Close your eyes, Dove," like lyrics to a song I never knew I needed. I zero in on the word 'Dove,' or did he say 'love'? A diluted English accent and a concussion make it difficult to decipher. I drift to sleep listening as he begins to sing, and for a moment, I am warm in the arms of a stranger—a stranger who saved me.

"*Family wounds run deep, but so does the love that binds us through every storm.*"

CHAPTER 1

Emory

It has been one week since the accident—that dreaded car accident that imposed itself so selfishly on my life. Not much has changed. Who am I kidding? Everything has changed. My mom now spends every waking moment with her new boyfriend, Peter—he is brawny, and as a police officer, it's expected. He stands about six feet tall with fiery red hair so bright it makes his emerald eyes glow. Don't get me wrong, I don't want to sound like I am complaining, it's just been years since our mom was able to express herself to anyone who wasn't Evelyn or myself. She had been so miserable after our father disappeared.

I want to say, we were only ten when he left. It was a Tuesday in the middle of spring. Evelyn and I had just walked in from a long day at school, to find our mother passed out at the edge of her bed.

Her face flushed, her eyes red from crying, snot pouring from her raw, crimson nose. We woke her up, trying our best to be gentle.

When she finally told us what happened, my sister and I could barely keep from crying ourselves, fearing it was our fault for his leaving. As a form of reconciliation, we would receive letters sporadically. Nevertheless, they stopped just as quickly as they started.

Jumping forward a few years, we discovered our mom wailing on the kitchen floor, and that is where the abhorrence for our father stemmed. Every night after, she would sit up staring at his photo, crying for the gods to bring him back. Occasionally, I would still catch her, teary-eyed, looming over his portrait. One would think, after that, a hatred would form. Instead, when my sister or I would show distress or disdain, she would tell us, "It's not your fault. He loved the two of you so much," or "Don't ever speak of your father in that way." You know, the way you would if a loved one had died, or something along those lines. In my mind, he was off somewhere, living life without the responsibility of twin girls.

Evelyn was born precisely five minutes after me. We were different in many ways. I loved to keep my dirty blonde hair at shoulder length, so it fell strategically around my heart-shaped face. My sister, on the other hand, was adorned with stunning Brunette hair that trickled down her back, making her already shimmering sapphire eyes brighter.

She stood a whole head taller than me and had no problem keeping her athletic build just that—fit. I was of short stature with a solid build. We also shared the unique connection where we could sense each other's pain. Our mother didn't believe us at first. That was until the night of Evelyn's first major incident.

It happened a few years ago, we were maybe eighteen. My mother and I were dancing in the kitchen, singing to fifties hits. We were swirling and twirling as it belted from our stereo. She grabbed my hand, spun me twice, and dipped me just as the song ended, then faded out. A familiar melody took its place—it was Evelyn's song, which would often be played during her absence when thoughts of her would arise, and the sense of missing her became overwhelming.

The sorrowful melody bled from the speaker, invading my ear canals, until I acknowledged it was "Kentucky Rain" by Elvis Presley. Once it sank in, a sickly feeling twisted my stomach, and tears prickled the back of my eyes. Then, like a semi, it hit me—claws from the darkest demon, long and sharp, ripping the self-made water from my ducts.

I cried so hard that Niagara Falls would have been overshadowed in National Geographic, from the outpouring that bounded down my face. As I felt the panic ripple over my skin like the shockwave after an explosion, I was jolted back to reality and then pivoted left, facing my mom, and the terror painted across her angelic porcelain image. My voice broke. My mind was frantic. I pleaded for my phone. The need to get a hold of her was dire. I had to make sure she was safe.

Once at the hospital, the nurse relayed the news to us. It was a five-car pile-up, yet she walked away unscathed. Our mother never doubted us after that. So, you can only imagine the betrayal I felt when I heard Evelyn had checked herself into rehab. I was floored. I didn't even know she had a problem. All I knew was that she blamed herself for the accident. I tried to reassure her it was not her fault, but she wouldn't listen. I don't remember much. All I remember is:

It was December 21st, the first day of Yule, also known as Mother's Night. My father was Asatru, meaning he believed in the "Old Ways," at least that's what I remember he called it. Our mom continued with celebrating the wheel of the year to symbolize "keeping his memory fresh." That night, a friend of ours was having a baby shower. Evelyn and I stopped at the store to get a gift, then headed over. She lived just over the bridge on Bird in Hand, about an hour or so from our house in Dover.

It was cold, even for Pennsylvania weather. The snow fell in sporadic spirals, sticking to the already blinding, white knolls. The party was great. A handful of ladies showed up, and we drank and had a merry time. I may have had a little too much to drink, and that is where things start to get fuzzy. Lily's voice rang out above the dwindling hustle and bustle of the late-night function. "Hey Emory!" She pulled me aside." The storm is picking up, and it's starting to look pretty rough outside. Do you and Evelyn want to wait it out? See if it lightens up?"

I peeked over her shoulder and out the frosted window that was displayed across the living room. When I looked back at Lily, I gave her a gentle nod, then ran off in search of Evelyn to inform her of the situation presented before me. I found her upstairs, sleeping next to the toilet in the guest bathroom. At that moment, I called out for Lily. I knelt alongside my sister as I tried to wake her.

When I realized she was still breathing but not waking up, I assumed she was more intoxicated than I was. Once Lily was within earshot, I asked if there was a place for Evelyn to sleep it off. Lily's husband, Brent, carried her to the couch in the den and laid her down softly. As I sat in the chair beside her, I too succumbed to sleep.

I am awoken by the buzzing of my phone, on the cushion beside me. I pulled it out of my pocket to examine the bright LED screen, squinting through the sleep that crusted my eyes. I barely made out the word 'mom' before I was berated by her not-so-quiet, blubbering on the other end. "Where are you two? Are you okay? Why didn't you message me?" Like nails on a chalkboard, her voice exacerbated the migraine that was once subdued.

I groaned, "Sorry, Mom. We will be heading out there soon. Must have fallen asleep. We just wanted to wait for the weather to clear up until we knew it was safe. See you soon. Yep, love you too. Bye." I hang up as I reach over to shake Evelyn awake. She released a low growl as she turned to face me.

I jumped back at the sight of her, and man, did she look like shit. I wondered if she was still drunk. No matter—we had to head out. "Do you need me to drive? Mom is freaking out, and it would be best to hit the road." She rolled to her side, making it easier for her to carry on a conversation with me. Her eyes were like an ocean bleeding the blackest ink as her makeup ran down her face. "That bad, huh?" I asked. She used the sleeve of her sweater to wipe her nose.

"Yeah, but I'll be alright. I know you don't like driving distances." I visibly sank into my chair at the shame that settled on my shoulders. I've always been afraid of driving. I would only drive when needed, although I should have listened to my gut.

The last little bit came in flashes. I waved goodbye to our friends as my sister slid into the driver's seat. I remember Evelyn's smile, the overhead light illuminating her exhaustion.

A sheet of snow covered the windshield.

The blaring of the car's horn.

A screech.

A crash.

The icy water as my head met the dashboard.

My vision was getting dark.

All I had left was my ability to hear and an incessant need to know what just happened.

"Obsession blurs the line between protector and predator."

CHAPTER 2

◇ ◆ ◇

Oliver

I remember that night like yesterday. What the Hell was she thinking, allowing her sister behind the wheel? Why wasn't I there sooner, and who was driving the other car? Too many questions and not enough fucking answers. I can't believe I forgot about the party.

So much was happening already, emotions were whirling like the tornado did through Oz, and guess what, we weren't in fucking Kansas anymore. Emory wasn't the only one I admired—there *was* another... that word still sits stale on my tongue—*was*. I felt my body shudder for a moment, the misery and dread absorbing what little emotion seeped through my tough exterior.

I'll tell you now, I was not about to lose someone else. I couldn't be there for her because *they* needed me. Their situation demanded I hold them and love them. I didn't want, nor did they deserve to *die* alone. My emotions vibrated into a confused mess that night, the feeling of control slipping from the death grip I thought I had on it.

Why the *hell*... did it have to be *that night*?
Of all *fucking nights*!
I guess when it rains, it *fucking pours*!
But hey, as it was said in "*The Crow*",
"***It can't rain all the time,***" right?

The car was already submerged beneath the frigid water when I got to the shoreline. Pieces of the bridge floated on the surface, mocking me for being late. I am never late, always there, but that night was different. That night... was tragic.

Without a second to lose, I leapt into the lake after her. The visibility was like trying to see with a plastic bag over my head, and my body ached with the cold. By the time I found her, not an air pocket remained, and her sister was nowhere in sight. Her damn near lifeless body tussled mildly as the course of the water pushed around her.

I fought with the seatbelt until I reached down, unsheathed my knife, and cut the safety strap with one single swipe. I jostled her— until she was untethered from the condemned wreck, coiling my fingers around her coat collar as I deadlifted her to the surface.

Finally, I settled her down on the snow-covered bank. Once I was sure she expelled the water from her lungs, I stared at her for what felt like forever. I watched as her chest rose and fell, a small plume of air visible against the icy atmosphere, dissipating just as quickly as it appeared. It's been a long time since I've felt that way—fighting back tears as a mixture of fury and trepidation boiled beneath my skin.

If she wasn't lying there, the vexation that mauled at my moral compass may have been too much for me to hog tie and shove back into the darkness, it was trying so hard to escape from. The efforts of my sanity and sense of 'what's right' were futile in preventing the thoughts of retribution—finding the driver of the other car, and slowly waterboarding them in the lagoon, I just pulled my little bird from.

Just the imagery alone tantalized my occipital lobe, leaving it itching like a crackhead looking for its next fix. The muffled, hallucinatory screams, a haunting imperceptible echo, teased my auditory cortex. The pure glee that radiated through my being, where their life was in my hands, under my control, and at my whim... was orgasmic in a '*rage-fueled*' kind of way. My self-control was hanging on by a thread, and that thread was her. I couldn't leave her alone—not there... now, nor ever again.

I was half-tempted to teach her sister a lesson as well—however, that all changed when I realized the speed of the other vehicle had increased. Once the cars collided, the other driver slowed to a painful crawl across the bridge. The girls hit the icy lake below, and the other car sped off in a way that assured me it was no accident.

It was at that moment that her sister no longer occupied space in my cerebrum. My propensity for violence roused with a gluttonous hunger. I recall grinding my teeth, an animalistic growl emanating from my core, stirring like a witch's cauldron inches from overflowing. Just before my anger was about to spill over, the negative emotion vanished, interrupted by a small coo from my dove.

I turn all my attention to her, singing a song I heard that fits her perfectly like the dresses they wear at the Gala, "This Little Bird" by Jewel. Surprisingly, it calmed us both that night. It was more mainstream than what I was used to, but I knew it would fit in her playlist. Unable to do much, I lay beside her until she was taken away. That night... that night changed *everything*. I spent days next to her hospital bed. Seeing her like that infuriated me but solidified my feelings for her and my resolve: to never leave her side again.

Now, she sits in her room on the second floor, first window to the left. I've been watching her for so long that it's second nature. Thumbing the envelope in my coat, I wait for the right moment. I pull a cigar from my breast pocket (*Al Capone dipped in cognac*), lighting it. I puff and watch as she combs her fingers through her hair. My heart aches with how I long for them to be my fingers. Sadness exudes from her striking gray eyes, reflecting in the vanity mirror. "What troubles you, darling?" I mutter beneath my breath.

As I survey my surroundings. I see a pile of rocks stacked in a perfect mound at the base of a tree. Examining her once more, I make my move, grabbing a pebble to toss, hitting the glass on the first try. She is at her window in seconds, as if she had been waiting for something to happen. She looks around, scanning for the culprit. When she lays her eyes on me, my heart flutters like the beating of a bird's wings. My cock pulsates as our eyes meet. For years, I've watched from the shadows. I only involved myself when she was in danger.

The night at the lounge, for example, when she went out with her friends on her twenty-third birthday. She looked breathtaking in that red gown, tied around her neck like a docile snake, the front descending downward past her breasts.

A slit in the side climbed its way up to the top of her hip, barely concealing her womanhood. It was the first time I ever looked at her as more than someone I wanted to keep safe. No, I wanted her. For years, I have loved her, protected her, and vowed no harm shall ever befall her. Yet, tonight was different. I went from 'loving her' to 'being in love with her,' still, I knew it wasn't the right time. I looked on as she laughed and drank. At one point, she even sat beside the pianist and sang along to the fervent cries of the sixties jazz tune. The night went on without a hitch till this silver-tongued cad happened along.

He made her smile, offered to buy her a drink, and managed to smooth-talk her friends. I looked on as she went back up to sing a jazz take on a modern-day song. I was enamored with her. I almost didn't catch him slipping something into her drink. Long story short, I ended up having to strangle him over her confused, drug-induced body. That was the first night I openly killed for her.

Her personal candle snuffer, eliminating the air that feeds the flame of the lives that dare look at her wrong.

I fed on the pain and fear expelling from his eyes—eyes that should have never had the privilege to gaze upon such beauty. A moment of recognition washed over him as if he could see my smile in his death throes. His veins protruding from under his skin, in their last attempt to plead with my humanity, dick thrashing, frozen erect from the lust I denied it to satiate. His body gyrated and contorted as he clawed at his throat for air. "Die, you sick fuck. You don't have the permission to breathe in the presence of what is mine." I whispered snidely in his ear.

He dared to glance down at her, begging with the last breath he could muster. "Help me!" He wheezed. She was heavily fatigued, her limbs weak as she tried to get up. I hated seeing her in that state, confused and defenseless, although nothing could extinguish her beauty.

As his body grew limp, she looked up, and that was the first time our eyes met. The anger stirred in me again at that realization, making me squeeze tighter, so tight a cobra would be envious. I had hoped the first time she saw me would have been special—but no. I prayed it would be under different circumstances. Instead, fear is her first impression of me, thanks to this waste of human life.

I was able to get her far enough away from the scene of the crime so that it wouldn't be tied to her. Not long after placing her on a couch in one of the private rooms, she was found by her friends and brought home. I followed to make sure she made it back safely. Later, it came out that he died of erotic asphyxiation, alone in a very precarious way. That was five years ago, and still, I would stop at nothing to protect her. This world will burn in a blazing inferno before I ever let anyone hurt her.

*The night of the accident, I **failed** her. It will never happen again.*

As I stalk to the mailbox, she keeps her eyes fixated on me. I open the door, my eyes never leaving hers. Her hand rises to rest against the glass, and my body quakes with the thoughts that rush through my mind. The depiction of her petite hands around my shaft, knowing with my size, she'd have to use both. One on top of the other —even then, there would still be an inch gap before they touched. Cuffing myself, I envision it being her. My full length is visible, so hard just from the thought of it. Thankfully, I am shrouded in the darkness of the night.

Once I awake from my daydream, I realize she is no longer at the window. I flick the cigar butt, jam the letter into the empty box, then slam the door as I turn to walk away. Moments later, I hear her sing-song voice call for me to stop, her vocals reverberate off the empty streets as she demands I turn around. "Oh, my precious dove." I chuckle to myself.

I feel a strange urge to oblige, as the thought of taking her right here in the street arises. The illumination from the streetlamps cast a surreal glow, adding ambiance to the chilly air that almost feels electric against my skin as it slips beneath my coat. The tension between my little bird and me thickens with each passing second. Her persistence to catch me is inspiring, a mix of curiosity and something deeper, something unspoken.

The envelope in the mailbox may bring light to the darkness she has been locked away from for years—the same darkness I have become so accustomed to.

I must force these feelings to the back burner, the weight of them heavier, knowing the contents of that letter.

The words contained within it will put me on full display. No more running, no more hiding in the shadows. Now is the time to claim my little dove.

The desire for her is burning within me. I knew that surrendering to it at this moment would undermine everything I had strategically planned. My actions had to be calculated and *precise*. Her safety, her happiness, even if she hasn't realized it yet, depended on my restraint.

I can hear the faint echo of my heartbeat, matching the rhythm of her approaching footsteps. "Stop!" She calls.

I resist. "This may be the first time you beg me to stop… but it won't be your last," I whisper as I peek over my shoulder. She is jogging after me, her breasts bouncing as her feet hit the pavement. Her attention is redirected when a car comes around the corner. I take advantage of the moment and slip back into the twilight.

―◇　◇　◇―

"Sometimes, the answers we seek are hidden in the shadows of our own fears."

―◇　◇　◇―

CHAPTER 3

Emory

A small tap on my window pulls me from the thoughts clouding my brain. I hurry over to catch a man in a long overcoat standing beneath my window: a bright cherry, the only color against his blacked-out form. Dragging something from his pocket, he strides toward the mailbox, relieving it of the lock that holds it closed.

The door bounces slightly as he stares up at me. The bud of whatever he is smoking, gingerly shifting from red to orange, then pausing for a moment on yellow.

What is he doing?

I place my hand against the window, craning my neck, trying to get a better view.

What is he waiting for?

Does he want me to meet him?

His gaze never falters, so I push off the glass, grabbing my coat as I stumble down the stairs. Fumbling with the locks on the door, I finally managed to jar it open.

Fuck It's cold.

The man is halfway down the street before my foot makes it past the welcome mat. I call out for him to stop. When he doesn't react, I follow. In my pursuit, he manages to look over his shoulder, his body nothing but a silhouette against the streetlamps.

Who is he? My view is obstructed by a vehicle rounding the corner. The car pulls away, and I am left speechless—he is nowhere to be seen. *Did he get in?* He vanished as if he were a ghost. *Have I met him before?* My thoughts wander as I try to discern his identity. Reality brings me back as my mother's black SUV approaches from the opposite direction. I swiftly return to the mailbox to retrieve the letter and hurry to my room. I close my door the same moment the front one opens.

I can hear my mom's laughter from downstairs. Knowing she was content is a pleasant change. The man's voice is quiet as they exchange a few words. After listening for one second more, I could tell it was Peter. I look back at the parchment in my hand, breaking the seal. A waft of Whiskey, Honey, and a slight tinge of smoke tickles my nose—a scent I won't soon forget.

Retrieving the letter from within its wrap, I allow the packaging to drop to the floor. Suspense builds as I unfold it, then begin to read:

My Dearest,

I hope this message finds you in good health. You and your sister have always meant so much to me. I would like to speak with the two of you if allowed the honor. My home address is featured below. Stop by anytime.

As I read the words on the page, my face distorts. Confusion builds inside me, a Trojan horse presenting itself with innocence.

Who is this guy, and how doeshe know my sister and me?

Further down the page, the address shows he lives in Owings Mills, Maryland. That's a twelve-hour bus ride if planned right—a choice I would have to make since my car was totaled. Also, Evelyn's rehab center is somewhere around there. Glancing at the bottom of the letter, I see the name of the sender.

Sincerely,
Alfred Tobias Selby

My heart drops, and I can feel liquid pooling in my eyes. *Daddy?* Haziness eclipses my vision. Blinking away a single tear, I allow it to cascade down my face. My father was everything a child could ever ask for. When he left, our hearts were shattered. I stare at the calligraphy on the page until my mind transfigures it. A tidal wave of reminiscence crashes down on me, while a tsunami of emotions rushes through my senses.

Before I can register what to do next, the house phone chimes. I can hear my mom's voice as she addresses the person on the other end. It could just be the note, but as she starts to speak, a pit forms in my stomach—a sudden feeling that my entire world is about to change. That gut retching twist you get when the vibe feels off, or even the angry butterflies that start in your belly and travel upward, trying to burst from your throat as fear takes hold of you.

Her voice is muffled as it travels through my bedroom door. Growing louder, providing little assistance in the clarification of her words. Sneaking into the hall, I hear her hang up, aggressively, I might add. The familiar sound of the phone slamming against the receiver repeatedly indicated it wasn't a good call.

Sobbing filled the house alongside an occasional scream. When she spoke, her speech was incoherent, broken, and shaky. "W-Why! Not m-my baby! W-What am I g-g-going to do... what am I g-going to say? H-how will I t-t-tell her s-s-sister! I got to go, I must go!". All is quiet for a heartbeat. "I can't be here right now," she breathes.

The change in her voice was petrifying. One second, she is screaming in defiance. The next—she sounds defeated. Peter whispers, his voice barely audible over her lamenting. "Shh-shh-shh, we will figure this out together. Just breathe." The front door opens, then shuts again. I watch from the top of the stairs as the headlights signal the car pulling out and leaving.

What did she mean?

"What did she need to tell me?" I choke on the words as they escape my mouth. Thoughts of my sister flash before me. They range from memories we shared to the number of horrible things that may or may not have happened to her. Visions of us making mudpies and swinging at parks morph into her slumped over in an alley. My face burns red-hot—a kaleidoscope of imagery goes from light to dark, happy to sad, pink to blue. Before I know it, my hands and knees hit the floor, and I am drenched in tears.

A sinking feeling hits me, and suddenly, the presentiment of something bad happening becomes more inevitable. I inspect the letter clutched in my fist—an idea molded in my forethought. I gave myself little time to contemplate the drastic plan before I was out the door to the bus stop, annual membership in hand. I waited for the bus, and as it neared, I glanced in the direction of my childhood home, then climbed aboard.

The doors close behind me, sealing the chilly air outside—a small draft touches my back through my coat as the doors meet. I insert my bus pass into the machine, experiencing a mix of emotions. Waiting for the green light, but nothing happens. The bus begins to move. *No light?* I must have missed it, or the ticket machine is malfunctioning.

As I continue to the rear of the bus, I observe the remaining seats along the way. It is quite empty, due to the late hour. I focus on my intended destination—typically, this section remains unoccupied until now. A man, attired in vintage clothing, extends over the back seat. He appears to be one of those cosplayers I have heard about.

His fancy clothing is reminiscent of the characters from the series "Peaky Blinders". A Newsboy cap conceals his face entirely, casting shadows and warding off the light—complete with a dark trench coat that covers his three-piece suit. I have always considered such attire to be both elegant and attractive.

I locate a seat near the middle of the bus and sit down, leaning into the fabric. The bus departs as I peer through the window, my eyes swollen from crying and my body fatigued. Eventually, I fall asleep, but it was interrupted by a recurring nightmare that is deeply ingrained in my mind. I am jolted awake just as the bus screeches to a halt, and the driver's voice interrupts the silence, announcing our arrival. I nearly miss it before his words register. The individual, seated at the back of the bus, appears to have disembarked as the seat is now vacant.

As the bus begins to pull away, I scan for a rest spot. Then, looking at my phone for the first time since I started this journey, the reality of it all hits me, so I settle on a bench, mere feet from where I stood—pulling my backpack into my lap and digging around for some much-needed snack-age. A shadow catches my attention, flickering in my periphery, as I finish the rest of my beef stick.

My heart begins to race, pounding so hard I can hear it—my very own horror movie soundtrack. Before I can investigate, I am distracted by the squeaking brakes as the next bus appears. I slink over and give one last look behind me, adrenaline fueling the fear that I might see the mysterious shadow again. Instead, I am face-to-face with the guy from the first bus. His Newsy is tilted slightly to the right, hovering over his cornflower blue eyes, darkened by the deep gray handkerchief that covered the rest of his face.

My head falls back, resting on my shoulders, as I gaze up at this tower of a man, and his chiseled features—like some marble statue from the Greco-Roman era. Catching myself standing there, mouth wide open, I force my petrified body to react by giving it a little shake. Upon boarding the bus, he sits in the front, as I head toward the back, halfway to the finish line of my repetitive process: Scan my ticket. Take my seat. Settle in. Fall asleep.

My body starts to shiver. Immense darkness engulfs me. The air is crisp and disappearing fast, as water is quick to take its place. I coerce my eyes to open, my vision blurry as blood streams down the bridge of my nose. I try to scream or move, but my body is non-responsive. Plunged into darkness again as my eyes are forced shut by fatigue, I find myself gasping.

Once I can reclaim my sight, it's the same thing all over again—there's that voice. This time, the thought of it being my father brings a sense of peace. Then, I wake up, with sweat beading on my forehead, and my skin is clammy. If only we had waited a little longer, if only I had given Evelyn more time, I wouldn't be on a bus to Maryland to save her.

When I get off the bus, I start the standard walk to the next stop. A few paces in, I notice the echoing of footsteps mirroring that of my own. I pick up my stride to see if the phantom steps will match. They do. I turn quickly to face what or who it is. The only thing I see is the fog swirling with the cool winter breeze. My walk becomes more of a sprint, with only another block to go.

Just then, a man steps out from beside a building a few feet in front of me, his silhouette ominous but familiar. He lifts his hand just enough, and the streetlamp highlights his leather glove. His palm face up, stops at waist level. Two fingers beckon me to come closer. My heart quickens, like Russian racehorses at their first derby, the beating of their hooves galloping toward my nether regions.

I should not be turned on by this.

This man before me, who is he?

His stature matched that of the man who left the letter in my mailbox. Now that I am closer, he seems too young to be my father.

Is this the man from the bus?

Has he been following me the whole time?

Does he work for my dad?

I heard him release a small, low chuckle, then realized I was biting my lip. He is giving mad dark romance vibes—the red flags are at DEFCON 4, signaling me to run away. Instead, I do the opposite—I walk forward.

"*Desire, when left unchecked, can become both a sanctuary and a prison.*"

CHAPTER 4

Oliver

Hm, oh, little dove, you should not look at me that way.

I feel a profound tremor from her stare, her eyes round and doe-like. *Why does she do this to me?*

I must force restraint on myself. I cannot act on these feelings, but damn, what I wouldn't give to force her to her knees right here in this alley, is an extremely compact list. *To fill her luscious mouth with every inch the gods have blessed me with.*

Clenched shut in protest, my teeth go cold as I suck air through them while the intrusive, but true, thoughts stampede through my mind.

Her face glistening with tears, as her lips stretch wide to take me.

Shit, my mind is running away from me. Ugh, but joy of 'getting

off' to her screams, as they ricochet from

every brick, is riveting

A small laugh escapes my mouth when I notice she is gnawing at her bottom lip. *What are you thinking, little dove?* I grant her a few steps toward me before I vanish into the darkness of the alley.

The pitter-patter of her feet makes me smile. *That's it, chase me.* I release a laugh so maniacal that it even gives *me* chills, as the shadows morph into my fun house. "You are no match for me in the darkness. I. Am. A shadow." My voice drops to a baritone.

"Wait!" She calls out.

"Run, run, run as fast as you can." I pause for a spell.

Am I taunting her with a nursery rhyme? Yes, I guess I am.

The air was thick and eerie, so her voice rang out crisp and clear, "What do you want?" She belts out more of her interrogation, and my body shudders. My inner fiend is drooling at the mouth—growing more excited with her persistent mewling.

I dart behind her, into another blackened corridor, whispering against her neck as I pass. "You. I. *Fucking*. Want. You!" There's a detectable hitch in her breathing—shown by the vapor of smoke her hot breath makes as it clashes with the frosty winter air.

Her ongoing hunt captures my interest, "Why... me?" She persists, making it that much more difficult to fight my urges. "How do you know me? Did my father send you?" So brazenly, she questions me.

Is she even the slightest bit afraid that she is alone in an empty alley with a strange man?

My outline moves, closely following her form—before I become aware of my actions, I find myself extinguishing streetlights, using whatever debris I find lying around. She keeps running, staying within the glow of the lingering torches. It went from her chasing me to my favorite game of all—prowling.

My senses heighten as her heavy breathing fuels the animal that is tearing at my instinct to remain calm. My darkest self, a barred creature—the constant reminder that I am not human. I am a ghost, a phantom, a shadow...her shadow, and she has starved me long enough. Unfortunately for her, she finds herself standing beneath the last lantern. As I situate myself before her, I brandish my blade and twist it, so the edge will randomly catch the light and shimmer in the dim glow that encompasses us.

I admire her face, her eyes darting from the weapon, then back to me. An image of exhilaration, subdued within her silvery eyes. I crouch, obtaining a single stone from the ground below. Her gaze follows the path of the rock. Upward, as it defies gravity, then down as it surrenders. Something my little bird will be doing soon.

Surrendering.
To me!

As the piece of gravel crashes into the streetlight, black becomes charcoal, and my vision evens out. I replace the knife in its holster, and all that is between us now is air—and opportunity. Seizing this moment, I dash toward her, stopping close enough for my breath to caress her lips—I inhale hard.

There goes all the air.

Her hands shift towards me, and I step back, letting loose a low guttural sound that rumbles from deep in my throat. "Not so fast," I feel the wind as her touch falls short of my coat.

"I can't see," she cries out.

"The better to tease you, deary." My words come out in wisps as I dance around her, relishing in her symphony of cries and ragged exhales as they seep into the night. Her heart is pounding like a bass drum, and her shallow breaths palpate on the offbeat. *She is so fucking gorgeous.* My questions are like a thick fog in my mind.

What is this 'Obsession'?

Would she allow me to devour her, here in this musky passageway?

"Where-" She begins to speak, and I am behind her once more. I wait to hear what she is going to say, "Are you going to hurt me?"

My hand wraps around her neck as I pull her into my chest. The erection forming in my pants is unyielding against her back, pressing into her cute little peacoat. A coat that is far too thin for this weather.

By the gods, I knew she was short, but damn, my build dwarfs hers. She must be no more than five feet. Leaning down, I place my lips on the helix of her ear, "Only in ways you'll be begging me for more." With purpose, I add a rasp to my voice, slowing my speech, pronouncing every syllable. The leather of my glove collared around her throat. My Index finger traces her jawline, before I apply a gentle *'you're mine'* squeeze.

She releases the most hypnotic moan, awakening the animal in me. I tear back the cloth from my face as I tilt her head downward, catching her by the scruff of her neck, and I begin to kiss her—hard. Her satin-like lips are cold against mine.

Damn that Jack Frost who kissed her first. If he were real, I'd kill him. It wouldn't be the first time I have taken someone's life for her. No matter, I am only at liberty to kiss the frost away, and as the clock ticks, I ponder.

Why isn't she running?

Why isn't she fighting?

My mind is going a mile a minute. Then something happens that silences the voices and throws me into a full primal state. She returns my kiss—without delay, morphing my obsession into a full-blown possession. Never did I believe I would be this close to her, let alone in this position.

I move my hand from around her neck to replace the one cradling her at the nape, entangling my fingers in her hair as I spin her to face me. The maneuver seems to anger the creature that slumbers within my little bird. She lunges at me with a fiery passion I only dreamt I could experience.

I tighten my hold on her hair, paralyzing her where she stands. A brilliant flame coruscates in her stormy eyes. I retrieve my dagger once again. This time, using it to command her to look at me, placing the blades' extremity just below her chin. A small, dark bead rolls down the spine of the blade

Shit, I didn't mean to draw blood.

Yet, she doesn't even wince.

Fucking hell.

She watches me, desire masked with a hint of horror, as I lick the sweet, scarlet stream from the steel, my eyes never leaving hers.

Even in the opaque veil of midnight, her beauty is radiant—her skin, ghostly in the moonlight.

My tongue flicks off the tine, her blood like candy, tantalizing my taste buds. My hand around her throat again, I guide her steps backwards, until she is pressed against a wall. Her hands spring up in a failed attempt to prevent herself from slamming against the brick. I trail my blade over her plush skin, contouring her facial features as I imagine the little pink lines that trace after. I follow along her creases and divots, down her clavicle, then further to the first button on her coat.

With a swift jerk of my wrist, the shiv makes little work of removing it. She gasps, reaching for the tiny plastic material as it plummets to the ground. I spin the blade in my palm, catching it between my thumb and forefinger—tightening my grip around her neck even further, preventing her from moving, practically making her one with the wall.

She shudders. At first, I thought it was the cold, but the heat radiating from her body says otherwise. I slide the metal over her, skating it from one shoulder to the next, then down towards her breasts, following my previous path. The tip of the steel disappears as her cleavage consumes it.

The glow from the moon summons a demon in her eyes, silently beckoning me to continue. Not breaking eye contact, I remove the knife, lowering it out of sight, and placing it between her thighs. Her legs wobble briefly at the sudden pressure on her leg. As the metal moves higher, she still attempts to steady herself. My skin tingles at the sound the steel makes while it drifts across her jeans—now mix that with the drumming of her heartbeat as it quickens. *Fucking delicious.*

Now this alone could have been enough to finish me, but I don't want it to end here.

It is in this moment that I realize the rhythm of my heart is matching hers beat-for-beat, and I lean in to kiss her afresh. I put the blade away momentarily as I collect her wrists and cage them beneath my hand, then, in reaching for the hilt of my knife, she does the unthinkable—she stretches, and pulls, my eyes widen as I see she is pulling *towards* me.

W-What, the hell is she doing?

Notes

"*Fear and longing often walk hand in hand through the shadows of our hearts.*"

CHAPTER 5

◇ ◇ ◇

Emory

I am running. Why am I running? The darkness follows me in tandem with the resounding crash of each lamp. The bulbs split into shards with the kiss of a pebble, going mock holly fuck. I shouldn't be okay with this, but my heart is more alive than ever, and adrenaline is feeding into it, giving my feet the '*will power*' to sprint through this dim labyrinth of stone.

A brick wall appears a few feet ahead, and a glance to either side confirms the thought that instantly invaded my head before my eyes could come to the same conclusion—trapped, like the little mouse he has made of me. Just when I thought I was in control, I find myself here, at the end of an alleyway... a strange man on my trail.

I twist on my heels, back against the cold material behind me. The vision before me is both entrancing and terrifying. He stands in the

shadow as though he were avoiding the light like demons to a salt circle —a delicious cocktail of balefulness and forbidden desire. The only light is above my head, and before its radiance is stamped out, the last thing touched by its beam... glints—bright, silver, mysterious. Then, all is pitch black, and I feel the wind as he rushes forward.

Reaching out, I try to touch him, grasping nothing but air as he steps away from my touch. Standing alone in this leaden alley, my sex is at war with my brain, a tornado forming from the circles my stalker is creating. Stalker... the word brings me closer to reality, and I ask, "Are you going to hurt me?" When he answers, I become weak in the knees.

"Only in ways you'll be begging me for more." A slight hunger hangs in his words. "My muse."

Something about it is familiar, and so comforting... *but why? Why is it that his voice has such an effect on me?* Everything after that was a blur of pure ecstasy. I can't see him—the moon doesn't provide me with that luxury. Touching him is out of the question, but my lips— oh, how my hands are jealous.

Time slips by as his blade dances over my body, peppering goosebumps as the cold steel follows my veins. I can hear iron scrape against something, before there is a firm grip around my wrists, slowly he corrals them above my head and entombs them beneath one of his massive hands. Then I hear the sound again, like the sound of a chef's knife on a sharpening block.

I clench my thighs in a failed attempt to hide my arousal, as the edge of the metal drags along my jawline — he pauses for a moment before he spins the knife in his palm again, this time grabbing it by the blade.

"It's no use trying to hide your sweet scent--it will always double-cross you." His lips meet mine as the hilt collides with my clit, the fabric and seam adding the perfect amount of friction.

As he feathers kisses over every inch of skin that he can get his lips on, something about it feels off. I can't place it. Was it a beard or stubble? It felt coarse against my flesh, like one of those silver Brillo pads used for specific dishes. The texture wasn't enough to distract me from my denim, so wet that it may as well not even be there.

I melt into the mixture of his scorching lips and the solid object pressing into my pants—the heaviness of his massive hand enclosing my wrists causes me to stop and wonder about myself.

Is this really the kind of stuff I'm into?

He breaks away, drawing the pommel to his nose, as a seductive laugh escapes him, pushing past the cloth that covers his face.

"Fucking hell." He snarls, and I catch wind of his breath--it is laced with a familiar scent that lingers between us—a subtle fragrance I knew I wouldn't forget.

Whiskey. Honey. Smoke.

"You!" I fight as the hard object between my legs starts to gain traction, making my limbs weak from its rhythmic motions.

Then, the sensation leaves me as he speaks, "I... what?" he sneers.

The knife handle returns, and he quickens his pace, causing my words to come out broken. "You-you were at... my house." My

voice is shaky with euphoria as my whole being defies the logic in my brain.

His face is iridescent beneath the night sky as he tilts his head to peer at me. His brilliant blue eyes are hooded by his damn near perfect eyebrows. The lower half of his face is still protected, coated in the shadows. Something, like a tattoo or scar, peeks out from the mask so fastidiously placed, allowing him to move and talk freely, all the while keeping him hidden. "Was I?" He teases as he canted toward me — his lips warm against my frozen neck. How is it he can scare me yet make me need him at the same time?

He is planting feathery kisses from my collarbone to my earlobe, in a desperate attempt to try and hinder me from speaking.

"Y-yes, and you've been stalking me... since then. From the bus to the alley."

Stopping at my ear, his words are like a gentle lick. "Oh, darling," he sighs between pecks, the warmth of his breath doing nothing to help the deception of my body in the argumentations of my brain. His dagger hilt, so firm against my sex, finds my clit again.

Why did I wear these thin ass skinny jeans?

Rotating the blade at a nectarous pace, he pushes me to the edge, my eyes close, savoring the pleasure. A small tear slips down my face as my brain signals its defeat, then the feeling and stimulation vanish, and I gasp in its absence.

"It's been much longer than that." His panting is mere wisps over my skin. "You're going to miss your bus," he pauses, and I feel him brush the tear away. "Dove."

My eyes spring open, the phantasmagoria a brilliant display as they try to adjust. Once my eyes become aware of my surroundings, I find I'm standing alone in the alley, discombobulated and cold.

I barely made it in time to catch my last bus. I do a quick comb over the terrain, finding that he was nowhere in sight. I would have thought I had dreamed of the whole thing—if it weren't for the damp spot on my jeans. I didn't even catch his name, but flashes of what happened exploded in my mind. What did he mean by '*longer*'?

How long has he been watching me? The taste of his lips still lingers on mine. Clearly, I've read too many books. I was too willing and accepting of what just happened. Still, how could anyone resist those cobalt blue eyes? The way they transmogrified into more of an electric blue... *can eyes be electric?*

This time I didn't fall asleep. I spent the entire ride watching everyone board, hoping to see him, to feel the burning his haunted stare gives me. My stop comes quicker than I expected, and I feel it's for the best, since I need to get back to thinking of Evelyn, and the reason I even ventured out like this.

The bus screeches to a halt, and I step off. It's just a short walk now to the address my father left me. As I follow my GPS, I realize it's morning and my battery is low. *Fuck I* didn't *pack a charger.* "I hope this place has one, and a place to sleep, or even if I'll have the chance to...." My voice falls flat as I stop at the clad wrought iron gates. One of them is a jar just enough for me to slide through.

Once inside the compound, the image before me is dreamy and not of this earth. A mansion stands erect, the epitome of an old Victorian castle.

A few shops form a semicircle around the main structure, as it stands tall in the center. The smaller buildings ring below it, circling it with the semblance of a personal mall. A single store stands bright amongst the husks of the other buildings. Faint lights battle to shine through the few opaque windows in the manor. The streetlamps offer a feeble gleam where they stand by the gate, adding to the ambiance of this Ghost Town. I approach the window of the well-lit shop and squint through the mosaic-stained glass to see inside.

Shelves stand from the ceiling to the floor and are lined with books. An elderly lady with alabaster hair is scurrying around, working to get the place ready to open. I rest my hand on the handle, applying minimal force. My hand drops, and the door squeaks open. The lady looks up, her heterochromatic eyes finding mine, and she smiles. Not just any smile, the kind of smile that warms your soul, the kind no one in their right mind wouldn't *"respond in kind"* to.

"Can I help you, love?" she says, in a slightly off, Jersey accent, like she may have lived in Europe when she was younger, then moved here. "Are you lost?" Her brows furrow as she steps toward me.

"I'm, um, looking for Alfred Selby." Her aged eyes widen as I say my father's name. "My name is Emory, I'm his daughter." I continue.

Her hands fly to her mouth as the cup she was holding crashes to the floor, and what looks like tea coats the stone in amber. Tears well in her eyes. "He told me you'd show. I didn't believe him, I am..." She pauses, thinking about what to say next. "I am Niven. It is such a pleasure to meet you." I give her a half smile.

"You must be extremely exhausted. Please come with me. I have a cot upstairs you can use." Walking towards me, the volume of her voice is imperceptible as she proceeds. "Then, after you've rested, I will answer all your questions. Does that sound good?"

Sluggishly, I nod. "Yes, ma'am, thank you."

She escorts me up the stairs to a little room in the back. It's cozy with a small bed, an end table, and bookshelves. I grin at the sight of there even being shelves lined with books in the room. Stepping in, I turn to look at Niven. "Is this your room?"

"No," She shakes her head gently, "This was my son's room." Melancholy befalls her face, pain radiating from her like she's been struck by a whip.

"What happened? I'm sorry, I didn't mean-" I stop short, seeing how my babbled apology isn't fixing anything. She brushes a solitary tear from her porcelain cheek.

"All is well, dear. I'll be fine."

"Thank you, Ms. Niven," I call back with a weary smile.

"Oh, please. Niven is fine." Niven lingers at the threshold for a moment before she closes the door behind her. Looking around, I find no photos, nor are there any personal items. Fatigue hits me like a freight train, leaving me no choice but to fall into bed, slipping into sleep as I wonder what might transpire when I wake.

QUOTES MOST DESIRED

"Am I taunting her with a nursery rhyme? Yes, I guess I am". -Oliver, Ch. 4

AYLA

"Addiction is a battle fought in silence, but recovery is a journey best traveled together."

CHAPTER 6

Christian

I've been in this nuthouse for a year now. The loss of one's mother can truly break a person. It was hard, to say the least. She was my best friend and all I had, especially when Dad had been drinking— he got... physical. He was never the best father, and I would never nominate him for *"Dad of the Year"*, but I blame that on my grandfather.

My mother passed away while I was overseas. I knew there was something off about that day when I was brought into the command tent and greeted by the chaplain, Commanding Officer, and Sargent Major. Let me tell you, that isn't something you want when you're knee-deep in the soil of a foreign country. Receiving that news not only brought me home, but it also brought me down, then it brought me here —the deadly concoction of her death and the transition back to *'the civilian life'* sent me spiraling.

It started small. Some weed here and there with my other fellow Marines—those thrown into the shark tank of ungrateful, wastes of life. Tending to the same travesties of humanity that inhale the air my sisters and brothers died for, all while complaining their coffee isn't done right. They take full advantage of the freedom brought to them by the blood of my kin, those worthless wretches with no understanding of what it means to *truly* lose.

The reefer calmed the voices but did nothing to ward off the shadow people. No solace for the constant sounds of the firefights or bombings I experienced during the time I was forward deployed. So, the more things I tried, the more the nightmares would morph, becoming accustomed to the drug of the week, challenging me to try something different, something stronger.

This place was like living in a Broadway masterpiece of dysfunction and filth. The smell, so potent it could knock a bloodhound senseless—heavy chemical cleaners mixing with human shit and piss. The sounds aren't much better. Down the hall, resounding in HD, are the screams and incoherent ramblings of those deemed a threat to themselves and others.

One relief I had was an orderly named Barney. Making it into his good graces was a Godsend. I attained this gem after I stopped a complete nutcase from splattering his brains across the common room with an IV stand. In return, he sneaks me smoky treats—cigarettes to most. On occasion, he levels up, bringing pre-rolled joints from a smoke shop for us to share.

Orderlies like him make the nights when the demons creep from the mind and into the shadows bearable and safe. Having someone like that on the outside could have stopped the high—the one that had me fading back into that nightmarish dream that caused me to go berserk.

The very night that got me off with a plea for temporary insanity and five years of rehabilitation.

I remembered feeling the pulse in my veins matching the frequency in the flashing glow of the alternating red and blue. Then I was restrained to a bed, blinded by bright fluorescent white lights, buzzing like a hive of angry bees as they passed above me. After everything was all said and done, I found myself here: a routine med schedule, a routine food schedule, and lights out by nine.

After all the time I've spent here, there has never been a reason for my leaving... until she joined the rehab center a week ago. Going on what now? Five, six months of sobriety, and I would throw it all away for her—little did I know that is what I would have to do.

Evelyn

It was all a blur. A fever dream, and it was my fault. I will never forgive myself. I must get better, if not for

myself, then for her.

These words have imprinted themselves on my psyche. Like an old hag nagging, they echo in the caverns of my mind... always the same words, never the same tone, a broken record struggling to correct itself.

I brought myself here. I dragged my rock kicking and screaming to meet this bottom, this low of all lows. I am an embarrassment to her. I brought myself here. I dragged my rock, kicking and screaming, to meet this bottom, this low of all lows. I am an embarrassment to her. My sister, so smart, intelligent, and all of that could be erased because of my negligence and disregard for my own life.

The stench hit me the moment I pulled open the double doors. Moans from lost souls ringing off the walls. If you close your eyes, you can imagine Hell just from the haunted howls residing here. "All Father grant me the strength to accept the things I cannot change, the courage to change the things I can, and the wisdom to know the difference." Habitually, I recite the words my father told me.

I always needed to be the center of attention. I'd piss everyone off to have it... good or bad... didn't matter. Attention was attention. Now look where I am, standing at the front desk of a rehab center, waiting for the receptionist.

My hair stands on end as a shadow forms, looming over me, the wind brushing against my neck as whatever it is exhales. I turn to find a man around my age looking down at me, his hands in his pockets.

"What's a pretty girl like you doing in a place like this?" My eyes are wide as I fight back the urge to laugh.

Does this corny shit still work on women?

My face goes red hot, as the corner of his lip lifts in a half smile—I guess so because I am smitten.

Two days pass, and the false wall I built has been broken. Putting it up was an attempt to put myself last. Or at least I thought I was putting myself last for once in my life, until he pointed out the opposite. "Why do you hide?" his voice appears out of nowhere. My shoulders kiss my ears in response, then I go back to playing with the mush on my plate.

"Not going to talk to me, huh? That's cool, I'll get it out of you eventually." He twists his foot on the ground, like he is putting out a cigarette. The way he teases is infectious, and I'm hooked, but I don't let on that it is working. His voice rings out again, pulling me from my thoughts, "Hey sugar, wanna get out of here?"

"What! No, I can't... I-I haven't-" Once the panic settles and I realize the smug grin on his face as he crosses his arms, glaring down his nose at me, I clasp my hands over my mouth. Laughing the loudest I have in, I couldn't even say how long.

I look up at him. "Well, there goes the neighborhood." In almost a whisper, I respond to him, pushing a piece of stray hair behind my ear as I glance up to meet his gaze—a deep chuckle is how he answers, and it sends tingling sensations so deep I could feel them straight to my bones.

He moves toward me, his face hovering over mine, and I am scrunched in my chair—his breath hot on my face. "I have encountered many drugs." I watch as shadows roll over his features like those cast by the clouds against the mountains on a warm summer day. "I have never been addicted to one before even trying it... until you walked through that door." He points behind him in the direction of the lobby, and my heart skips a beat.

Whydoes he make me feel this way?

Rocking back on his heels, he relaxes his face and, with a sultry *'follow me'* stare, he turns and walks away. A single glance over his shoulder, brows raised, his eyes boring into me, captivates my soul like a gem enthusiast finding a rare jade masterpiece—completely irresistible.

Christian

Evelyn... her name matches her beauty. Evelyn... uh... feels so good on my tongue. A name I could moan loud enough, even missiles would fall silent to its sound.

She tries to play shy, but I work my magic—I will have her speaking in no time, but only to me. Her smile melts my stone heart, and after looking back at her in the cafeteria, I knew I had her... finally, a drug I could get high on.

I lead her to the janitor's closet, and there, I'll get her to tell me her pain. Once the door shuts, that is exactly what she starts doing. I let her talk—she goes on about how she put her sister in the hospital, and their dad leaving when they were young. The story of her father disappearing was what, in my opinion at least, sent her down this path of addiction.

Her trauma is also my cue. Am I ashamed of the fact that I exploited her tragic background to slip into those gray sweatpants of hers? A little, but hey, 'gray sweatpants season' isn't just for women. While you all are staring at our front, we are wondering what shadows your ass casts.

Also, little reader, it was consensual. I used her sadness to my advantage, yes, but the difference is I made her feel the way she should have always felt—*wanted*. If you don't feel wanted, then they may just be using you.

As the conversation between us ended, our feelings got the best of us, and I found myself propping her up on one of the shelves of the supply rack. The way her breasts bounce as I drive my cock into her… is delicious. The soft rattling of the shelving unit as she braces herself… is hypnotic, like a metronome keeping me on beat. Our heat is building… condensation forming and mixing with the sweat on our bodies. "Oh sugar." My moans collide with her skin, echoing off the valleys where her neck dips. Soft but hungry, my hands wash over her.

Every inch. I must touch every. Inch. Ofherbody.

The moment we shared wasn't long, but it didn't stop us from savoring every bit of it. "Christy… Chr… Christy." Her cries made it difficult to last. I started naming different weapons in my head. My thoughts were taken over by the many names for the artillery I had back in the military. "I'm... gonna-" Her screams vibrate in my palm as I slap my hand over her mouth to muffle them. We don't want, nor do we need to be caught.

Not long after, my teeth sink into her shoulder as I climax. "Oh, my little drug." I pant, "What have you done to me?"

She had me on a high I never thought I would come down from. All was well between us, and we became remarkably close, inseparable even. Until one day, she was wheeled out, looking like a zombie, strapped to her chair. That's around the same time I found a letter, and then I knew what had to happen.

It took days to plan, hours to implement, and she was too weak from the meds that the Doctor had been giving her. I had never seen him before--his green eyes deep like the forest I wanted to bury him in. I would have remembered those eyes, the distant mystery and absence they carried, but also, I couldn't read his body language or the lack thereof. The way he conveyed himself was with a false sense of bravado and the *demand for respect* attitude, like some entitled high-born.

"Evelyn, sugar... come on, baby ... you gotta wake up. Damn it!" I snap my fingers in front of her face. "Come on, baby, we gotta book it." I look around. The alarm klaxons are screeching, and I can hear some of the nurses as they chatter like anxious chipmunks. Their voices heightened and alert due to the events transpiring before them.

I grab Evelyn's arm and throw her over my shoulder, leaving the other exposed for ramming—if necessary. Dodging nurses from pillar to post, like a recruit in basic training, body-swerving the Drill Instructor swarm. The double doors leading out to the front parking lot come into focus. Just as we approach it, two steroid-pumped rehab bouncers block it.

That didn't scare me, though, because what they have in bulk, they lack in brains. I open a room to the left, and by my luck, it's a supply closet. I put Evelyn in a wheelchair, before I throw on a pair of scrubs, clipping a name tag to my patch pocket—one that I lifted off a male nurse as they rushed past me to stop the other wards from rioting.

After placing restraints on Evelyn's limbs, I comb her hair out of her face using my nails. "I'm so sorry, sugar. We are pulling chalks on this hellhole." Her glazed eyes stare absently past me as if she had been lobotomized. Surveying the room, I take a broom handle, snapping it in two. Then, I unscrew the bristled head and throw it to the floor, all so I can slide both halves into the back of my scrubs, pinning them to my backside with the waistband of my pants.

Once I pull my hoodie back on, I sneak us back into the hall, snatching a fire extinguisher from the nearby stairwell. Discreetly, I stow it in the pouch of the wheelchair behind Evelyn, and we make our way to the exit—calm and collectively. "Hey fellas, this is a late transfer, gotta get her back to police lockup," I say to tweetle Dipshit and tweetle Dumbass. "Which Wagon is ready for her?" I glare at the one who keeps eyeing Evelyn.

"Bus three is gassed and ready," the other one interjects, cutting the tension in the air with his sharp response. "Keys are in the cupholder."

"Thanks," My voice is airy as I push her past them. Coming within proximity of the guard that was eyeing Evelyn, something clicks, and I remember he is due for a karmic surprise. He is the one all those stories are about, involving his *nighttime welfare checks* in the female ward. Without hesitation, I take the broken broom handles from my waist, stabbing the splintered side into the other guard's fat ass gut.

He recoils, I crack him on the back of his neck, then uppercut his forehead as I bring the pieces together, causing him to collapse instantly.

My focus wasn't on him, but I still had to incapacitate him—I don't need to be interrupted in what I must do next. Turning to the Dipshit left standing, I slip the extinguisher from the back of the wheelchair, lifting it before me like an AK-47. With all my force behind it, I lunge forward, causing the bottom of the tank to meet his face and break his nose. I bathe in the crimson reward of my victory from it bouncing off him—like the recoil of a M1A1 50 Cal sniper rifle.

Before he can recover, I retrieve the broken broom handle from the ground by Dumbass and commence beating Dipshit with it. I don't stop until his arms are useless noodles flopping at his side, unable to shield himself from the events that will inevitably follow.

Attaining the fire extinguisher once more, relieving it of its protective seal, I saunter over to him. Crouching down beside him, I lock his throat between my thumb and forefinger, then lift him off the ground until his legs dangle. "This is just a quick check on your welfare.... that's what you told them, right?" My inner beast whispers.

Without waiting for his retort and with no respite, I ram him into a wall, then jam the hose down his throat. Using a little pressure, I slide my hand up his neck, enough to secure and stabilize the hose. "Don't want that to fall out now, do we?" I fumble a little to get a good grip on the tank. When I have it, a menacing smile graces my face. "Say, Ah!" After pulling the pin with my teeth, like a mother. Fucking. Grenade—I squeeze.

I hold it until the gauge reads 0 psi. "That's for touching what doesn't belong to you." Releasing him, like it's my turn to serve in tennis, I kick him center-mass, "40-Love!" I shout as I deliver a blow with such force that my foot goes through his chest cavity. His crystallized organs shatter on impact. As I stare at him, my vivid imagination and prior knowledge hold the door open for the reel playing in my head of what the rest of his frozen insides look like.

Shit, I hope he wasn't an organ donor. I just ruined a perfect specimen.

I grin at my work, then I step through him and turn—completing our escape.

NOTES

"To watch over someone is to carry both the burden of their pain and the hope of their salvation."

CHAPTER 7

Oliver

A person like me will never know what secrets are held in the heavens. Nevertheless, I would be ok if my little bird is the closest I get to Nirvana. In all my years, with all my darkness and wrongdoings, no one has ever silenced the demons the way she does. She makes me... *want...* to be a good person.

I watch as she boards the bus, scanning for any sign of me hiding in the shadows.

Not this time, little dove.

My thoughts are coming down from the '*high*' she put me in when I finally make it back home. Stepping through the threshold, I am greeted by the spasmodic clattering of countless fragments hitting the metal siding of a small trash can.

I clear my throat, redirecting her attention, "All is well. I just broke my tea glass." She calls out before she looks at me.

As our eyes meet, I notice hers are red and puffy, and she is using body language to communicate something to me. She is yanking her head in an upward motion—it looks like she is having a seizure as the wrinkles on her neck go taut every time her chin lifts.

My brows furrow, crimping to the center above the bridge of my nose. I step toward her and cradle her face in my hand, inspecting the vermilion hue that is spreading across her face. Her eyes shift toward the spare room, then back to mine.

It was then I knew my little bird was safe in the nest. "Welcome home." She mutters, her voice shaky from crying.

"Thank you, Mam." I respond, sliding my hand to her shoulder as I stride past, bee-lining a path to the staircase. I get to the top, making it to the door in record time, and I crack it just enough to see her sleeping soundly—*she is safe now*.

It's far past lunchtime when I hear the old door squeak open from upstairs. A cheshire smile stretches across my face, nearly touching both ears as I follow the sound of her footsteps down the hall from the first floor with my eyes. I find they are faint but perceptible against the wooden floor. I peer through the bookcase I ducked behind—gazing with awe at the gloriousness of my little bird.

She clears her throat. "Ehm, Ms. Niven." She barely grumbles. "I mean, Niven. Would you happen to have any coffee?" Her flaxen chestnut hair falls chaotically upon her shoulders.

"Oh, good afternoon," Niven responds as she waltzes around the corner. "I have a dark roast and a nice Irish sweet cream. Will that do?"

Emory smiles wearily. "Yes, ma'am, thank you." Niven disappears again as Emory swivels, taking in the scenery around her. She strides from bookshelf to display case, reading some of the titles aloud. "The whole Hannibal series by Thomas Harris? Fantastic." She whispers with something like a gleam in her eye. I watch as her fingers dance over the spines, like keys to her fictional piano.

I have just the place where you and I can talk." Niven rounds the corner once more, a piping cup of liquid in each hand. "Follow me, dear."

I stalk after them. As they travel across a narrow room toward the back of the building, they pass through a hidden door and vanish beyond a false bookshelf that swings open to a restricted section—one that requires adult clearance.

Nestled just past the shelves of mature tomes, tucked discreetly behind double doors framed in mahogany and carved with gothic detail, lies a personal library —the nook—where every publication is a signed first edition.

Emory, with her coffee and Niven with her tea, settle into the gothic chairs under the only light source aside from the unlit candles— the fading sun. Knowing the torches will soon roar to life the moment the sun's luminosity dips past the horizon, I find a place in the shadows to obscure my presence from their view--permitting myself to be mesmerized by my dove.

"Any New Year's resolution?" Niven asks, the rim of her cup just below her lips, as she embraces the heat emitting from its contents.

I haven't really had the time to think of that." Emory answers in a dismal tone, "It's been one thing after another this week."

"How so?" I look on as Niven presses for more answers. Frustration boiling, as the urge to charge out of my hidey-hole and ask her '*what gives her the right to pry?*' gets stronger—I digress.

Then, Emory speaks, and every bit of that washes away. "Well, for starters, Yule started with a bang." Her giggle, although forced, was angelic. "And a crash." She continues, "Not to mention one of my worst hospital visits to date. Then-" her words begin to trail. "Then a phone call, something about my sister, and from the tone of it, it wasn't good. That's what led me here."

"Oh?" Niven's forehead wrinkles with confusion. "Why would that bring you here?"

Emory stands and walks over to the reflective Palladian window, a clear view of the manor pictured before her. Delicately, she idles her fingers over the glass, as if afraid smudges will appear in their absence and ruin its elegance. "My sister's rehab center is close to here. I figured-" Her speech was hopeful as it fades into her next statement, "Since he wanted to see us—my father that is," she stops, quickly glancing back at Niven, then returns her gaze to the foreboding architecture looming mere feet in the distance. "That maybe he would help."

The library door tolls, interrupting her. "Excuse me, dear, duty calls." Emory gives a brief nod. "This is where I leave you, no worries, I'll lock the door to give you privacy."

Niven leaves the Nook after a swift gander in my direction,

then disappears through the archway, closing the double doors—locking them behind her. Emory waits for the sound of the lock to turn, giving time for Niven's footsteps to fade away toward the storefront. Once they get to a secure distance, she turns back to the window, her reflection a somber representation of longing.

I admire her. The way her messy hair gleams in the light from the setting sun. The innocent way the glow creeps across her skin, adorning it with an orange tint. Her hands move to her lips, and mine instantaneously begin salivating, building the desire to be pressed to them again.

A chain reaction starts as butterflies fight like rabid beasts in my gut, and my ears perk up to her gentle whisper. "Who are you?"

Her voice is like a siren's song, looking to lure me to my death. She bites her lip, and the pulsating in my slacks grows stronger. My body is frozen, bewitched by her beauty as her fingers dance from one corner of her mouth to the other—pining, longing, bleeding through her pores.

Is she talking about me?

"Where are you now?" Her fingers slide down her chin. "Are you lurking somewhere, watching me?" She traces the faint lines left by my blade. Answering my question as if, eerily, she heard me.

I shake my head. That is impossible, so I speak, as to test it, "Yes, my dove. I marked my territory, and by the gods, don't you look *stunning* in faint red lines," I know I am whispering to myself, there is no way she can hear me at this distance. Her dainty fingers trickle further to the hem of her blouse. I stagger back from the look in her eyes. I have seen this look... Is she.... I watch on with an-tici-pation.

She raises her free hand, clamping it down around her throat, and my blood boils to the surface. "Yes, there you go, little bird. Now, just a little harder." Her fingers coil tighter as though on demand. The indents are so deep that they expose her heartbeat, revealing its quickened pace. The hand that once rested against the cold glass of the window is now cupping her right breast.

For.   Fucks.   Sake.

She has no bra on, and her nipples are already peaking, casting small shadows over the low bits of her perky, perfect breasts. "What I wouldn't do to have those perfect tits pressed against the window, while I railed you from behind, little bird." With a low, gravelly tone, the words are out before I can stop them. She takes a sharp breath. Either she heard me... or she pinched a little too hard—At this moment I couldn't care less. She is here, and she is divine.

I pause for a moment to see which of my thoughts would play out, that's when the hand around her neck slowly moves—making its descent. Assuming she doesn't hear me, I keep my tone low and famished, and in my mind, I fictitiously guide her pleasure. "Slowly now, little dove. Feel the heat beneath your touch." Humming as I fight the urge to follow suit, "Close your eyes. Imagine your touch is mine."

Her movements glide past her chest, over her solar plexus. "Stop!" Adding a feral undertone, because if she could hear me, I know she would listen. "The right is lonely, dove. Give your glorious breast a little tease before you bypass it."

My mouth is watering like a man with a sweet tooth at a cheesecake factory. "Roll it between your fingers. Pinch and pull. Pinch. And. Pull." My vocal cords vibrate as my tone drops another octave, "That's my girl. My little bird," I take a deep breath, steadying myself. "My dove!" Her hand shifts, allowing her right breast to settle into her palm.

They look so much bigger in her tiny hands.

She pinches and pulls like she is told, and I am too caught up in the moment to realize it. I can feel my chest tighten as this seductress steals my breath away, all leading up to the moment her hand plummets over her belly to the button of her jeans. She has the clasp and zipper open sooner than I can stop her.

"STOP!" Her hand freezes as her eyes shoot open. "Too fast, little bird." My breathing is heavy, and my pants are stressing as my dick fights against the fabric.

"Who's there?" Her voice is soft as her eyes dart in my direction. When I don't answer, she huffs with annoyance. Then defiantly, as if to coax me out, her fingers dive beneath the fabric and begin slowly rotating. She massages her chest a little longer, pinching and flicking— my heart and cock both ready to explode.

When I think she is close to finishing, she slams her hand hard on the glass pane. Her back is to me now and arching with her ecstasy. She moans, "Who are you?" The deliverance of her pleasure is more frantic, and at this point, I can take it no longer. I leave my place behind the bookshelf, closing the gap between her and me in two strides.

Strategically, I place one hand over hers as it struggles to supply her release, the other closes around her neck. Her hand stops for a moment, eyes open, and slate-gray with hunger. Massaging the top of her fingers through her jeans, I assist in guiding her satisfaction, lowering my face until my cheek meets her temple.

"Oliver." My voice deepens. I breathe into her ear through the cloth on my face, then I shove my hand past the material—forgetting I took my gloves off, I am welcomed by her skin so soft against mine. I proceed to use my hand to maneuver hers, pressing down onto her middle and index fingers, making them disappear inside her. "Or Ollie." My breathing is heavy with excitement. The fabric on my face is aiding little to not at all, becoming my number one nemesis.

"Whichever you prefer, my dove." The sweet aroma of her arousal fills my nostrils as I roll my fingers over hers, assisting her, thrusting in and out. "Do you want release, little bird?" She nods, rubbing her cheek against the material concealing my face.

"How bad?" *Oh my... fuck.* Her scent of honeysuckle and vanilla is inebriating, and on my exhale, I growl in her ear. "Tell me, dove."

"S-So, bad... please." She begs, making my dick throb between the crease in her jeans as they hug her ass

"Be a good girl for your phantom," My tone is breathy, "Let go in... three." I take my time counting down, absorbing every bit of her. The way she moans. Her invigorating fragrance. The seduction in her tone as she calls out demands that up until this point I have only imagined.

This moment was better than anything my lonely mind has ever conjured. "Two-" I let out a roar, pausing for just a moment, before giving my good girl exactly what she's been waiting for. "One." Her body convulses as she climaxes, and I inhale audibly, "Is that all for me, little bird?" I watch as her fear turns to desire—then she omits.

"Oliver," her soft saccharine voice saying my name, and the way her ass rubs against my erection forces me to unload in my pants, my body trembling with my release.

New craving unlocked: Emory fucking Selby with my name on her lips.

Notes

"Curiosity can be a lantern in the dark--but beware what you illuminate."

CHAPTER 8

Emory

I stare at the scenery before me, surreal and intriguing by nature. The cold surface of the glass beneath my fingertips did little to convince me that I was actually… here… in this library on the foreign grounds owned by many from my father's side. I wonder what part Niven plays in all of this. Could it be that she is the groundskeeper?

Once it is apparent that Niven is far enough from the room, my mind drifts toward less important, but still demanding, questions for my journey—ones that still need answers. The man from the alley, and all that transpired beneath the tenebrous shroud of midnight, comes to mind.

What was his name?

Who was he?

Was he watching me even at this moment?

Then an idea begins to form in my mind—the utmost, horribly rotten, bratty, pettiest idea that has ever taken hold of my mind. Let's say he is watching me now, and judging by his actions in the alleyway, he feels something too. With that said, my idea is: I *will* get mine, even if it is self-administered.

Just as I expected, I hear rustling, and gentle whispers emerge from behind one of the shelving units in the nook. Although they are hushed, they only get louder as I call out to my shadow stalker and touch myself. How he got in here doesn't matter to me. If he wants to be a shadow and hide in the darkness, too afraid to step out into the light, I am going to treat him as such.

I pinch and pull, making sure to fall just short of his calls, giving him the illusion I can't hear him, as I exact my revenge—forgetting one simple fact as I stand awash in the citrine glow of the setting sun.

Shadows only grow and get stronger in the light.

Without warning, his voice is right in my ear... and with his grungy tone, he startles me, and my lust for him skyrockets... too much to bear after the way he left me in the alley.

I must fight the urges.

*This is **your** revenge—don't stop Emory.*

Don't let him leave you like that again.

His hands are on me, this time as an unforeseen guide to pleasure. I am unable to prevent the climax that escapes me, leaving my panties sodden. I knew he'd be here, but how did he find me? Those *were* his barbaric chants I heard, like a puppet master's orders to his marionette. I listened, thinking it was all in my head.

He said he was a shadow, could that be true?

Did I manifest him here giving life to this illusion?

I look up, and our eyes meet. I watch as a ravenous look darkens the blue in his eyes to an ultramarine. I feel something firm plastered to the small of my back, and my bratty side arises again.

How does it feel to be left longing, asshole?

The thought makes me want to snicker, but my heart has other plans. My brain wants to kick his ass, but my libido longs to devour him. Somewhere along the war path of the two, my heart intervenes, making the executive decision.

"Oliver." His name rolls off my tongue, seizing the saliva that converged at its tip, leaving my lips against the will of my command. I notice a slight irregularity in his breathing.

Did he just?

His broadness pulses as I feel my lower back dampen. At the same time, he fastens a large hand around my jaw. His thumb presses lightly at the bottom of my right ear, while the rest of his fingers fold around my chin, his middle finger brushing my left ear. Then they constrict, and he murmurs, "I blame that on you, dove." He motions to his pants, and my mouth falls open.

*He just jizzed his pants and **blamed** me.*

He trails his thumb over my lower lip, cradling my face, before he forces my body against him. His eyes soften, and that familiar scent blankets me—in this moment, I choose to lean into his hold, recalling the warmth from the previous night. I touch his hand on my waist after fastening my pants, interlocking my fingers with his.

Why does this feel right, letting him in?

Just as I move my other hand towards his face, his presence vanishes. The lock on the door turns over, signaling someone is outside. My heart sinks, while dismay and confusion congest my mental focus—as the emptiness of standing here alone hits me. Niven stands in the entryway, a small book in her arms. "You will not believe what just got here—are you ok, dear?" I look around, not acknowledging her at first, trying to find my pursuer. "What are you looking for?" Niven vocalizes, dragging my attention back to her and away from the shadows.

Did I imagine all of that?

"Nothing," I shake my head slightly, "Just lost in thought, I guess."

"No worries, I'd like to show you the new additions to this room." She turns, and while her back is facing me, I do one last sweep of my surroundings. Her voice nearly frightens me when she speaks again, "Then I have a few things to discuss with you about your... accommodations." She hesitates for a second, "Are you sure you are, ok? You look like you've just seen a ghost."

I shake my head slightly. "No, I am fine. Shall we?" I move my arm forward, palm facing up, as I motion for us to start moving.

Niven smiles, "Very well, follow me." She responds with excitement, then she proceeds to guide me back to the front of the store. I take one last look at the room before following her.

As we step into the main section of the library, a box sits

open on the counter. "Is this what you wanted to show me?"

Her laugh is infectious as she strides over to me, whispering. "Shhh, don't tell anyone, but I like a good spicy book here and there." Retrieving a book from the depths of its cardboard housing, she holds it out before me. Her hand covers her mouth as she giggles like a schoolgirl.

I pull the cover into view and read it aloud, "Yule be Mine: A Krampus Novella." Glancing up at her, I give her a little smirk, "Is this?"

Niven's eyes widen. "Shh, keep it down," she does a quick scan before she laughs again. "You never know who is listening."

Wait, does she see Oliver too?

Oliver—it is only befitting that a man as perfect as he has a name to match. He may appear flawless, but everyone has secrets—I will find his flaws, but until then, I will focus on finding Evelyn.

It's pitch black by the time we exit the library. Niven is securing the doors as I take in the layout of the grounds. "This way." She beckons after she turns the key. Then, lighting a small lantern, she looks at me to make sure I heard her.

"Of course," I answer. Then, like a majestic creature, she walks in the direction of the manor, her long flowing skirt trailing behind her. I follow her footsteps closely, matching step-for-step. It doesn't take long before the mansion looms over me—the Victorian features materializing like turning the page of a pop-up book and watching the three-dimensional paper figures take form.

"This is Selby Manor." She gestures at the foyer, the instant the large wooden doors swing open. I step through the entranceway, and the vaulted ceilings, along with the Grand staircase, stretch and display themselves in panoramic view.

The Selby, who owned it, made it their mission to keep it immaculate.

As we step onto the deep burgundy carpet, which sprawled out like a runway, Niven sighs a little, "You will be staying here for the duration of your time. The other shops are either closed or waiting for renovations." As she speaks, I can tell she is avoiding making eye contact. "I will be in the library if you need me at any given moment."

Our eyes never meet, and I can see that sorrow has crept into her brows as her gaze falls from the portrait that hung dead center—looking over the stairs. "If I hear anything from your father... sorry, if I get any news from Sir Selby, I'll let you know." She clears her throat and leads me further through the portal of the present day and into a pristinely kept past. "So, you will remain on the east wing of the manor."

"Why the east wing?" I interject.

The wheels are visibly turning as she tries to conjure a response. "The west wing is condemned." She says, with a lack of certainty. "The floors have wood rot in some places and are unsafe till further notice." She finishes her response with a snap, giving me the impression that there is more she isn't telling me.

Sighing, she gives a tired half-smile in an ineffective attempt to hide the terror seeming to consume her. "I will show you to your room, and Mr. Gaston will be here early to help you with your endeavors."

Making our way up the grand staircase, I glance around Niven in the direction of the west wing. My hope of catching a glimpse of what ailed her was null and void. We take a right as we reach the ledge, causing my view to be blocked by a suit of armor standing guard at the mouth of the dark hall.

Turning my attention back to where Niven is guiding me, we pass by several doors down a candlelit hallway, where the wallpaper and trim appear to be straight out of medieval times. Finally, we stop in front of one and enter a vast room with a four-poster bed--the large windows expand over the view of the abandoned estate grounds.

"Thank you." I flash a genuine smile.

Niven responds, "This is where I bid you farewell till morning, dear." Niven lowers her head in a bow, then closes the door. Her footsteps vanish into the night. I sprint like a child and jump, landing face down on the California king-size bed, the old wood frame creaking with the long-forgotten attention I was giving it.

After I was done making snow angels in the middle of the champagne-colored sheets, I investigated the rest of the room. The espresso wood furniture, complete with a wardrobe, vanity, footlocker, and chaise, is enhanced with rose gold embellishments. A second glance, and the windows aren't windows at all, but French doors that lead out to a balcony.

On the other side of the room, alongside the vintage wardrobe, is a lavish bathroom. The walls are lined with mirrors, and the cabinets have the same traits as the furniture. The most astonishing feature rests smack-dab in the middle of the room. Sitting there, isolated and beautiful, is a pearlescent claw-foot tub with rose gold feet.

As my exploration ends, I settle back on the bed, closing my eyes. It isn't a second later that a small knock echoes off the walls.

"Come in," I call out.

The door pushes open as I get to my feet to greet whoever enters, and Niven walks in with a plate of food. "Oh, thank you, I'm not hungry though."

"I understand, all this excitement can make one feel like that. I wanted to bring it up anyway." She smiles, but I can see it is masking her sadness. "No matter, maybe tomorrow. Goodnight, Madam Selby."

"No, please, it's just-" The door shuts before I can finish my statement. I look back at the bed, the sheets tousled from my earlier escapades, and it appears so inviting. I allow my shoulders to slump as I stumble to the bed and cocoon beneath the blankets, drifting off to sleep.

Sweating, panting, struggling, drowning, freezing... saved.

I wake up in a cold sweat, the comforters damp and knotted from my late-night tiff in my dreams. Sluggishly, I melt out of the bed as the sunlight reflects off the grooves in the wood on the floor. Walking over to the vanity, I grab the antique brush and run it through my hair a couple of times.

Checking to see if the wardrobe harbors any clothes that would fit my physique, I find a collection of 1930s dresses, ranging from exotic prints to floral patterns, occupying the inside. I see an emerald day dress with a modest top, and as I slip it over my body, the soft fabric feels as though clouds were touching me. It stops just past my knees with a slight flare and a high-waist belt.

The stunning image I see of myself in the floor mirror makes me want to accessorize. I start by adding some perfume in places where it matters.

As I walk back over to the vanity, I fix my hair into a thirties up-do, apply minimal makeup, and adorn myself in costume jewelry I find in one of the drawers. I am leaving the room when I hear voices coming from the first floor. The woman's voice, I can tell, is Niven's, and the other is a softer male tone. The damp air muffles their sounds, making it challenging to decipher any intelligible words. I try to be quiet, but my heels keep clicking, releasing a soft remnant on the solid wood floor.

When I finally make it to the top of the staircase, Niven spots me. She looks at me, and with a smile that stretches across her face, she introduces me, "Madam Sel—Sorry, Emory." She announces, reaching her hand in my direction. I flash an agreeing grin back to her, as my eyes lock on the back of the man she was speaking to.

Could it be him?

Could it be I wasn't imagining things in the first place?

"Please join us." Her words reach my ears in slow motion as the gentleman next to her swivels on the spot.

My eyes take in his features, from his black dress shoes to his charcoal trousers. A Pearl River button-up shirt is superlatively tucked in and strapped down with suspenders. The sleeves are rolled to his elbows, revealing strong but not muscular forearms, while his tie secures his collar taut and takes on a bone-colored hue.

Scars sit like tattoos on his skin, like he had been attacked and needed to hold his arms up in defense.

My heart skips a beat when I notice the cloth that conceals his face. "Madam. Emory. I'll get it right, I promise," she corrected herself before continuing with her introduction. "This is Mr. Gaston, the groundskeeper." She places a hand on his shoulder, "He is also highly knowledgeable in technology and, as mentioned, he would be more than happy to assist you with whatever questions you have."

His eyes finally meet mine, and the crow's feet in the corners of them, caused by smiling, fade and are replaced with a look of desire. He looks at me like Jack did Rose when she stood in the same spot on the Titanic. Like butterfly wings, my heart flutters, and if our ribs weren't made to be in cages, then my heart would have been on the floor, clawing its way to him—begging to be shackled to him for eternity. I catch my mouth before it falls to the floor, as I straighten my stance. Taking on a fallacious sense of self-confidence, I float to the foot of the stairs, doing my best not to stumble.

He clears his throat, his right eye shadowed by his Scally cap, "Pleased to have finally made your acquaintance." His voice is like a hot knife through butter—smooth yet raspy when he hits those lower octaves. A voice that is flawless with every note that floats past the material shielding, what I was sure were perfect lips, from my voracious gaze.

Regardless of the rest of his beauty, it's the feature nestled between his cap and the hem of his mask that beguiles me—his eyes. Those eyes that I have come to thirst for, that make me more dehydrated than a lost slave trudging the far-reaching, desiccated Egyptian deserts.

As I take my place between the two of them, I reach out my hand. "The pleasure is all mine... *Mr. Gaston.*" I put an accent on the name, raising an eyebrow in tandem.

"Oh, please," he chuckles. I can imagine an animalistic grin slide across his face... like a zipper opening to release a demonic creature.

"Call me Oliver," he says, with a bow, taking my hand in his, and I can't help but let my mind wander as he plants a gentle kiss atop my knuckles.

This man will be the death of me.

Notes

> "*Forgiveness begins with understanding the wounds we cannot see.*"

CHAPTER 9

Evelyn

The haziness of my vision is fading as Christian's face appears before me. "What... happened?" The words are a mere whisper as they push past my lips. With my sight slowly clearing, my surroundings become more refined by the second. My body is shaking with the cold, and my breath is visible before me, like little crystal clouds escaping my lips.

"Where am I?" He is brushing my hair out of my face, his sea foam eyes drowning in sorrow. As I address him, "Christy-" A calloused finger seals my words in, not allowing me to finish my statement.

"We got out, sugar." His voice was soft and sincere.

A smile starts to form on my face until the words register. *We... got... out?* "Out of what?" One glance, and it looks like we are camping, but it is more than that. No, this is a homeless encampment. "Christian, where are we?"

He drops his gaze, so he doesn't have to see my disappointment as he responds. "We aren't staying here. I just needed you to rest until the drugs wore off. They were dosin' you, babe." His words hit like a freight train. I try to stand, stumbling and groggy. "Careful, sugar." His hand is on my elbow in lightning speed, bracing me as I take a few more steps.

Interlocking my arm with his, we wander around the fire barrels—he tells me what led him to the choice to leave, and more importantly, why he took me with him.

"So," I begin, as he wraps his arm around my shoulder and lets out a deep giggle, I proceed, "I was like a zombie?"

"Yeah, it was kinda hot, at first. I felt like we were in that movie... *"Warm Bodies,"* He starts to kick pebbles on the street, "And it was, for a moment. I got to save my zombie."

I snort-laughed at his comparison. "You just compared us to a zombie romance." Nodding, he takes my hand and kisses the back of it like I am royalty.

"Anything for you, little zombie."

Something about my new 'pet name' sends chills through me that not even this wintry weather could match. "So, what does that make you? A Necrophile?"

"Yo, that's funny, little zombie." He chuckles, and the image of John Travolta in *"Grease"* springs up in my brain, and he continues with his 'greaser' persona, "Wanna find a decent place where I can *crack open a*
cold one?"

"Christy!" I smack him on his shoulder. "Ew, that is gross." A tee-hee leaves my mouth.

He doesn't stop there. "Come on, don't you want to help me with my *'mourning wood'*?" I gasp at his audacity. "Hey, Necrophiles are people too... we're just looking for some*body* to love." He turns me to face him with a half-ass smirk plastered to his face.

Pulling me close to a cut-out between two buildings, he steps back, his beat-up sneaker disappearing into the darkness. "Come, little zombie. Step into my freezer."

I keel over in laughter. "Okay, the other ones were bad. This one... HA! This one takes the cake."

He grabs my wrist, yanking me into his arms as the crevice devours us, engulfing us in shadow. My back smacks into the stone as his lips crash into mine. His hands cup both sides of my head, then work their way to clasp fists full of my hair. A waft of cinnamon and pine fills my nose as his tongue forces mine into a slap-box battle.

Cinnamon and pine—yes please, it's so much better than the clean linen smell that will forever haunt me.

I place my hands on his chest, his pecks prominent beneath the hoodie he wore over stolen scrubs. His hands start to dance over my body in a frantic attempt to lift the hospital gown that drapes over my sweatpants. He hikes the material up, so it rests in the curve of my lower back—my ass supporting it.

Once his goal is achieved, he takes hold of my wrists, raising them over my head to finally flatten my hands against the brick wall, before entwining his fingers with mine.

Getting the hint, I leave them raised as his fingertips slide down my arms--the sensation is diluted by the coat I am wearing. "Sugar, I am going to get you so high that sobriety will look easy." His gaze is screaming dominance.

"Let.

    Me.

        Be.

            Your drug."

He spins me to face the wall, one hand trapping my wrists above my head, while the other makes little work of pulling my sweats aside.

"Lift your ass, sugar." I rise to my tippy toes, pushing my stomach away from the wall, doing exactly what '*my drug*' demands me to do. "That's my good *fucking* Zombie." Running his cold hands over my bare skin, "I'm going to give you the best brain you've ever had. Ready. Breathe in." Before I can even obey, he slams his cock deep into my pussy.

With a strong hold still on my wrists, he moves his free hand around, placing it on my lower belly. This placement allowed him to thrust. Harder. Deeper. Compelling a small whimper to escape me. "Oh, Christy."

"Oh yes, sugar." His voice is like an earthquake —a rumbling echoing in the empty alley, "Please, please, please, please." His voice was softer with every plea. "Say my name, baby."

I call his name--soft and broken. "Chr-is-tian." Again, I am spinning. This time, as my back leaves the concrete wall, he picks me up.

I wrap my legs around his waist, as he folds my arms around his neck, then my back meets the stone once more. "I want you to come for me, sugar." Using his body to pin me, one knee jams between my legs like he is putting me on a pedestal. I feel him shift the material of my pants, moving them further down my thigh until they are bunched at my knees, and my bare ass is exposed.

He shifts my body slightly off center, the cold air invading my vagina as the warmth of his leg moves. My breathing hitches when he drops his hand through the hole he created, \and my body bucks when I feel him start to rub the head of his dick on my clit, before he pushes it inside me. I try to look down and watch, but as to purposefully be my enemy, my pants are in the way as my knees meet my chest with every thrust.

"Fuck Evelyn," he moans before he shifts me to where I have one leg over his thigh, the other cradled by his forearm—slipping closer toward his shoulder as his free hand moves to collar my throat. It's slow, at first, while he gets his footing. "Come on, baby. You ready to 'pour some *sugar* on me'?"

Because I wasn't prepared for him to crack a joke, I broke out in a fit of ugly laughter. "Yes, Christy, I am." He chuckles along with me. I speak once more, "Anything for you." He takes my final words as an invitation for him to go harder. Faster. Deeper.
Just what I wanted.

His hand leaves my throat, traveling down my chest, and stops at my pussy. He rotates two fingertips around my clit, then slides them back and forth, until finally he inserts them, cupping me in his hand, adding more girth as he moves them in coordination with his cock. His palm pressed into me, rotating methodically over the bundle of sensitive nerves. That was the final step. He is doing it so well. I can no longer fight the feeling, and I come almost instantaneously.

My breathing is jagged as I feel his cock pulsating in me. Breathy, I try to ask, "Christy, did you-" He nods, removing his fingers from me and bringing them to his lips. Inserting them in his mouth, he releases a low vibrato followed by the sound of him sucking them clean. "We didn't have-" I try to continue.

He talks over me, cutting my statement short. "You." He puts a hand behind my right knee, still aloft on his thigh. "Taste." Entranced by his words, not expecting what comes next, "Fucking. Invigorating." As he finishes his statement, he forces my back higher on the wall, wrapping my sweatpants around the back of his neck, making his face—*my seat.*

Suddenly, he begins licking and lapping, pushing anything that attempts to escape back in. He pulls away briefly, sticking his tongue out into the frosty air. I look down and watch it glisten with my essence. Then, after a moment, he returns, and the sensation from the cold on his tongue was like a wintery takeover as he works his magic down there.

With my fingers gripping his hair tightly, I meet my second release. He enhances it with a growl at the realization he finished me a second time—the vibration in his tone better than any toy I have ever owned. "Sugar. Spice. And everything is nice." He says each word between licks before lowering me, forcing our eyes to meet, "Tell me you'll be my girl… let me be the chemical X that completes you?"

"You-" I use the arm of my sweater to wipe his face as I giggle. "You want me to be your Powerpuff girl?"

"I mean, weed is the only enhancer I would be ok with still doing, so you can say that." He flashes a charming smile, but it doesn't bless his face too long. We are interrupted by a noise echoing from further in the cutout than I would dare go. "Stay here, sugar." And with that, he is gone.

After he emerges from the darkness of the alley, I notice he has a new addition. Draped over his shoulder is a woman, and as they slink past me, he gives me a look, one of anger and sorrow.

We stay for a moment more, dropping her off at a tent the others said was hers. "Adelaide," She doesn't budge as he snaps in her face. "Adelaide, hun… wake up." Her eyes open to reveal crisp, honey-colored eyes. As she looks at Christian, finally, she speaks, "Do I know you?" Her voice is raspier than one who has smoked their whole life.

He gives her one good look-over, then replies, "Not anymore." As he turns to walk away, he kicks something hidden beneath the sleeping bag in the tent, causing him to nearly face-plant on the stone floor.

"My father's Louisville?" Leaning down, he picks up the baseball bat.

"Why does she have your father's baseball bat?" I inquire.

Without even looking at me, he answers, "That is a question for another day." He examines the object a little longer before he brushes past me to leave. "Come on."

"Where are we headed, anyway?" I try to break the silence that fell between us. "You didn't disclose that earlier."

"Don't worry about that, sugar." He says with a sharp tone, "I've got a plan."

A bit of frustration slips as I try to push for more information. "Don't be sus now, Christy. Where-" I am cut off by some crack head looking for a fix, but I'm not scared, Christian won't let anything happen to me. *Right?*

Christian

"Fuck you, man!" I throw my arm up in front of Evelyn, "We ain't got your fucking shit!" Evelyn is watching me with her dazzling baby blue eyes, boring holes into the side of my head—she is scared, and I know it. It may have been cold, which doesn't help, but a shiver from the frost and trembling with fear are distinctively different. If the Marines and an abusive father taught me anything, it was that.

The vibration of her horror soaked deep, rattling my bones and awaking an anger that had long since been caged. The bat in my hand was getting heavier as my urge to swing grew. It's been a long time since this bat and I felt as one, and it wouldn't be the first time it helped to make a problem disappear.

In a flash, the tweaker lunges at her like a rabid animal, and I couldn't stop myself. I shoulder Evelyn. Propelling her out of the way, taking her spot in front of the doped-out addict, as he grabs the length of the bat. We push and shove in a life-or-death tug of war, before I sweep my leg forward, and my foot meets his calf. With a quick jerk, his feet leave the pavement, making room for his ass.

His backside collides with the cement as I raise the ligneous object above my head like I'm calling down the power of Grey Skull. Then, yanking my arms back down, the weapon meets his head. Simultaneously, he drops his hand hard, and laughter erupts like the barking of multiple seals. My heart moves to my throat, but I swallow it back, relieving it from its failed attempt to flee.

The horror that plagues my eyes, as I turn my gaze, broke me. I follow his dark, empty stare. A barbed grin smears over his face, and I see he has plunged a needle so deep into her ankle that it dimples in her skin.

His eyes dart back to mine as I stay focused on the syringe clutched in his cracked-out hand. I watch as he slowly pushes down on the plunger, the liquid leaving the vial and invading her body—poisoning her. "No!" I roar, turning to face the monster—the bastard that just signed his death certificate. He doesn't even care that he is about to get his brains smashed in. He erupts in laughter again, and I kick him square in the jaw.

Choking on his blood as it pools in the back of his throat, he leans forward, spitting on my shoe. He would have already been a dead man, but her groaning catches my attention, "Sugar!" I shout, diving after her. Catching her as she collapses.

"Christy," her eyes rolled to the back of her head. "Christy, is that you?"

I check her pulse, it's quick, but something I must allot more time to, for the purpose of allowing the drug to rear its ugly face. I prop her up against the brick wall, then turn to oppose the victim about to be consumed by my wrath. "What did you give her?" I stalk toward my prey—a predator on the prowl.

"You will tell me." I smack the bat against my hand. "I will not. Ask. Again." His laughter quickly turns to panic. His words start to pour from his lips.

It begins like a stutter, then a bout of diarrhea from the mouth. "It was a... please no... Are you going to kill me?" I look down my nose at him—the tip of the bat pressed hard into his bony chest.

"Christy," the state of her voice grinds like a key stroking against the lock that hinders my demons. Their bonds loosening with every falter of her speech. "Chri-" She falls quiet, my sugar... my drug—*is silent.*

Evelyn

The pain shot through my body like poorly done acupuncture. Spreading, stabbing, like venom crawling through my veins. He is drifting further away from me. I reach for him... for Christian.

The ground?

How did I get to the ground?

My hands come into view, and I am distracted by my fingers as they distort and elongate before my eyes. Crying out his name, fighting. "Christian!" His name is sweet like caramel on my tongue... sticky and hot.

Why isn't he listening to me?
I've been screaming for him, I don't know
how long--time feels irrelevant

The colors around me begin to sing. As they grow brighter and more vivid, their songs reach octaves that put tinnitus to shame. The ringing in my ears and vibration in my skull—caused by the many voices that all speak at once—morph together until the words become an incoherent rambling.

Churning in my stomach aids the sudden onset of dizziness. While the crawling under my skin... the tingling... makes it feel like it's moving molecule by molecule, barely holding the door shut from the nausea that's been rapping at it like the police with suspicion of foul play. My chest and throat start to burn with the acidic intrusion of vomit and stomach bile, while the feeling of my airway closing triggers an all too familiar sensation.

Sweating, panting, struggling, drowning, freezing... free.

Christian

One glance in her direction, her eyes have closed, and her breathing is shallow. It takes every fiber of my being not to run to her and hold her, to kiss away her pain. To be there when she comes to and tell her, *"Everything will be alright"*. My eyes burn with the lashings my tears are giving, threatening to pour out--her pain. I can feel it.

How did I let this happen?

Where did he come from?

I stand there staring at her, lost in the guilt of my failure. It's only when the pleas slowly, meticulously, fade to a chuckle, soft at first, then steadily transcending into a vile fit of laughter.

It was that moment my demons laughed back, "You dare laugh in my presence after what you did?" Still facing Evelyn, I raise my head to the sky, silently apologizing to God for the ultimate sin I am about to commit. The shackles that thwart my past ghosts in the

shadows of my soul, *shatter*—the behemoth has been *unleashed*. I take a long-drawn-out turn back to the miscreant that caused her suffering, and with the most sinister tone, my dybbuk snarls in response, "Now. We. Play."

"*True beauty is revealed in moments of vulnerability.*"

CHAPTER 10

Oliver

My Heart stops the moment she does. She stands there perched at the top of the stairs, and instantaneously, I forget how to breathe. The green from her gown is radiant against her ivory skin as she walks down the stairs with such elegance and grace, presenting a bout of confidence I've only seen in her once—when their dad left, that moment made the rest of her life such a challenge. She had to step in, step up, and be the strength.

She had to pick her mother up off the floor and keep her sister from slitting her wrists. The thought of rejection was too much for Evelyn to bear. That spoiled brat—Evelyn had always been envious of the connection Emory had with their father. She would always act out in hopes of attention. It didn't matter what kind. Evelyn often exhibited attention-seeking behavior, which was observed in various aspects of her interactions with others.

She tended to dominate conversations, frequently interrupting others to ensure that the focus remained on her. Evelyn often shared exaggerated stories or personal achievements, seeking validation and admiration from those around her. One would assume her behavior called for constant reassurance and approval, which stemmed from her underlying insecurities.

While her actions would be engaging and entertaining, they can also overshadow the contributions of others. This led to potential frustration boiling down to numerous arguments with Emory and their mother. Evelyn was selfish, always trying to outshine Emory, but not this time. Evelyn's antics would never be enough to divert the attention from the beauty Emory has stepped into, especially in this moment.

She waltzes down the steps like a queen entertaining her people. The intensity of her presence is like a temptress, drawing me closer with every step she takes. Her every movement resonates with an elegance that discredits the history her chaotic bloodline carries in the secrets of past lives. She stops between us with a short, sweet greeting. I can barely hear it over the thumping in my chest. For years, I have walked this earth, but this feeling is new to me.

We stand there, our eyes locked, and an unspoken bond forms a silent agreement that transcends words. The air around us seems to hum with a shared anticipation—the promise of a destiny intertwined. I bow to kiss her hand, and the world narrows to just the two of us. Emotions swirl inside me as they connect with her energy—an intimate dance of souls lost then found again. Her skin is \soft, and the air around is staticky as I catch a slight breeze of honeysuckle and vanilla—intoxicating.

I never want to be free of this scent.

I extend my elbow in hopes she will take it, and with the utmost heart-melting smile, she does. I look back at Niven and smile at her, accompanied by a gentle nod. "You two enjoy and behave yourselves." With a twinkle of her fingers, she waves goodbye, like she is Angela Lansbury herself, then she prances away as though the bed is about to leave without her.

Emory's pulse is subtle on my arm, a steady bump-ba-bump. Then, as Niven fades further away, disappearing in the distance, it finally hits her—the realization that we are alone, and I can sense her heart rate quicken. "Shall we?" I question, and she answers with a grin. Her desire for a deeper understanding boiled deep within her, seeping from her eyes, while the energetic atmosphere radiating from her was almost seamless in hiding her false aura of bashfulness. I gesture towards the exit, and once I receive her consent in the form of a shallow dip from her chin, I lead her out the door.

I start by showing off all the glorious shops her family has built throughout the decades. At the far left of the gates, there is a barber shop with a worn sign that reads '*Selby Barber Shop*'. It is the second building added to the manor after the Selby family bought it. "This shop was built for your grandfather."

I swing my arms from back to front, clapping my hands together as they meet before me. "After escaping to America, your great-grandmother wanted to make a name here." We stop at the storefront as I continue, "She wanted to leave something behind that would last through the ages."

She peers in the window, then asks, "Why isn't it in use now?" The look in her eyes is the same look I'd expect if she were to see me and my truths... *pity*. The state of these shops isn't too far from the condition of my soul—aged and hollow, and having no words worthy of using to answer her—I shrug.

I led her inside the old barber shop. My sight converges with my mind, bringing pictures frozen in time back to the moments in the past when it was once bustling with activity.

Where lively banter would fill the air, now it stands in silence—echoing back the void within my own heart. I, too, was once lively, but now I roam alone—a guardian of this ghost town. The scent of aged leather and aftershave lingers, a wraithlike reminder of days when the chairs spun with stories and laughter. Moving along, her curiosity piques around every corner we turn, as she investigates every piece as if peeling back layers of history intricately woven into the fabric of existence. It was only recently that the shops shut down for business, but longer than that, they have sat empty.

Much like me, the stores were abandoned, languishing for any nod at life. The antique equipment sits idle, clean, and perfect. Straight from the 1930s, as though we have leapt back in time, and I can't help but watch her. Being this close to her, with her acknowledgement and acceptance, is a feeling so surreal to me.

If only I could stop the world in this moment forever, even though I know that is too much to ask for. Soon, she will have to make a choice. She will either choose to spend a lifetime and thereafter... *with me,* or she will disappear as swiftly as she arrived. Never again will I be allowed to lay eyes upon her beauty, forever a memory stamped on the pages of past time.

Once she is done surveying the barber shop, we move on to the tailor, where the most lavish dresses and suits hang—A display of true talent. As we walk through the shop, the elegance of the garments matches the grace with which she moves. I admire her expressions as I am sure, she is envisioning herself in each beautiful piece, mostly because I am doing the same. Her eyes sparkle with curiosity and intrigue, drawing her deeper into the stories of her family's past.

Each item we encounter is like a hidden chapter of her lineage, awakening a connection she never knew existed. She listens intently as I recount tales of her grandmother's mastery with a needle and thread, her eyes wide with wonder and excitement. Her enthusiasm is contagious, and I feel a swell of pride in being the one to guide her through this journey of discovery.

We travel deeper, passing fitting rooms and registers, as her questions grow more eager with each revelation. "Your grandmother was very skilled with a pair of scissors, needles, and thread." Stopping short, she glares up at me.

Then her gaze switches back to a stunning flapper dress—navy blue with silver glitter that sparkles like stars. "I never knew her, never even knew her name." Desire encompasses her, "Just that she was beautiful."

"She was beautiful and still is." Without thought, the words are out before I can stop them. "I believe she is even more admirable now than ever."

Just like that, as if nothing else in the world mattered, she begins bombarding me with questions, "You know her?" Her eyes are like saucers as the excitement surges through her veins. "Does she live here?"

I stagger a little, trying to appear frightened, pausing to give myself a moment to recover a response. "Yes, your family has been a big part of my existence." *Don't ramble.* I tell myself in thought. "Yes,

I know her. As for her being here, not currently, but she does live here."

"Well, when will she be back? Does she know about my sister and me?" My brows furrow as I try to hide my sorrow. There is so much I wish I could tell her, but it just isn't the right time. No, there is so much she still needs to know before questions can be answered. She must have noticed my hesitation, as she responds, "I... I'm sorry." I use the padded side of my fingers, moving her chin to guide her gaze to mine, while stroking my thumb over her bottom lip.

"The time will come when all your questions will have an answer." With a long face, she nods, releasing a small sigh. I press on, "For now, I will be able to sleep better just knowing you are familiar with the grounds."

Suddenly, an idea sparks. One thing I know will get her mind off the subject at hand. "I have something I need to show you." I flatten my hand in front of her as I give her a semi-bow.

This can go one of two ways: It can strike a match of anger or open the flood gates of sorrow.

"For me?" She raises an eyebrow. A small smirk, like a shy little mouse in search of some cheese, creeps across her face.

"Are you going to take my hand?" A dark tone vines its way up my throat, "Or am I going to have to make you?" Then, the moment we shared in the alley comes into focus, occupying all the space in my brain. I struggle to fight back the intrusive thoughts that only get stronger as she takes my hand with no further questions.

I lead her to the next shop, and warmth floods my heart as I hear her gasp. Turning to face her, I see her hands clasped over her mouth, tears welling up in her eyes. "For real... can we enter?" She focuses on my face, waiting for my response.

"Of course, dove. It's your family's shop." I pause before I say my next words, "Your father's shop."

She looks up at me as I open the door, then barrels past me. It is nice to see her childish side, even if it is only the flicker of a moment. Closing the door to the toy store, I chuckle as she runs straight for the little wooden dolls.

"Lolli, oh my Sweet Lolli." She picks one up with blonde curly hair and a teal dress adorned with daisies and accessorized with white bloomers. "My Father made my sister and me matching dolls like this." She starts her story, but what she doesn't know is that I am already aware of this tale. She continues, "It was funny. Evelyn and I fought over their names at first, wanting to name them the same thing. So, our father, being the smartest man I have ever known, split the name in two. Lolli and Poppy."

I knew every bit of her life, and still, I drag a stool over, and rest one leg over it while the other touches the floor. With my elbow on my knee, I canted forward, illustrating my interest and eagerness for her to continue.

Quotes Most Desired

"Shit, I hope he wasn't an organ donor. I just ruined the perfect specimen." -Christian, Ch. 6

SLICEOFSANTIAGO

"Childhood memories are the roots that anchor us, even as we grow into storms."

CHAPTER 11

Emory

It feels like a dream to hold this doll in my arms again. My face starts to burn with sadness. I remember how the garage used to smell of cedar and herbs, while my father hunched over his table. His whittling tools are displayed before him, while a sage aroma fills the room from the incense burner, riddled with ashes, that sat perched beside him. The memory of the day he laid the dolls in our lap materialized before me.

Evelyn and I were five, I think. I'm not too sure. Our mother told us when we were older that she couldn't figure out what was wrong with us. If I remember right, with us being so young, it's not a direct memory. Later in life, she told us that while our dad was working, we wouldn't eat and we would sleep all day. He rushed home from work, quickly putting us in the car, no care for buckling us in.

Our bodies rocked with sudden turns, our mothers' arms wrapped tightly around us as the car came to a stop, and red and blue lights lit up the car. A shadow bounced within the lights as an officer came around to the driver's side. I could never remember the conversation, but it ended with a police escort. I remember that , on the other hand .

We spent eight days in the hospital with severe kidney infections, according to our mother's recollection. She told me that Evelyn had no issues with the nurses, but I went through three. According to the doctors, I had... what they called... rolling veins. My hands were bruised from the seven veins they popped before the last nurse decided to put it in my arm. Every day we spent in the hospital, our father always came to visit. When the last day arrived, he brought us each our doll.

Waking from my memory, my surroundings come back into focus. I realize I have been crying, and Oliver is holding me close and tight. His scent fills my nostrils and transposes my woefulness to adoration. "Hey, little bird, do you want to play a game?" His strong, deep voice breaks the silence.

His hand rises to my face to wipe a tear that beaded and rolled down my cheek. I look up at him, still holding on, "What kind of game?" My eyes dart around the toy store. Handmade toys line every shelf, and I'm searching for some board games or even a card rack—there are none in sight.

"Oh no, little dove," the bestial tone of his voice returns, sending delicious chills down my spine. Shing. I feel a sharp object skate over my skin, the familiar goose bumps superseding in its wake. I shudder as his voice comes forth again, "What do you say?" His words billow over me like the fog on that night in the alley, the object skidding up my throat, stopping to allow my chin to rest on the point like a balancing bird toy.

"What's the matter, little bird?" I open my mouth to respond, swallowing my words back instead. "Cats got your tongue?"

Little bird. My dove. I love his pet names for me.

With only a brief glimpse of the blade, I am startled by his snarling, "Run!" Oliver releases me as the demand leaves his lips, and I topple backward.

Stammering as I repeat him, "Run?" Unprepared, he lunges at me, sending me into a full-blown sprint. I dodge around displays and shelving units, still unfamiliar with my surroundings. My heart is like a pinball clattering around my chest.

He speaks again, his voice loud with the echo of the empty store. "I'm all for the game *'cat and mouse'*, but I've never been a fan of shy mice. "I can hear him tapping things with the knife.

Cling,
Clang.

He is looking for me, talking to give away his position. I can't tell if he is doing it to give me a head start or if it's his way of telling me:

'You can't run, nor can you hide'.

He continues, "No, mice scurrying is unnerving." More taps of metal on wood. "However, the flutter of birds' wings," I hear him inhale, then exhale as he speaks. "Now that's something I can lick my teeth to." I push my legs together and hold my breath.

What is wrong with me? Why am I so turned on right now?

Here, birdie, birdie, birdie." He stalks, still hitting things with the knife to signal where he is. I survey the exits around me, and there is a door toward the back, blocked by some display cases. I peer from behind the counter, shielding myself from his devilish stare. I notice his back is turned, and he is guarding the other exit. Giving no more thought, I bolt in the direction of my escape—the back door. Knocking one of the 3-foot nutcrackers from the countertop, catching his attention as the hollow wood sings from the collision with the tile. He is after me in the blink of an eye.

What? How? How did he make it across the building that fast?

The door opens to reveal a stunning courtyard that starts at the manor and stretches outward on both sides--a fountain shimmering at its core. Frantically, I take it all in, scanning the terrain until I lay my eyes on a hedge wall with an opening carved out to resemble an archway. Without a second to lose, I book it in that direction.

Before I can catch myself, I am eating dirt, tripping on a decorative stepping-stone protruding from the ground a little more than the rest, stopping my escape in its tracks. I can't even take a moment to assess the damage before '*My Cat*' yowls. "Little dove--**When** I catch you. I **will** devour you. If you make it too easy, then you **will** be punished."

"Torrential downpour," I mutter under my breath, as I place my hand under my dress. Feeling the wetness coat my fingers, I pull them into view... watching as they glisten beneath the late afternoon sun with my sticky stimulation. Wiping my hand off on the underside of my dress, I lift myself off the ground and brush the dirt from my knees, then head through the archway. As I turn in, an unworldly sight unfolds before me: a sanctuary of flowers, as a canopy of trees above allows minimal light to shine through, and slight beams that slip past the leaves to bless the flowers, aiding in their flourishing.

I spot a bench surrounded by an assortment of Carnations, and as I make my way over to it, I am bewitched by the black walnut seat, bestowed with intricate carvings. The backboard is adorned with a detailed dove, and something is written between the span of its wings. I tilt my head, while waving my hand, trying to move the overlapping branches and brush.

Suddenly, a hand covers my mouth to muffle my scream, as an arm coils around my waist, spinning me like a ballet dancer. "Too easy," he hisses, sliding his hand down my leg to the hem of my dress.

I fight against him, pounding on his chest with my hand. As my battle pursues, I scan for something, anything that would get him to let me go. My eyes find it like a heat-seeking missile locating its target.

That damned mask.

That might work.

No sooner had I grasped at the material shrouding his face, no sooner did I find myself plastered to the ground, his daunting shadow encasing me in darkness.

A rumble like an earthquake emerges from his throat. "That was not very smart, little bird." I slightly curse myself for wearing jewelry, as he slips his thumb through each bangle on either wrist, "I guess we shall see how strong you are." Again, my arms are lifted above my head, restrained by one massive hand while the other oscillates and glides down my body.

He leans in, whispering against my neck, "You're either going to be strong." He pries my legs apart, the war drum in my chest bashing louder. His fingers are tracking up my inner thigh, but instead of fighting more, I succumb and welcome it. I listen to his voice, "Or you're going to be smart." The tingling in my body stops as he does. Euphorically, I open my eyes and see his wide-eyed expression, for a moment, then it turns primal.

He rubs one, then two fingers at my entrance. His voice shudders and morphs between sighs and grumbles. He practically roars as his fingers slip inside me. "No. Undergarments? You are a naughty bird." What I used to think was a diluted English accent is now, clearly, a Cockney accent, and not diluted by any means—now he isn't trying to hide it. His fingers thrust in and out, pushing me higher. "Alright, dove."

I moan in response, while he continues, "I'll give you one more chance, make it this easy next time," his pacing is rhythmic, as he says, "And you'll need a safe word. For the punishment-" all sensations vanish, "I have planned for you." His voice fades, leaving me here, horny in a puddle of my emission.

Ugh, edging must be his kink.

Why does he keep leaving me like this?

Suddenly, his voice materializes out of thin air, and again he is standing over me. "Run... and this time make it real." I stagger to my feet, incredibly precocious. My knees buckle as he draws his knife once more—painfully slow, a serial killer who has finally got his victim alone. Pulling the knife into view, he rocks it back and forth, giving the impression that he is examining it. Then, his eyes are on me —a Kubrick stare sharper than the dagger he wields, then he inhales. Slowly, like a leak in a hose, he hisses, "I. Said. Run!"

All I can do is stand there in awe, his brilliant blue eyes changing and shifting into something else, something hungrier. Darker. Void of everything except the hunt. He charges forward, and before I can blink, he cuts my waist belt. A grimace smears over his face, one so evil, you would think a demon possessed him. "Run!" He shouts.

I start running again, leaving the garden behind. The courtyard comes into view as I pass through the cutout in the shrubbery. I am taken aback, as the fountain reflects the warm colors of the sunset in a breathtaking phantasmagoria of light—a single beam directs my sight to the base of the estate, where I find a set of bulkhead doors. I run to them, and as my hands fall on the warm wood, I let out a sigh of relief to see that the hatch is already unlocked.

Lifting the piece of wood, I stop to peek over my shoulder. Before entering the darkness, I take a final glance up at the sky. I push the chase to the back of my mind, overshadowed by the looming uncertainties surrounding the well-being of my sister. I see the sun and moon both present, knowing that one will soon disappear to allow the other to shine—my body shudders at this morbid truth.

NOTES

"Sometimes, the monsters we fear are only reflections of our own pain."

CHAPTER 12

◇ ◆ ◇

Oliver

Where did she go? I gave her a head start, allowing her more time to be creative. I walk through the courtyard behind the estate when I am, damn near blinded by the sun reflecting off something. Walking over to the cellar doors, I find the lock cut and thrown haphazardly to the ground beside it. Inspecting it, I can tell this wasn't my doves doing.

I open the cellar doors and proceed deeper into the obsidian shadows that retreat from the slim orange glow of the setting sun—into a darkness that callously inherits the dwelling as it evades the light peeking from behind the trees. Sadly, the hunt will have to wait, for this takes precedence above all.

I close the doors behind me, knowing the shadows will mold to my advantage. "Whoever is here will regret it." I stalk about in the pitch blackness of the cellar, making sure to offer little to no noise. All is quiet, then a sharp pain erupts in my gut, then another in my left shoulder blade. The stabbing and slashing were habitual, as searing pain forms on countless parts of my body. I throw my arms up—an attempt to block myself from my invisible attacker.

Splintering pain charges its way to my elbow, and my clothes begin to stick to me. A warm and thick substance coats my skin as the scent of Iron fills my nose... *blood.* I keel over coughing, as the syrupy liquid saturates my body. "Oliver!" I hear her scream.

The clicking of her heels echoes off the cobblestone floor. "No... *run!*" I manage to get out, but she is already at my side. I don't want her to see me like this, but it is too late.

Her hands touch my shoulder, and I wince in pain. "I'm so sorry. Stay there. I'm going to find a light." The warm hue from the bulb flickers on in no time, doing little to frighten away the darkness that clung to the musky walls. She gasps the moment her eyes find me kneeling, fist on the ground. I switch my gaze from my bloody forearm to look at her. "Are you going to help, or just stand there like a deer in the headlights?" I manage to strangle the pain, forcing the words from my throat.

"I-" She is shaking like a leaf. I need to distract her. My body quivers and sways as I get to my feet. Deep red lines have formed, indicating the cuts and their location. I start to slide my suspenders off my shoulder, making her believe that I'm trying to clean things up. Once I have relieved them from my slacks, I lung at her, pinning her against a Wine rack, and using them to capture her wrists and '*suspend her*' to one of the empty wine bottle compartments. I chuckle at the pun in my head.

so 'suspense-full'.

I reach behind her as she shrieks, "What are you doing? You're hurt, why-" She pulls and tugs, as I chuckle at her—amused by her efforts. I allow her to finish her question, "Why are you doing this?"

"Because I can." The tension my smile has on my face dampens the intimidation in my voice, "It's no use. I used to be in the Navy," I pull the strap taut. "Tied a lot of. Knots. In my day." I pull a bottle of 1812 Bordeaux from behind her waist—she winces from unknown intentions. "Now, since you made that so easy, we can just *'hang'* for a bit." I look her up and down. "Well, you can." *Ha! So punny.*

"Wait, are you not hurt? Was that all just a ruse to catch me?" I don't answer her. I begin tearing the decorative foil off the bottle, popping the cork with my knife, then I start lathering my wounds in the alcoholic beverage. The opaque liquid joins the blood and turns the dry parts of my gray shirt burgundy. There she goes, biting that lower lip again as she follows the crimson droplets down my body.

I use my thumb to pry her lip from between her teeth—a smear of blood from my hand tracks after, staining her skin a cherry red. I stand paralyzed as her tongue extends, tasting the little crimson line. I set the bottle down on a nearby barrel, as my eyes shift between her and the knife in my hand. Facing her again, I put the honed edge to my palm, then clasp my hand around the blade—the tapered end and handle leaving indents in my skin.

As I slowly slide the steel across my flesh, I study the emotions that flash and contort her face: worry, fear, and lust. Once the full length of the metal has left my skin, I slam it into a piece of the wine rack above her head—the steel bending slightly from the pressure. Cambering toward her, I elevate my right hand, now coated in red, and level it with her eyes—they widen with desire. Tightening my grip on the knife handle, as I thrust the other hand at her, engulfing her mouth beneath it. I observe as blood from the cut drips scarlet down her chin, while promptly, I feel her tongue rolling and lapping at the blood coursing from my palm.

I release my grip on the blade's handle to coil my fingers around the neck of the bottle sitting stagnant on the barrel. Slipping my head into the shadows, I take a long swig, leaving next to nothing in the bottle. "Mehm," I clear my throat, "Bitter... like my soul."

Then, coming back into the light, I trace her jawline with the closure of the bottle, watching as the remaining edge of the foil produces paper-thin raspberry stripes in its wake. With my hand still over her mouth, I bring the glass to my lips—gnashing my teeth over the malleable metal, I tear away the embellishments that give the brand its uniqueness, and without it, it's just an opaque glass container with a paper label. Once free from the close-fitting hold the fine metal had on the glass, I allowed it to fall in a downward spiral.

By the gods, I am obsessed by the look on her face—the one of

curiosity when she can't make out my expressions.

Especially in times she feels it should be easier.

Praise the All Father, for the shadows in which I reside.

With my hand still clasped firmly around the bottle, I drop the arm holding it, allowing it to fall out of the sight of us both—she flinches, as the cold glass touches her skin. I held her gaze as I rolled the crystalware from the top of her knee, up her thigh, and to the hem of that gorgeous green dress.

Smiling wide enough for it to reach my eyes, I give her a simple grunt—the only hint to my mischievous thoughts, she's going to get. Without wasting another second, I drag the bottle over her thigh, stopping briefly to tease her—swirling the opening against her clit.

Rolling the cold bottle back down the other side, I stop where her thighs touch, prying her legs apart as I force the bottle upward.

Ready or not, littlebird—you'regoingtocome.

"I have questions, and I hope you have the right answers." She gawks at me, confusion and longing doing the Lindy in her eyes— flailing and gyrating like a joyful couple on the Ed Sullivan show. "I am going to remove my hand, then you will answer."

She manages a nod as I take my hand away. "Did you make this easy on purpose?" My hand is fully detached now, and my dick jumps at the sight of her mouth glistening with the brilliant carmine red that pooled from the laceration on my palm.

"Answer me first!" She shouts, "Are you hurt? Is this part of the - "

I cut her off, nearly smacking my hand back on her face, enough force to make a pop. "Wrong answer," I say as I rotate the bottle between her thighs, the friction causing her to spread them further apart. I stop just as the opening kisses her vagina, then I begin rocking it from clitoris to opening, allowing her body to provide the lubricant.

"Now, my dove, this time you'll just nod." Mixed emotions flicker in her eyes as I proceed, "Did you make it easy on purpose?" Her eyes widen with expectancy as she takes a moment to think about her answer, before shaking her head. I roll my neck in an attempt to loosen the tension that builds up with her lack of following the rules.

"Wrong answer, little bird." She squirms a little as I slowly apply pressure, and the neck of the bottle starts to disappear. My hands get warmer the closer they get to her. I move my hand to the shoulders of the container as her body shows me all that she can handle.

Now coated in her discharge, I move my hand to the butt of the bottle to get a better grip, and I begin basking in the moans that escape from under my palm as I fuck her with this container. "Oh. My. Dove." I breathe, accenting each word at the apex of my thrusts. I am nearly hyperventilating, impressed by her consumption.

"Did you. Make. It's easy. On. Purpose?" The words barely leave my mouth. She nods in response this time, and a low rumble breaks free from my throat. "That's. My good girl. Now. Do you like me *fucking* you? With this bottle?" Her eyes are slits, narrowly open as her body trembles, while my wrist slowly oscillates the object bombarding her entrance.

Her eyes roll to the back of her head as she answers with another sultry nod. I switch to my dominant hand, freeing her mouth as my other arm wraps around her waist. I pump the bottle a few more times —my need to *'collect'* stronger than a bee's demand for pollen. "I want you to come, dove," I whisper before I remove the bottle, lowering my gaze to find it glistening with her essence.

Strategically, I push my shemagh aside, I bring it to my mouth —licking it clean, before my free hand tangles in her hair, clutching firmly at her nape as I yank her head back, forcing her gaze to meet mine. After giving her a devilish stare, I return it, pumping the neck of the bottle in and out of her. Faster. Harder. Her whimpers and moans echo off the cellar walls.

Using my knee, I prop up one of her legs, spreading her wider. Then, without warning, I extend one finger... then two, resting them parallel to the backside of the glass neck. I ache for her, as my erection presses hard against my pants. Just the thought of my fingers against the glass being the same span and height as my dick makes it challenging to hold back—from the shoulder to the mouth of the bottle, and the extra width my fingers add, puts it so close to my actual size.

Damn the gods, this woman would be able to take ALL of me with no issues.

"I want you to finish for me, my dove." I continue to pump, her noises becoming more hypnotic. I switch up the pace. "Do I need to count you down again, little bird?"

Without warning, her response nearly stops me cold. "Yes... my shadow."

Oh, fuck.

My cock was throbbing for her—to feel her.

By.
The.
Gods!

"Three... just for you, my dove. Only for you." I start the count, "Two... for our souls, lost and hopeless to find love." I move the bottle faster, mostly because I am turned on as well, "One... the only one for me is you, come for me, little bird."

On my command, she does, and I feel compelled to reward her —so I do, "Good girl." I whisper, breathy against her neck, and she deflates in response.

No words.

No arguments.

I very gently remove everything, and I admire the bottle as it sparkles like a thousand diamonds. I lift it to my lips again, cautious to keep my face from view. This time, I don't just lick it, I tip the bottle—the mixture hits the back of my throat, and I am in pure ecstasy. "By the gods, your taste is far beyond the expectations I set for it." As if possessed, I lick my lips, "It's as intoxicating as your radiant gray eyes and shimmering smile. With that said, my dove," I lock my eyes with hers, "Nothing will ever compare to your heart of pure gold."

"May I?" I extend my hand out to her, and she looks at me, confused. "May I escort you to your chambers?" She nods with a small smile, and I release the straps that bound her, catching her as she fumbles weakly with exhaustion, then we leave the cellar—all the while I stare at her in awe.

Please, please let me be enough for her.

The water roars to life, echoing off the mirrored walls of the bathroom, as I turn the handle on the tub. She is lying on the chaise, while I mix scents and shampoos in the water—my very own cauldron of aftercare, rivaling that of my ancestors from back in the olden days.

"Need any help?" I hear her whisper. Turning my head, I see her standing at the entrance to the bathroom, and frustration races through my veins.

"I told you to lie down." I scold her, "You should be resting." A small smile touches her face, and I relax my shoulders. Reaching out to her from my perch on the side of the tub, "No fear, it's nearly ready." She walks over and starts timidly undressing. I jump to my feet to stop her.

"Please allow me." I stop her, "The whole point of aftercare is for you to relax *after* and let me *care* for you."

"I-" She breathes, barely forming a sound, then nods slightly. I move quickly, positioning myself where I am towering behind her. I unclasp the dress, running my rough hands on her smooth skin, as I tend to the zipper on her side. Releasing the fabric, I watch its descent, astonished by how it ripples at her feet.

She is mesmerizing.

I circle her, taking my seat on the edge of the tub again, hand outstretched, beckoning her to accept it. She stands there like a lawn ornament, her arms covering her nudity. A small red patch on her knee catches my attention. Dried blood and dirt cover the wound, clinging to each other in forsaken matrimony.

Her hesitation is palpable, but she takes my hand, and I lead her gently into the warm, fragrant water. "The water smells wonderful. What is it?" She inquires.

"It's one of my mother's old recipes. She used to call it bath tea." The cloth on my face, for the umpteenth time, has become the bane of my existence. I want to feel her tender touch against my face.

The tension in her limbs melts away as she lowers herself into the bath. Cautiously, I watch—ready to catch her if she were to slip. Once submerged, her eyes close in silent gratitude. I dip a soft rag into the water, wringing it out delicately, before beginning to cleanse the

dirt and remnants of the garden from her angelic skin. The steam rises around us, enveloping the room in a cocoon of tranquility.

Folding the rag, I place it gently on her forehead, guiding her further down, as I watch her body vanish beneath the suds. The edge of the tub meets and cradles her neck, then her breathing steadies. Her chest now rising and falling in coordination with the rhythmic dance of my hands, while they follow her curves with compassion and purpose.

Each touch is an unspoken promise of care and devotion, a ritual that binds us in these moments of serene intimacy. I dip my hands in the water in search of her legs. In retrieving them, I place one on my thigh while she tugs the other away from me and leans it on the opposite side of the ceramic basin.

A perfect view if it weren't for the damned bubbles.

I feel as though she can read my thoughts, because right at that moment, she begins to sway her leg. A force that causes the bubbles to make a clearing, it has the resemblance to the eye of a hurricane—the suds, like the clouds, to the heavens--separate. The scent of the water is visibly soothing her, as it whispers secrets of ancient times, carrying the essence of herbs and flowers—a testament to the old ways of healing and connection.

She opens her eyes, meeting mine with a look of unspoken trust, and in that gaze, I find a profound sense of peace. The world outside fades into insignificance, leaving only the sacred space we share, grounded in the simplicity of our presence together. Bewitched by her beauty, I don't notice her hand—or the sound the water makes as it rolls down her elbow, forming craters in the bubbles, on its return to the reservoir encompassing her.

Without warning, I feel the steam strike my face as the material slips away. Rage breaks through like a primordial demon whose binding circle has finally been broken after centuries of rotting in damp and dusty catacombs. I grab her wrist with strength even I was unaware I possessed, and lift her from the bath, in this moment, "I Remember," from *The Phantom of the Opera* fills my skull. I hold her up until her eyes are level with mine—they don't meet immediately. No, she does a full once-over of the monstrosity before her.

It doesn't last long before the fury melts into desire as her face changes from fear to sadness. Still holding her elevated, I watch as the water sways in response to what I assume would be her other hand. The murky liquid, scantily covering her lower half, as music continues to play in my mind.

The warmth from her hand follows the scars that garnish my once-hidden face, from the judgmental eyes of this cruel world. My heart is beating like it would after running a marathon, now that the horrific side of me is on display for the world to see...

lucky me

It is only my universe before me. ·

Hatred and fear take my soul as a single tear leaves her eye, joining the dew forming on her cheek from the heat that hung in the air, like wayward souls down the river Styx.

Her touch is like a thousand butterflies' wings. "What-" she stutters. "What happened to you... Who hurt you?" Watching her sorrow shift to ire, her eyes blazing with a newfound loathing. It strikes me at my core, like a ferro rod to kindling. Her voice, though trembling, carries a strength that defies the frailty of her form. "Tell me," She demands gently. Her fingers are tracing the contours of my scars with a mixture of reverence and pity.

"Don't-" My face hardens. "Don't you dare pity me."

The soft presence of chamomile, accompanied by the calm of lavender, plays its part wondrously in the percussion for the ghostly melodies of our shared silence—now a haven for unspoken truths. The steam wraps around us, cloaking our vulnerability in its ephemeral embrace. Her eyes, as if speaking for her, long to probe deeper into the crevices of my past. The look indicates that she wants to know the weight of my pain and the shadows of my memories.

Her empathy, like a salve, soothes the raw edges of my soul. Dissolving it into the warm, fragrant air. The compassion she holds corkscrews around me, like the ribbon of an antediluvian scroll—binding us together in a tapestry of shared sorrow and proliferating hope. The sacred space we inhabit, once a mere physical boundary, now transforms into a sanctuary of healing and rebirth—where the fragments of our brokenness are not hidden but exalted.

"*Redemption is found not in perfection, but in the willingness to try again.*"

CHAPTER 13

Christian

Dusk has fallen, as we finally make it to our destination in one piece. It's only been a few hours since she was narcotized by the contents in the needle that the crackpot jabbed her with. Only a little bit longer, and we will be able to move beneath the veil of the night sky— the moon lighting our way. "Evelyn, sugar," I shake her, knowing she won't be coming down anytime soon. "Sugar, baby, please. At least look at me." A small flutter of her lashes is all I receive.

Damn it, Christian, think.

I lay her down in front of a tall shrub so I can peer through the wrought iron barricade before me. "Don't worry, sugar. He must help, he said he would." I notice the gate has already been pushed apart, and the lock is broken.

Fuck, finally a break.

I grab Evelyn's arm, sliding her over the back of my shoulders in a makeshift 'fireman carry,' then weasel the two of us through the opening. The ghost town that materializes before me is silent and devoid of light, with no sign of life whatsoever. As I carry Evelyn, we cross the massive grounds of the estate and up the stairs to the front entrance of the mansion. Before I knock, a blood-curdling scream reverberates off the pavement.

I step back as the screams continue, then dash around the back of the building. A cellar door comes into view, and as I lay my hands on the wood, I see the lock is broken. "That damned soul. This was, more than likely, their point of entrance." I huff as I try to change my hold on Evelyn, shifting her weight so it's easier to carry her. Then, like a lighthouse to a lost ship at sea... a beacon of salvation... far in the distance, shines a small, warm light.

I walk up to the building, glancing briefly inside the windows— avoiding the ability to be seen. It harbors a quaint little library, as the front stretches into a half-circle. Windows line the walls around the display of a little café, which sits snug in the upper corner, while the bookshelves disappear behind the barista's bar. I find a safe place to lay Evelyn's head, nestling her into some leaves beneath a winter-kissed bush.

I brush away the matted hair on her forehead and plant a soft kiss. "They'd better help you, or they'll be the ones screaming. I will burn this entire plot to the ground and rebuild our lives from the ashes." I reach up and squeeze the handle of the baseball bat hidden underneath my hoodie. "If I get even the slightest feeling that he will turn you away, they will join the other souls soaked into the wood of this bat." Tears bruise the back of my eyes as they torturously threaten to break loose, causing me to pull the Louisville from its homemade sheath and lay it on the cold ground next to her.

I hold Evelyn's frosted hands in mine, before I slide the hoodie from my shoulders to use it as a makeshift blanket—with hopes it will provide her with warmth. I watch as a figure peeks between the bookshelves. A petite old lady is restocking and putting books back in their designated places.

As I am here, I knelt alongside Evelyn. I recite a prayer I learned in basic, "Oh Father who art in heaven, hallowed be thy name." I look up to the sky, and proceed, "Thy kingdom come, thy will be done... on Earth, as it is in Heaven."

Looking back at her, I start to sing, stopping when I notice her crystal blue eyes are open and staring at me, pleading with me. Red and glassy, but that didn't matter—they were open.

Evelyn

What is this darkness that I am cloaked in? What are these random splashes of blues and purples?

The splatters appear like watercolors on canvas, then dissipate into the fabric of the void that surrounds me—it's like I've been lost in the ether and walking through the passages of time. Moments my soul remembers but my mind doesn't recall—fading in and out like the memoirs at the end of documentaries, that read, "In memory of…"

Suddenly, I am paralyzed, and my body is stiff, as a helpless feeling shackles me within myself. I can't open my eyes, nor move my limbs. I am petrified as the same words echo habitually in my brain.

It's your fault.

You are worthless.

You were never as special as she was.

YOU. DID. THIS!

Air whips around me as I fall, and the oxygen leaves my lungs while I panic. A cold sensation, like being plunged into an ice bath, encompasses my body—I still can't move.

Anxiety hits me, seizing control of my other senses, and that's when the scenery around me becomes more vivid. Then it hits me, and I remember this night--the only difference is she's staring at me. With fear painted on her face, she sits there, the depiction of an old oil painting—forever etched into the history of art.

The next instance, she begins to scream, but no words come out. "Emory!" I shout back, only to find it was in vain—I sit frozen, as my face catches fire from the tears that plummet downward. I look away from her, allowing them to fall, allowing myself to feel.

Just as I do, the voices are back, and this time they are right in my ear. Maneuvering my gaze back to her, all the emotion in her face has drained. She is just sitting there, straight-faced, glaring into my soul.

"It's your fault." She speaks, and the noise dies down around us, even the water as it rushes in through the car window... Is silent. *"You are worthless. You were never as special as I was."*

Finally, I scream. "No! That isn't true! You aren't her!" But that didn't stop it. Whatever demonic entity or dark part of my spirit that was trying to manipulate my memory of her continued with its torment.

"YOU. DID. THIS. TO. ME!" This creature wearing her face yells back at me, but I know better. Emory would never say that to me, but the figment of my imagination proceeds, repeating the last sentence, louder and louder.

Then silence, once again. I open my eyes after having previously closed them in a failed attempt to shut it out. I see Emory in the passenger seat, her head slumped as blood pours down her face—the true image I had from that night.

I can move now, so I duck under the seat belt strap. Leaning toward her, I slide my lower half from the belt—my body is now free, but she doesn't budge. Reaching across her body, I attempt to free her as well. When her buckle won't release, I try to pull the material over her head the same way I did mine.

No use, it's locked in place.

The mechanics are stuck, giving no leeway for the material to retract any further, and the water is rising fast. I yank the fabric in hopes of breaking the locking mechanism—to no avail.

I grab the belt where it meets the car, and just as I am about to pull, a voice, not belonging to Emory, speaks. *"You did this to me, Eve."* This voice was soft and cryptic, and there is a '*darkness*' about it. The words come out muffled, like they were being spoken underwater—the water has barely even reached our chest.

Immense pain.

A moment of silence.

My hair is standing on end.

Then, that creature is yelling again, an invisible force banging my sister's head against the dashboard as it hollered with her face.

"YOU. KILLED. ME!

"YOU. KILLED. ME!

"YOU. KILLED. ME!"

I pull myself through the car window... only to fall back into the darkness.

Longing for solid ground.

Out of my mind.

Scared out of my wits.

Trapped within myself.

I hear singing from a familiar voice and open my eyes to see Christian, but he isn't alone. There is someone behind him, and I am trying to scream, but the only thing I can manage is a tear.

Christian

"You will be better soon, sugar." A singular tear slowly trails down my cheek, a prisoner free from its restraints, grasping its freedom for the first time. I couldn't express the happiness and relief that filled my body as she sat there, her eyes open, looking at me. I will not allow this to happen to someone else.

*I **will** save her.*

*She **will** come back from this.*

*We **will** be sober together.*

*We **will** raise a family together.*

All while watching the gray consume the color in each other's hair.

My mind shifts back to the sight of Adelaide, so far gone she didn't even recognize me. It hurt… at first—until it dawned on me

151

that the person she loved all those years ago has died and since been 'reborn'. My past existence, the skeleton of who I am today—sallow-faced and higher than the bells of Notre Dame.

I hear a chime from the store in the distance, pulling me from my thoughts. Shortly after, footsteps are crunching in the frozen grass behind me. I turn to defend us and hopefully ask for help. Expecting it to be him. Expecting Evelyn's father—it wasn't.

"The truth, no matter how painful, is the first step toward freedom."

CHAPTER 14

Emory

I am floored. "What happened to you... Who hurt you?" Anger barrels through my veins. I trace the bright red lines, disfiguring his face like overgrown vines on an abandoned, dilapidated building. His eyes switch emotions like a television would switch channels.

"Tell me," I demand, but I am sure it looks closer to a rabbit baring its teeth.

"Don't you dare." His expression goes cold, and his brows furrow. "Pity me." He forces through a clenched jaw.

A few moments pass before I can speak again. "I'm sorry. That wasn't my intention." I soften my tone, "I just... have a tough time believing there are people in this world who are so cruel. So... vile."

He sighs with his whole body, as if he were a hot-air balloon releasing all its heat. "It's getting late. You should get rest." His voice begins to trail off as a loud ringing gradually drowns him out. A black mist slowly closes in around my vision as though I'm looking through a straw. The compassion that coursed through my hand was now flooded with an urgent need to leave his face. I feel my nails, sharp like razors, to my soggy, pruning skin as I claw at my throat.

No, not now.

"Oliver." I manage. Then, I am engulfed by the mistress of darkness, as she casts me into her pitch-black void of loneliness—her chasm of endless shadows. Now, when all feels lost, a light appears, its intensity increasing like that of an approaching train within a tunnel— moving swiftly along the railroad tracks.

Everything is so much more vivid this time. The water appears cool in color, as I wave my hand, parting the liquid with my fingers—a lucid dream, maybe? I feel I am in control. I try, first, to take charge of my eyes, looking around, surveying the environment. Things I don't normally remember take precedence, as I realize that the car is already fully submerged—not an air pocket in sight. I look over where Evelyn should have been, my chest burning as the tears I am holding back scream at the sight of the empty driver's seat. Seeing that I am alone, I begin wondering if she was going to save me.

Suddenly, as though my lungs were a bale of dry hay, a scorching sensation emerges. I pull at the belt that traps me here, and panic when the realization sets in that I am not going to make it out of this. My chest metaphorically catches fire from the lack of oxygen. My mind goes frantic, knowing that the actual process of drowning is going to be much worse. I try to redirect my brain and wrangle together my thoughts, when I am distracted by a school of hair curlers as they float and bob around me. Then, that is when it happens, flashes of core memories sprint a marathon before me—character-building moments that everyone involved would be affected by.

Is this my life flashing before my eyes?

All I can do is watch—I know in my mind I am crying, only my tears refuse to make themselves known, as they mix with the rest of the liquid that surrounds me. They are brief moments, enough to strike right where it hurts the most. Scenes that hit the hardest. Moments that, later in life, I thought we would look back on and laugh at. If I don't make it out, the tears that would have been joy will forever be tears of heartbreak and disgrace. Silly memories that would have given us belly-giggles will be the very ones she will be crying over if I don't make it out of this car.

I can see it now, memories like when I broke Evelyn's favorite perfume in a fight after I found out that she kissed my first boyfriend, will bring her shame. Every time that scent touches her nose, she is going to break down, and tears will flood her face. She will wish that I were there to break her perfume again, because at least I would be there.

Or the time after graduation when mom took us out for sushi. I couldn't believe we were able to convince her to join us in a game of "Poison" (where each person picks a piece of sushi to put wasabi under while the others look away. Then, you take turns eating the sushi till one of you gets the '*poison*'). If they ever go out for sushi again, people will witness a vulnerable moment as they both sit there... silent while tears soak their faces. An empty seat... harboring nothing but a memory of a time we all shared, haunting their happiness unbeknownst to the invisible bystanders, never again will they feel whole.

I must fight!

Just as I sit here. Trapped. Watching this panorama of my life as it flashes before me, I hear a loud thud echo like sonar. Then, the water starts to shuffle, as I observe tiny bubbles dance past me--completely unaffected by my presence. My vision blurs for a moment as my body is hauled from the wreckage. It was then that I realized I couldn't feel anything, not physically at least, but my vision was fully enhanced, as were my emotions. With that cognizance, I look at my rescuer, but before I can lay my eyes on him, I am awoken by a scream resonating throughout the manor halls.

Falling out of bed, I fumble to my door—enervated by my nightmare. Slowly drawing it open, I wince at every squeak from the old hinges as I step out into the hallway. It was, at this moment, that the squeaking hinges were traded for creaking floors—damned *old houses*.

Finally making it to the banister, I hear the main doors slam shut. I gasp, startled by the thunderous resonance they produced. While my attention is now directed to the orientation of the noise, I turn to catch a glimpse of the culprit that caused it, something shimmers in my periphery—a mist floating up the stairs.

It stops at the entrance to the west wing. Staring, I witness the anomaly morph and configure, as something forms from it. Or is it someone? A ghostly man appears in its center, looking around, and like smoke with a mind of its own, the diaphanous mist swirls through the air. Colors shimmer as they reflect off the light penetrating through the streaks that tendril outward from the form.

I lean forward, trying to make out any of his features, when my heart stops, from the floor sounding beneath my feet, forcing me to shut my eyes. A moment stretched on to an eternity, and I am *petrified. Mortified. Stupefied... then left mystified by this unknown force.*

Slowly, my heart starts to quicken again with the fear of whatever that was, and the possibility that it is now positioned in front of me. My hair stands on end, as I drop my head down now facing my feet, then I whisper to myself, "It's all in my head."

Alas, my body freezes, and my eyes skyrocket open. I can feel its gaze on me, and the air is now frigid, beginning to spiral around me. I finally got the courage to look up, but the apparition is now standing at the other side of the grand staircase, and curiosity shoves its way forward to the driver's seat of my brain. I follow it— Niven's voice echoes in the hollows of my mind,

"Stay out of the west wing."

What is so special about the west wing?

I stalk after it, making it to the mouth of the hall. My body is shaky as I stare down the corridor of the west wing—no signs of the entity that led me here. The floor is warping, as the wallpaper is peeling and cracking, like a raisin in the sun. The ominous atmosphere, accompanied by the lack of light, was giving slasher vibes. To a point, I felt that if I made it halfway through, a psycho killer with a knife was going to come after me.

An unearthly feeling sat stale in the air, and the suspense of taking my first step loomed over me. Finally, I scrounged up enough nerve to walk forward, and just as I did, the walls were set alight with a flash of lightning, followed by an obnoxious roll of thunder.

Creeping my way down, making sure to watch where I stepped, I can see what Niven meant by 'condemned.' There is only one door that isn't either locked or boarded over, and cobwebs hang thick in the corners, while spiders sway—catching things and eating their insides. I push the oakwood back, entering a bedroom significantly smaller than the one I occupy. There are two doors to the right as you walk in. One is open, revealing a bathroom, while the other is closed. To the left sits a couch and massive amounts of medical equipment.

The dressers are lined with old photos and vintage-style candlesticks. The windows are covered in thick velvety curtains, green in color. I listen, and when I feel it's okay to proceed further, I make my way to the dressers—taking one of the cold, metal frames in my hands. I glance at the faces peering back at me through sepia-colored eyes. A woman is perched on a railing between two men—her arms draped over the one with a striking resemblance to my father. Assuming that this man was my great-grandfather, I observe the surroundings. They all look to be in 1920s England.

His full beard and deep, cowled eyes are predominant beneath a wide-brimmed hat. My eyes then shift to the other man, and there is a familiarity in his hooded eyes. His face is clean-shaven, and an amicable half-smile creases his face. Then it hit me, and I nearly sent the frame plummeting to the floor, as a gasp escaped my mouth.

"Oliver?" It's got to be an ancestor of his. The resemblance is uncanny. It's impossible to be him--the scars are missing, as is the cloth that kept them shrouded. The thought of the gashes carved into his face angers me all over again, bringing back the glimpse I got before I blacked out from heat exhaustion. I found myself with more questions—the list growing the longer I linger here.

Standing there... photo in hand... questions forming clouds so thick a butter knife wouldn't cut through. Another blood-curdling scream rings out, frightening me, causing me to jump and pulling me from my thoughts. It's the same scream I heard earlier, only this time it emanated from behind me—from the only door that remains shut. I swivel, facing the door that potentially conceals this poor soul, pleading for help. More questions entangle themselves in my head.

Who is this poor soul?

Should I help?

Placing the frame back on the dresser, as I migrate towards the sounds—low moaning, the faintest scratching, and a rhythmic pounding every so often. My entire body is screaming, 'This is a bad idea.' I reach for the handle when my wrist is grabbed, and I'm spun on my heels. Oliver is looking down at me, his face hidden once more. His deep blue eyes bore into me like tiny daggers, each hitting a pressure point. Jerking my wrist to his chest, he draws me closer, no words—he didn't need them, though, the pain in his eyes and brooding vibe was enough. Not to mention, his body language was loud and clear.

He guides me out of the room, giving a slight glance at the dresser.

Is he making sure nothing has changed?

I never break my gaze—not even once. As we pass through the threshold of my room, he stops. "What were you thinking?" His deep voice breaks the silence.

Stumbling with my words, I reply, "I—I heard someone screaming."

"And that gave you permission to roam about?"

"Well, no, but-"

"But nothing, Emory. Something terrible could have happened to you. You do NOT know this place, and you were told not to venture into the West Wing." His aura is radiating betrayal, but why? I stand there, muted by my confusion, as I listen to him, "What even gave you that idea in the first place?"

He turns from me, facing the balcony. "Nevermind, that isn't what is important right now. Do not go wandering about anymore. Do you understand?" I hear him, but I am still stuck on the way he said my name. That is the first time he said my name, not the little pet names he is always calling me. I stand there for a moment, enamored by his use of my government name.

"Did you not hear the..." I fumble my words as he stalks toward me. It doesn't, however, keep me from continuing. "Scream?"

He interrupts again. "Do. You. Understand?!" He emphasizes each word. I let out a long, drawn-out breath.

Rolling my eyes to the back of my head, "No," I respond. "I *do not understand*." Putting even more accent on my words as I can.

He straightens his back and looks down his nose at me. "Are you being... defiant?" He pauses, giving the end of his question an 'oh really' inflection.

"Again, no." I straighten my stance, convincing myself of my confidence on this matter, "Defiant would mean you owned me, and last I checked... no shackles are holding me here."

The noise that left this man's body in response was alone, enough to discredit my statement. "They may not be physical. But mentally, I have you.

Hook.

Line.

And sinker."

He is in my face now, his nose mere millimeters from mine, "I am the only one who knows where your sister is." Deviance flashes in his eyes, adding a charge to the electric blue they adorn. He lets this statement sink in before he steps back. "However, if it's restraints you want, little bird. I can fucking give them to you."

Just like that, I forgot about the screams I heard. My mind hyper-focused on the image of me being chained at his feet. A plate of grapes beside him as he sits on the chaise like a king does his throne, feeding me like a captive Egyptian princess. Then, the image flutters—all the information my brain has received in a span of an hour, skips from one topic to the next. I get whiplash from the extensive emotions that rush through my system.

*Ugh, can my body, **please** make up its mind? Hot from the way he speaks to me. Bothered by his hesitation to elaborate on my sisters' whereabouts.*

Finally, I can convince my thoughts to focus on the images I had of my sister slumped in the alley, and the image that sent me on this path. I burn them in my brain, trying to form a constant reminder of why I came here in the first place. Squinting my eyes, I try to remember the differences in her face, but the only thing that comes to mind is her weary smile, barely visible in the dim overhead light in the car the night of the accident.

"Now that we have settled back on common ground..." he waits for me to come out of whatever trance I was in, then continues,

"What all did you hear or see?" The cloth dances on his face, as I imagine him licking his teeth—waiting for my answer.

Hesitantly, I do just that. "Common ground?" His words do more than pull me from my stupor--they infuriate me, "What makes you think anything you said put us on *'common ground'*." His head tilts with one raised eyebrow.

Fuck, this man can read me like a book, and he knows just how **spicy** *I like them.*

I sigh as I surrender, "I heard someone screaming and followed it to that room." Stopping as I felt him shift closer, "Not seeing anyone, I took advantage of the situation and went for the door. That's when you found me."

"Screams, you say?" I feel his hand brush my cheek, "Was there anything else you heard?" Holding that same hand in front of me, he smears the tear he collected between his thumb and forefinger.

I didn't even realize until now that I am crying, "Yes, in fact, there was." I raise my hand to my face, using my wrist to clear the rest of what little liquid remains. "Scratching. Moaning. Who was on the other side of that door?"

He relaxes his shoulders. "Please, get some rest. We have a long day ahead of us." He turns on his heels, right before he saunters out the door, without another word or answer to my question.

"*Sacrifice is the language of love, spoken in actions more than words.*"

CHAPTER 15

Oliver

Flashback a few hours

After Emory collapses in the tub, I lay her in bed and slip a petite, black nightgown of silk over her frail form. As she lay there, my very own… sleeping beauty, I tucked her under the covers. Kissing her forehead, I catch a glimpse of a pen that lay stagnant on her nightstand. Rummaging through the bedside table, I grab a notebook from the drawer. The lines form letters as they curve and swoop. Words appear on the paper before me as I scribble a moment more. Glancing at her peripherally, I steal one more glance—her body shimmering with the residue from the bath as it mixes with the beads of sweat forming on her pores.

Her breathing is irregular and shallow with spurts of gasps, but this is normal for what she was going through... for what her body was going through. By the looks of things, it's only going to get harder from here on out. Tomorrow, I'll tell her everything... and I hope she decides to stay. Upon leaving her room, I linger for a tick outside her door.

I fear that I won't be enough.

Although that is all I long for.

I want to be enough.

*Please let me be **enough**.*

I raise my fist, so close to slamming it against the oak, but the image of my sleeping beauty stops me. Not having the intent of waking her, I place my palm on the wood instead, then I make my way to the library to speak with Niven.

As I walk through the empty manor, my attention is drawn to the mouth of the West Wing. My chest expands as I take in a deep breath, then head to Niven. My plans for late-night escapades end abruptly before they even have a chance to start, the instant I make it to her side. "Mam, what happened? What's wrong?" Strands of her hair are popping out from the tight braid she always has neatly kept. At first glance, I notice it was loosely hugging the left side of her face.

The sound of her breathing is jagged, as though she has gone for a run. "He fought me. I fought back." I reach up, wiping a bloody tear from her cheek. She straightens beneath my touch.

"There is no need for you to pretend in front of me, Mam. All will be taken care of soon. Have you gotten any word from Mr. Selby?" That seems to be the straw that broke the horse's back, for in that moment she relinquishes whatever strength is holding her and falls to her knees.

Once I took care of Niven, providing her with a hot cup of tea and tending to her injuries, I stormed off in the direction of the west wing. Rage was building with every strike my feet made on the pavement.

Trying to simmer down as I push open the door at the end of the hall, my heart stops, and all my efforts go to hell in a handbag when I find Emory snooping around. After dragging her away from that door, a bunch of questions barrage my mind. The halls seem darker as I lead her back to her room—more than likely, due to my anger and frustration. I am in disbelief that I found her so close to opening that door. I remember, as I was dragging her out, I noticed the dresser—the dust had been disturbed, and finger smudges lay present on the silver. I said nothing as she stared at me the entire way back to her chambers.

As we step through the threshold, a small disagreement breaks out, and I say some harsh things—although most of them were necessary. She stands before me—spewing lies to my face. Beating around the bush, while she only gives me the bare minimum of the information I seek. Honestly, I can't blame her. I can only imagine what must be running through her mind. Not to mention, I have been withholding information, just the same, which might as well be a form of lying. Now I lie in wait for the questions she may spring on me. Working on the many ways I could answer them—weighing my options.

How my heart longs to tell her that Evelyn was here, but I don't. Instead, my brain convinces me it was a better idea to leave her standing there in the middle of the room, after I told her I knew where her sister was. The fact that I knew she had laid eyes on that portrait was only part of my hesitation to walk away. However, my mind outweighs my heart, and I choose to give her the time to make her assumptions before the truth comes out tomorrow. Before this world, as she knows it, crumbles, and all that she saw as normal becomes nothing but a distant memory.

Now I sit in my study, knowing that the answers she seeks will soon be revealed. The weight of the night's events presses heavily on my mind, and I can't shake the feeling that an unseen force is guiding us toward an inevitable confrontation. When I saw the door was secure, I never ventured back to the room in the west wing. I saw no purpose. The manor sat silent, save for the occasional creak of the old wooden floors and the shadows that seemed to creep—moving along the walls with a life of their own. Dust swirls in the night air as though dancing, and I can't help but hear the Moonlight Sonata in my head as I watch the specks waltz in front of me.

Resting my shoes atop the desk, my thoughts drift to the promise I made to her—one that I intend to keep, no matter the cost.

I promise it will all be over soon.

The clock ticks relentlessly, and I know that dawn will bring a new set of challenges. For now, all I can do is wait and prepare for the storm that is surely brewing on the horizon. I drift into a daydream of a past that once belonged to me:

A friend of the Shadow Raven, forever shall he slumber:

Wherefore dost thou—even on thine deathbed thy lie—extend thine, heart, out for me? Wherefore must it be that an angel such as thee be forsaken with a life as fleeting as a brook? I beseech upon thy skin of snow, thine hair now bereft of its chestnut hue—I pledge to cherish what doth remain of thee, as thou departests, leaving a fresh bride and a progeny to be.

As the stars dost twinkle bright in the dark and hallowed night, I muse upon a thought most fair. Eternally shall I be a thorn upon the stem of thy Rose—her steadfast defender, bounteous provider, a shoulder for her weeping—a brother evermore in her thoughts.

The illusion of what once existed fades into shadows—one of the many miserable moments in my past life I am doomed to endure. Observing my clock, I watch as the hands tick and tock. The silence is finally driving me crazy, and I can take it no longer. I am most positive she is racking her brain all the same. I did leave her with some very unsettling news. Not to mention, I am aware she saw the photo, and that is a story for another day. The only question now is 'How am I going to explain it to her?' I sink into my chair before I stand, pushing it backward. One, then the other, I roll my shoulders and adjust my posture, preparing to make my way back to her room.

As my hands fall upon her door, I shove the solid oak open. I am astonished to see her standing on the balcony. Slowly and with light footsteps, I sneak up behind her, wrapping her in my arms. Still, the rain falls like crystals from the onyx sky, as little beads cling to the overhang above her. To their luck, they have no eyes, for if they did, I would gouge them out with a spoon for stealing glances at my dove.

I can only imagine the glow in my eyes… as the radiance from the lightning in the distance pirouettes through the droplets that cling to her ivory skin. Her breath hitches as she feels my arms envelop her, and I sense a slight resistance from her before she yields to my embrace—a quiet reassurance in the storm.

"You need to rest, Emory," I whisper—my voice is barely audible above the precipitation. She turns to face me, her eyes searching mine for answers. The truth hangs heavy between us, a silent promise of revelations to come.

Running my hand from her cheek down her arm, and stopping at her wrist, I lead her back inside—away from the tempest. I know that tonight is just the beginning of a journey that will test the limits of our resilience and trust. "There is something I need to tell you."

"Oliver." She looks up at me, catching me off guard, as tears from the sky sit like diamonds nestled in her lashes. "May I go first?"

I nod. She lifts her hands to rest on my shoulders as I hold her elbows.

I am ready to listen.

"I didn't tell you everything. I did hear screaming, that part was true... but..." She delays a moment, long enough to release a slow breath. "There were photos... old ones, and because I never got to know this side of the family, I got curious."

"And?"

"And I saw a picture of a woman with two men. One of them—clearly, my relative. The other..." She bites her lip. I couldn't tell if it was shame or intrigue. "The other looked... like you, or a relative thereof."

"What if it were?" I cling to anticipation for her answer.

"Oliver, please tell me we are not related." I can't help but burst out in laughter. "Why are you laughing?" I try to sound serious, but I fall r*elatively* short.

Pun intended.

She, too, must have realized how ridiculous that would be. "You see a photo of a man that looks just like me and immediately think we are related?"

"Well, it's not like it is you, right? You'd have to be like 125 years old,"

I interrupt, "122, actually."

Her giggles are soft like those of a little Sprite. "Or maybe," She takes on a Dracula accent and wraps herself in an invisible cape, looking at me over her arm. "You're a vampire." It was when I didn't answer that her seriousness returned. "You're not a vampire, are you?"

I shake my head with a smirk. "No, dove, I can assure you I'm not a vampire. However-" Tilting my head back, with an eyebrow raised, "I would love to taste your delectable blood again." I can't help but burst out into the deepest belly laugh I've ever had, before the tidal wave of earnestness returns. "But the truth is just as complex and perhaps even more unsettling." I fight with my inner self, not to give anything away.

I want to tell her the full truth, but she just isn't ready yet. "The man you saw in the photograph is indeed related. The resemblance is uncanny, almost as if time has looped back upon itself—like a twisted reincarnation."

Oh, the irony.

Her eyes widen, and I can see the wheels turning in her mind—processing, computing, and reevaluating. "So, you just walk around wearing your Great Grandfather's clothes?"

"What are you implying, dove?" I can see that only the truth will work for her—she will continue to pry until the facts are all that's left.

She is too smart for her own good.

"Fine, what I need to tell you is..." Pausing, I try to find a way to continue, ideas clouding my better judgment, "What I need to tell you is tied to your family's legacy. A secret that has been guarded for generations. A truth that would shape our destinies in ways you can scarcely imagine."

The storm rages outside, casting eerie shadows through the room—I fight myself on the fact that the time for half-truths and evasions is over. I know in my heart she deserves to know everything so that hopefully we can overcome it together. We can face the ghosts of the past and build pathways of hope for our future.

I am going to do it—I am going to tell her the truth.

I walk over to the bed, patting the space beside me. All the confidence in me is fading as she takes it, sinking further into my gut with the caving of the mattress from her presence. So, I did what any 'Love-sick' man would have done... I began to tell her a story. "I will start by saying this—I will be changing names for the sake of some characters' reputations. Also, you must listen carefully, because it hides the truth about who I am." She gives me a look—raised eyebrow and all. I smile back before I continue:

There was a man who fell in love, and she happened to be the talk of the town—one of the most sought-after women in England. Her hair was blacker than a raven's feather. Lips as red as blood. However, the most interesting, well-known feature she possessed... was her name. It was only fitting that someone so beautiful, so forbidden, would be named after one of the rarest, most expensive flowers. Unfortunately, she was engaged to the man's worst enemy.

The reason they were enemies was, at this moment, unknown. The man knew the kind of monster his precious Petal was engaged to.

He swore, by the gods—old and new—he had a plan to free her. To rescue her from him and the arranged marriage her father put her in.

*The man never longed to be a hero—he only wanted to be **her** savior. He knew that his demons were far scarier and more feared than those that the Monster of a man could ever possess. One evening, the man heard screams—in following them, he found the Monster and his beloved. The Monster was attacking the woman, causing bruises and little pools of blood to form. The man could take the abuse no longer— so he intervened, pummeling the Monster within an inch of his life.*

After that night, the man and his beloved were free to live and love one another, so long as the man promised her father that no harm would ever befall his princess again.

As my story draws to its end, I realize she has fallen asleep. Glancing at the grandfather clock, "Only five in the morning?" I shuffle out from underneath her, allowing the weight of her body to fall into my arms. With one swift motion, I pull her to the top of the bed and cover her up.

I look at the previous note I left and decide instead I'll leave something better. I make haste, running to the garden in a hurry. I pluck a Juliet Rose from its stem and press it to my nose.

Please, if you can hear me now, let her choose me.

Back in her room, I place it on her nightstand, this time leaving the words:

Find me in the garden, where for centuries I will stay. There you'll find a clue to where I am today. Read the plaque, but don't delay —Come, find me at the dress display.

Smiling to myself, I exit the room. Making it back to the library in record time to find Niven pacing. Before I can open my mouth to say anything, she speaks. "Please forgive me, sir."

"For what, Mam?" Confusion contorts my face. "You've done nothing—as far as I know."

Liquid forms in her eyes until the tears jet down her cheeks. "The girl who showed up with the red head..." Her pause was concerning. "She is sick, and I don't think I can help her." She wipes the sweat from her brow, "It looks like she is reacting to a high one that doesn't agree with her, I might add." I can see she is saddened, as she continues, "Who are they, Ollie?" I glare at her, not ready to give her that answer—she backs down. "Fine, but there is something off about the guy's aura. I also saw a scar on his neck..."

I look down at her as I speak. "What does that have to do with anything, Mam?"

She sighs. "I am unsure, but it looks like a brand that was burnt off."

Of course, Evelyn took something, and we can't figure it out. It's looking more like I will have to take care of my unwanted company sooner rather than later.

Things are about to get interesting.

"Thank you for informing me. If you get any more information," before I could finish, the luminescence from headlights shimmers across the shelves.

"To choose between life and letting go is the hardest
decision of all."

CHAPTER 16

Emory

As my eyes flutter open, their movements are quick like butterfly wings. I allow my vision to clear before I rise like the dead to sit upright on the edge of the bed. The last thing I remember was Oliver telling me a fairy tale.

Scanning the room, my gaze pauses for a moment when I notice a rose that is pinning something beneath it, and I lean over to see that it is a piece of paper. The calligraphy is stunning, like the script you find on scrolls at the Vatican—or something like that.

Is this how it's always going to be, receiving mysterious letters from this... man?

I chuckle slightly as I twist my torso to reach across the bed and confiscate the objects. Once in my hand, I smell the flower, grinning from ear to ear, as the floral scent invades my sinuses. Then, I open the note and read it.

Leaping from the memory foam mattress, I spring to the wardrobe, with as much excitement as a child has on the morning of their birthday, knowing the entire day is going to be about them. Learning my lesson from last time—and the fact that it is still measurably dark outside and horrifyingly cold in the room already—I find something a little more flexible and less revealing. Throwing my hair up in a loose bun, I set forth from my room on an expedition to the garden.

Just as I am closing the door, I hear crashing and a sequence of loud thuds. Fighting the urge to investigate, while my legs are incapacitated—like hinges that have gone a long time without oil, exposed to the weather. Finally, I can move, and I find myself skipping down the grand staircase. I can't help but glance back.

I knew I shouldn't have. As I turn, I feel a rush of air—cold and staticky—causing my hair to stand on end. Then, a fog begins to rise and shift around me. I am glued to my spot, unable... to... even... breathe. My eyes dart from side to side, lingering long enough to recover their focus, then blur again. Suddenly, a face manifests before me.

What am I seeing right now?

Is it looking at me?

The phantom being is gone just as quickly as he had formed. I backstep, bruising my back on the banister. Before fear has the chance to cripple me again, I turn and sprint out of the manor to the garden. Making it to the archway, mesmerized as the rose bush materializes in front of me.

Aw fuck.

A vine protruding from the earth trips me, but I catch myself, landing on my hands and knees. Once I steady my breathing, I pick myself up and brush myself off, walking forward to the lone bush of roses that matched the one left in my room—progressively growing in the distance.

Now, at its base, I observe the stone... my eyes fall on the scripture—I drop my voice to a low octave, my words are breathy as I read it aloud.

"T'was an age of miracles, it was an age of art, it was an age of excess, and it was an age of satire."

--F. Scott Fitzgerald

Such a beautiful memorial. Hers and my great-grandfathers' names are forever etched in stone. Upon looking closer, hidden in the shadows of the well-kept rose bush was another placard. Careening closer, I read:

"Eternally shall I be a thorn upon the stem of thy Rose."

Here lies:

Oliver Albert Gaston

1899-1929

Adrenaline rushes through my veins as my heart rate quickens. Flashes of every image I had of him flooded my mind, distorting it, detaching all rational thought. I am startled by a shuffle in the bushes. Swiveling, I position myself so that I can flee—if necessary. A sudden scream breaks the silence in the now rancid air. I bolt for the archway —that is, until a man breaks through the darkness, nearly knocking me to the ground. Thankfully, I still had a quickness about me in my impaired state and moved before he could.

Enthralled by the events that are playing out before me, I watch as he trips on the same vine I did—and hits his head on the stone beneath the roses. Goose-bumps kiss my skin when the same fog I encountered inside coils and builds at my feet. Wind brushes against my side as the misted man approaches, his posture indicating dominance, his action portraying something more monstrous.

I feel a mixture of fear and curiosity, coercing me to stay rooted to the spot despite the chaos unfolding around me. The ethereal fog intensifies, as does the tension between the two men. My heart tries to break from the cage it's trapped in as the earth stops for an instant. The second man emerges from the mist, as if he were made of it. He glances over his shoulder—his eyes piercing and sorrowful—paired with a presence both haunting and mesmerizing.

I take a tentative step backward—my breath shaky, as the air grows colder—and the spectral vision reaches out a translucent hand. Our eyes lock, as a rush of images swarms my mind, like angry bees after their hive has been knocked down. This man of smoke has features akin to those of my father, the same eyes, too.

Is he the ghost of my great-grandfather?

The only difference in his eyes was the weight of the sorrow they carried. It has come to my attention that this man isn't the only one taking on the appearance of being translucent—the other man looks as though he has a pulsating glow surrounding him.

I watched as the man who was the aggressor turned from me to focus his attention back on the man engulfed by the spectral light. The scurrying he does at his attacker's feet, as he tries to escape, has my stomach seething. The offender stalks after his prey with slow, beastly movements. This isn't just someone trespassing. No, this man has wronged him. Then, in the blink of an eye, his fingers convoluted around the other man's throat, lifting him off the ground.

The smaller man bucks and fights, but he is no match. Then, with all the force he can muster, the bulky one slams the other's back into the stone. Running his face over its surface, then tossing him back to the ground like a raggedy Andy doll. No words, no context as to why this display of anger has broken out.

He continues to land punch after punch. Then, finally, he speaks —or rather spits. "I will make you suffer the same way they did. You have robbed me of everything, you low life!" One good fist to the gut, and the human punching bag falls to the ground. However, the beating doesn't stop there. He brings his foot down on the victim's ankle, a deafening crack calls to the fading stars as the morning was fast approaching. "Good. For. Nothing!" Raising his foot again, this time— it's the knee—the sound of the kneecap shattering echoes through the air, slightly muffled by the surrounding shrubbery.

"Answer me, you fucking bastard! Oh, wait-" Stopping to chuckle, his tone drenched in sarcasm. "I must make sure you are deserving of that title. Bastard!" He turns his victim's face with his boot, as though using his hand is beneath him, or touching him is infectious. "Just as I thought, no mark. Your daddy wasn't one of them, was he?" My heart is racing as I witness these events transpire.

"I'm guessing your daddy wasn't the one damned by that foul bloodline." He licks his lips, "No. No, it was your mommy. Yes—that must be it—for the mark to be passed down, you must have the right family ties."

Family ties? Mark? What is he talking about?

"You must be born of a son to claim the family name." Turning his head, he pulls back his shirt collar, revealing a sigil burned on his skin—A circle with a cross in the middle, as tendrils branch from its edges. "So what? Did your misogynistic grandaddy tell you that if you hunted us down and finished us off, that he would welcome you back with open arms and brand you—then all would be well?" The man on the ground gurgles in response, as blood pours from his face—due to a broken nose and jaw from being raked over a rocky surface.

The assailant pulls something off his hip, slowly teetering his hand back and forth, as the object loosens in his hand and unravels—falling and coiling around his feet.

What is that? A lasso?

He swings his arm like a pendulum—a raucous sound arises as metal scrapes over stone. The man on the ground must have had the same recollection as I did because he quickly rolled to his stomach and attempted to army crawl in the opposite direction to get away as fast as possible.

"Oh no, little Beast. You aren't getting away that fast." He draws his hand back, then immediately snaps it forward. A loud crack pierces my ears just as a bolt of lightning flashes, gracing the sky with its brilliance. A roaring crash of thunder drowns out the screams that follow... steel meets flesh, ripping the screams from its targets' defiant lips. I watch as the other guy stalks after his target using the hydra-like whip as a torture device.

*Who did he have to kill to have this man so unhinged, so... **primal**?*

"You are going to suffer just as they did. I am going to make you beg to whatever Gods you pray to, baby boy. I will make you. My. Bitch." the guy on the ground whimpers as the other one drops to a crouch, recoiling three times—an indication of knee injuries. Then, ramming his hand to his victim's face, he smashes it between his massive fingers, then dips his head further, so his eyes are level with his victim's—he continues. His voice, a humorous cry, "You are going to wish you stayed away."

He begins to wrap something around the other guy's neck, and that is. When I recognize the face coated in blood—Peter? Staring at the sky in fear, I hear the other guy begin to hum the song "Edelweiss" before dragging Peter out of the garden and disappearing into the manor.

Chasing after them, my movements lagging… the hedge walls of the garden… appear to be… closing in on me. Finally, I break through the arch, and I glance to my left. To my surprise, I catch Oliver's eye. He must have been leaving the library or heard the commotion and was coming to see what was going on. I look around and notice the misted figures have completely vanished. Finally, I pull through my mental fog, and I run to Oliver's open arms—the icy rain stinging my face.

He doesn't shift as he catches me, and my face collides with his chest. A welcoming padded wall while his arms act as a makeshift straitjacket.

What I just saw was insane, and if I don't talk to someone, I am going to lose my mind for real.

"Oliver, I need to tell you something." I look up at him, "I am sorry I didn't meet you at the dress display. I-"

He places a finger to my lips, "Not here." His deep voice overpowers mine, and he takes my hand, guiding me into the library. A glance at Niven and she is terrified.

What is she afraid of? Did they see it as well?

I can't help but feel there is more to this than meets the eye, and everyone else knows so much more than I do. As we move deeper into the library, the weight of the chilling encounter settles heavily upon me. Oliver's grip is firm but reassuring as he leads me through the labyrinth of shelves. I take in the smell of aged paper as it fills the air, using it as aromatherapy. The distant echo of our footsteps amplified my racing thoughts, each one more frantic than the last. Sheltered among the towering books, I feel a fleeting sense of safety, but the haunting images of the brutal scene play relentlessly in my mind. We reach the nook, and Oliver turns to face me, his eyes searching mine for any trace of the terror I am struggling to articulate.

I draw in a deep breath, ready to confide in him—knowing that the horrors I have witnessed are far beyond any nightmare I could have imagined. The air is thick with unspoken words—I try to speak again, but the library's shadows seem to close in, forming a cocoon around us as I recount the events that will forever alter the course of this fateful night. "Oliver, I saw Peter?" his eyes broaden as his brows furrow--a strange amalgam of fear and rage.

Was there something he knew about Peter that he wasn't telling me?
Could he explain the mist figures I have been seeing?

"Justice and vengeance are not the same——choose wisely which you pursue."

CHAPTER 17

Oliver

FLASHBACK A FEW MOMENTS

I am standing there looking at Niven, "Mam, how much time do we have?" My voice drowns out the sound of the doorbell as I walk back into the library. "I will give it to the end of the day. If I can't find something to help her, then she must go to the hospital." She was shaking her head, and I know she would rather just call for help now. "I informed the kid that I will do all I can, but I can't make any promises." Headlights redirect my attention away from her, initially causing me to head back outside. I watch the driver's side door swing open as someone steps out, slamming it behind him.

Brennan!

He glares in my direction, and anger is plastered across his face. He snorts like an angry bull about to charge, before he turns and storms into the manor.

"Brennan is home, Niven." I step one foot back through the library entrance, giving her the heads up, "I am sure he isn't going to be incredibly pleased with what he finds in there."

Her shoulders roll back as she gives them a little shake, asserting her confidence. "I am not afraid of Brennan and remember you helped me." The corner of my lip curls up in a smile, "I'll stay here and keep watch, but you should head over and tell him what you've done." She will not be pawning this off on me. "It is only fair that you tell him what happened. He deserves to know."

"Sir, I can't do this without you, please?" I watch as her eyes pull together in sadness. "Just give me a moment, I will ask the boy to keep an eye on her." Before I can protest, Niven jogs up the steps, and muttering can be heard as the whispers bounce off the walls and tumble down the stairs. I disregard them and pace—waiting for her return. A few moments pass, and she arrives promptly with a nod of her head. "Ok, fine, let's make this quick."

Once inside, I speed off to Emory's room. Releasing a sigh of relief when the door opens and she isn't there, meaning she managed to make it to the garden before he showed up. Arguing erupts down the hall near the west wing, startling me, causing me to hasten to the noise. With prior knowledge that Brennan can be a lot to handle sometimes, I choose to keep my distance. Finding him Niven and him deep in conversation, I stay back, lingering just close enough that I know Niven can feel my presence—their voices are in earshot, as I listen just in case she needs me. Brennan would never do anything to hurt her, though I may not be as sure after she tells him what happened.

"I didn't know what else to do," she says to him, her arms crossed—face crimson with indignation.

"So, you bash his face in. Give him a few good lacerations, and lock him in my grandfather's room? Seems pretty thought out to me." His cheeks begin to brighten with anger, "Where did you put Charlie, Niven? Where is my grandfather?" Stopping to contemplate, he stammers a bit before continuing, "By the gods, don't tell me you finally put him in a home." He begins to raise his voice, then checks himself. Forcing himself to rein it in so as not to use a disrespectful tone. "You're like 80 something, how did you even-"

"Oliver... helped me," she interjects.

Brennan's eyes go white as he rolls them to the back of his head and scoffs, "Really, you're going to go with that old Ghost story?"

"It's not a story."

"Oh, no? Then prove it." Before she even had the chance to open her mouth, I grabbed the sconce from the wall and hurled it at his head. He is a trained killer with reflexes like a cheetah, so I knew he'd dodge it—and he does. "Who's there? What kind of game are you trying to play?" he calls out.

"Really? Brennan?" she interjects, "I don't have time for this. If you won't take care of him, then I will."

"Wow, calm down, ok." He backs down, trying to brush it off like a teenager would their mom, after she told them to clean their room. "Why has this scum got your old ass knickers in a twist anyway?" Niven gives him a look that instantly made him backpedal, "Sorry, why does he get you all worked up and ready to get blood on your hands?"

She straightens her body. "This will be a long explanation, so I need you to listen to all… of it before you react, do you understand?" He throws his head back and crosses his arms, flicking one hand out— A signal for her to proceed.

"I was in the library—where I always am." I settle against the wall as she begins to elucidate. "A phone call came through informing me of an order pick-up." Her chin pulls in as she fights her emotions, "It was December 21st, and I was waiting for the shipment of the special holiday edition of Harlequin books. I came up here to check on your grandfather…" Her eyes begin to blink rapidly, visibly commanding her tears back. "I wanted to ask if he needed anything."

The halls are quiet, not even the rats in the walls scurry, as her eyes begin to shimmer, and her silent battle continues. "I asked him if there was anything he needed. If I could grab him something while I was out?" There is a flash of white as she snags a handkerchief from her cardigan pocket—using it to conceal the quiver in her lips, before she puts the cloth beneath her lashes, to catch the tears as they form.

"Werther's candies. That was all he said before I left." She sniffles, "Upon my return home, Oliver was screaming, and… no matter… how many times… I called her name. Glindaline was gone." I watch as the house nurse's name sculpts a type of disgust on Niven's face that even an untrained eye could see.

Moving closer to her, I attempt to place my hand on her shoulder, but she moves away. "I charge up the stairs… barreling through the door," her speech begins to break as her body starts to betray her and shake against her will. "As I get in the room," she blows her nose, then continues, "He was… lying on the ground. I raced to him, thinking, maybe… he had just fallen."

More tears break free and glaze her cheek. "I roll him over... and-and..." Unable to hold it back anymore, she breaks, "He was... c-covered in b-blood... his eyes... were-were... b-bloodshot. He was b-barely... h-hanging on."

"Stop! What are you trying to tell me?"

"Brennan, p-please" Niven, begs, "let me... f-finish."

"No! What happened?

Stop!

Dancing around it!

TELL.
　　ME.
　　　　POINT.
　　　　　　BLANK!"

"Brennan!" she yells, tears pouring from her eyes, soaking the collar of her cream-colored blouse. "Can you just shut your f-fucking mouth and give me the-" Now in a state of hyperventilation, she begins to form a stutter, and her words are choppy, "I deserve r-r-respect and for you-you to j-j-just listen!' Brennan walks over as I finally lay my hand on her shoulder.

Reaching up, he wipes the tears from her face. "Mam, I am sorry. Go ahead, I will listen." He tries to pull her into an embrace, but she pushes away—finally at her breaking point.

She screams. The cacophonous sound of her lamenting reverberates through the old, empty estate—crestfallen and full of sorrow—she beats his chest with a hammer-fist combo, each hit producing a leaden thud. Her fight does little to prevent him from engulfing her in his overly muscular arms, allowing her to blubber into his abdomen. Niven isn't a short woman by any means, but Brennan is pushing seven feet—even an average-sized woman would feel minuscule in his embrace.

She pulls away only to say. "That beast m-murdered your grandfather in... c-cold blood." She puts the cloth to her nose, "Then he used his b-b-blood to write on the ground next to him." Now covering her face, making her next words echo with the wrath she was holding in, "Down with the Selby family! the whole time listening to him choke." Her voice is strained as it fights against the raspiness that inevitably follows her bellowing, "A poor, helpless old man." She whispers.

"He s-s-stabbed him thirty-two times!

Thirty-two

fucking
times!"

Her wailing can be heard in the heavens—they are so loud... so strident. Something in Brennan clicks—and as it does, his hands move to her jaw, firmly cradling her face, holding her in place at arm's length.

"What... was written?"

A look of confusion contorts her face, "*Down with the Selby family!* Why does that-" His face hardens as his grip falters, and his hands drop to the base of her neck and tighten on her shoulders. "Brennan? What's wrong? Ouch, stop it, you're hurting me," Niven lifts her arms between his and then brings her elbows down, striking Brennan, causing him to drop his hold and stammer backward.

His gilded gaze softens for a moment as he makes eye contact with her, "I am sorry. I think you should go back to the library… and… lock the doors." Pausing, he glances over her shoulder at me. "Take Oliver with you." He turns in the direction of the West Wing, "I only have one last question." His eyes have darkened as though he were wearing black sclera lenses. "How long has he been here?"

"He came back a couple of nights ago, and when he did—although you may not believe it—Oliver and I were angry… angry enough that he helped me channel my energy," She squeezes her fingers into a tight fist, "So it would allow him to harness it and manifest." Brennan's lip curls upward, causing his left cheek to rise, along with his doubt that presents itself so obviously on his face. However, his uncertainty drops and is replaced by disbelief when Niven slumps a little, due to me drawing in a pinch of her energy.

With what I took from her, I managed to make the lights flicker, adding a little aesthetic behind her words. She continues to fill him in, and as they speak, their voices fade away, and I slip into MY memories of that night:

The weather was insane, although nothing like the past few days: a cold spring with a shower or two of freezing rain—the real snow normally happens in January. This night was a devastating phenomenon.

I was sitting in that room with Charlie, a low crackling fire to keep him warm. As they went on, he carried out full conversations with me—even though he couldn't see me.

Not the way Niven could.

He knew I was there for him from the moment he was born, even then, as he was suffering from dementia, and most of the conversations were the same. That night, he was remembering stories about his mother. "All roses... pretty roses. Ring around the Rosie. Can I have a rose, Ollie?" He calls out to the empty room. "Mother has one, may I have one too?" For old times' sake, I obliged.

The ambient glow from the fireplace, as the flames pulsed and flickered, was the only light against the thick darkness that consumed the rest of the room. I got to my feet, standing in front of the chair adjacent to him, then made my way over to grab one of the many roses he kept on the mantle.

No sooner had my hand met the marble than the air began to shift. Suddenly, chills ran down my spine—we were no longer alone, and I knew it. Quickly attaining one of the roses, spinning on my heels, the tension lessening when I saw that he had fallen asleep—at least that is what I had hoped happened. Moving over to him, I placed one hand between his shoulders, the other on his forehead, guiding him back to avoid the formation of a kink in his neck.

That's when I saw it out of the corner of my eye, a figure darting and dodging—a failed attempt at staying out of what pinpoint light there was. I stood there listening to some shuffling that sounded a few feet behind him. My body was rock solid as I allowed my eyes to adjust. Slowly, rotating around his chair, still scanning for any sign of movement, my eyes met the gaze of the perpetrator. I knew they couldn't see me, so I glared at them—watching as they made their way to stand where I just moved from, giving Charlie the once-over.

That's when it happened. Charlie opened his eyes and threw himself at the trespasser. It all happened so fast. "I knew one day you'd come for me, Theodore." A loud 'shing' presents itself, followed by a groan of pain. The assailant's arm thrusts in and out as they begin to sink their blade into him repeatedly.

I was overwhelmed by the sheer escalation of the events that transpired before me. I lost count as his body fell... lunging, I tried to catch him—forgetting the obvious reality of my existence, I cried as he passed right through my arms.

A ripple of hope that there was still a chance he could be saved caused me to run to the window, but Niven's car was gone— surprisingly, so was the house nurse. I stood there, stunned, while the intruder was already out the door—I couldn't even recover from the tragedy I had just witnessed. Once my mobility returned, I ran to the door, down the stairs, and was able to catch the make and model of his car.

As the memory comes back, it hits me like a freight train. The way the car sped off that night was familiar. Then it clicked, not only did this intruder kill Charlie, but he was also the driver involved in the accident that had furthermore changed my Dove's life. My mind slips back into the memory of that night.

*Rushing back to his side... doing all I could do... cradling his old, fragile body in my arms—knowing that it was impossible... **unless**. The time slipped by, and morning crept ever nearer. I held him and cried—his dementia was too advanced for his soul to have any unfinished business. I am no stranger to the deep sense of loss.*

Words cannot begin to describe how much I suffered through my subsistence—he was my tether after his mother passed... the prodigal son, and my oath to her was to stay and protect him. He had always been a comforting constant in the labyrinth of my existence. The memories of that night will remain etched in my mind—a haunted image, an indelible mental scar that reminds me of the fragility of life and the ruthlessness of fate.

If it weren't for that night, Emory wouldn't be here today, because staying here with Charlie was the reason I was late. His death would be the first time I ever failed her and the last. Each day after felt like a tribute to his enduring spirit and the legacy he left behind—a legacy that shaped who he was and, in turn, who we are.

The echoes of his stories, his laughter, and his unwavering bravery lingered in the air—a silent testament to a life well-lived. And now, as the shadows of the past weave into the fabric of the present, we must confront the darkness that seeks to engulf us.

As I shake myself from the memories that haunt me, Brennan and Niven are breaking from a much-needed embrace. "You give him hell for me and your grandfather." I've never heard her so spiteful… so angry. As Brennan turns to go into his grandfather's room, Niven glares at me. Already aware of what the stare means, I listen as she speaks anyway.

"You make sure that bastard gets more than what he deserves."

"I can't stay long, I have to meet Emory in the dress shop," I peer down at her and give her a slight head bow, "But I will make sure he hurts for all three of you."

Her expression turns from hatred to confusion. "Three of us?"

I square my shoulders before I speak. "He was driving the other car that ran them off the bridge."

"Are you certain?" I nod again, as she continues. "Very well, I'll be in the library. Tell me every detail you can when you see me next." She pats my back on her way past me. Once she has cleared the doors and vanished, I turn to face the West Wing—following Brennan in stride.

The screams are deliciously loud as I enter the room. The door to the right is open now, and claw marks are carved into the oak like a wild beast had been trapped inside. Moving forward, Brennan is standing over the not-so-poor creature—a killer over his prey. "It was you, huh?" Brennan crouches in front of his victim.

Cracking every knuckle in sequence before he grabs the man's face firmly in his oversized hands. "Makes me wonder if you are the one who called the hit on me a year back." Spit flies, landing in Brennan's eye—a thunderous cackle bursts from his throat as he puts two fingers on the globe of mucus. Positioning them in front of the unaffected eye, he rotates his thumb, smearing the fluid between all three fingers. Then, in a flash, the back of Brennan's hand splits the guy's lip.

"Who are you?" Brennan demands. His anger is an anchor for the events that follow, while a sneer crosses his face. Once no answer is provided, Brennan begins to sway to the percussion of blows—back and forth—a metronome of lefts and rights. He delivers a powerful open-palm strike, but not enough to break his quarry's jaw—it's not his intention to keep him from talking.

His victim stops swaying and rocks back and lifts his face, unrecognizable, with both eyes bloodied. "I'm not… giving you shit!" He grunts between labored breaths. His voice is familiar—nasally.

A venomous smile stretches over Brennan's face, twisting up on one side, revealing his canines as he clicks his tongue. "I'll ask again, if not you, then who put it out? Hmm?" he reaches for his belt and unhooks a whip-like object—a cat-o'-nine-tails, to be exact. "Look, you already aren't getting out of here. So, might as well fess up."

Focusing way too much on the new toy he brought out, I almost didn't hear what he said. I have never seen one like that before:

Seven individual cables.

Eight feet long.

Braided steel.

Fraying on each end.

I am, briefly, distracted by the glint of a talon-shaped blade spinning in his hand as he circles the pathetic trash on his knees before him… torturously pressing it to his back. "Who the fuck knew where to find me?" Brennan raises his hand--the whip in one hand and a stunning blade in the other. I am torn by which weapon to look at, but that is decided for me when the tip of the knife catches onto the hem of the prisoner's jacket, stopping Brennan mid-interrogation.

A navy-blue button-up peeks out from beneath the hoodie—parting like silk under a seamstress's blade with the mere kiss of the tapered metal. Brennan chuckles, "Silk? That's a little fake and gay if you ask me." Then, proceeds to drag the knife up towards the nape of his neck. The point vanishes in his hair, where blood adds to its multiple shades of red. The pressure, although minimal, grazes his spine—the steel so sharp it causes a thread of crimson to follow in its wake.

Brennan shifts his other hand, the many tails of metal purr as they run across the wood, pulling them up to place them around his neck—draping them over his shoulders like a stole, before grabbing the man by the throat. Brennan's arms barely waver as he elevates him, and the veins in his arm pulsate with epinephrine—he lowers him where their noses touch.

"Not going to tell me?" He spits. "No biggy. Let's discuss which family, then."

Launching the man into the foot of his grandfather's hospital bed, Brennan shouts in German. "Steh auf, du arschloch!" The man stands, as told, then Brennan throws a quick jab to the man's throat, dropping him to his knees—clutching at it, gasping for air.

Clutching some IV tubing, Brennan snatches him off the floor and hauls him to the bigger room, shoving him to the floor, where a faint brown spot still torments my forsaken soul. Using the tubing, he ties the man to the mantle. He turns to face the rest of the room, before pacing over to the pre-lit fireplace—a fire, like a group of exotic dancers, throwing small ripples of light across the floor. "What family sent you, peasant?" he inquires, cleaning the underside of his nails with the blade.

When the room remains silent, he slides the whip from his shoulders, and an almost chain-like sound rumbles across the hardwood floor. "I heard you murdered my grandfather." Brennan cracks his neck, "So, your silence is not allowed. You will either answer my questions, or the desolate halls of this manor will spring to life with your screams." Then, he rolls his shoulders. "Old hallways, which have long since forgotten the vibrations of any sound, will now be charged by the melody of your pain."

"Fuck you, fucking Selby swine." He draws the length of the whip and flicks his wrist. The screech that erupts from the whipping boy's mouth, as the steel struck his back, sends a spark of energy up Brennan's spine—he shivers ever so slightly. "Ravel in A-Sharp? I figured you were more of a Mozart man."

Brennan laughs, mocking the higher pitch of the fool's screams. "I will only ask until the symphony of life has left your body. So, again... what family?" He stalks closer, "The Rougeou's... No, they understand what it means to cross me after the last time." He draws the whip back again, releasing it forward faster than I could blink.

"The Lee family... now, they love hiring me for cleanup. They tend to get... a bit messy." He turns, smiling, and the light plays maliciously over his face. Using his tongue, he lets out a... *tsk-tsk-tsk*. "The Downey family, then... it makes sense." He stops his pacing. "You reek like a bottom-dweller."

The man shuffles and looks over his shoulder. "Fucking filthy pigs, the lot of your inbred family." The man bellows back, "My Grandfather is Theodore fucking Downey, and he'll have your head for this!"

"Where are my manners, Downey, do boy?" This time, Brennan spins and fully extends his arm with a graceful motion. Taking a half-ass bow, as a low cackle transmutes into shouting as he comes full circle, "Did you *forget* your *fucking* place! Did you not *realize* where the *fuck* you are!" Brennan's body started to shake. "You may not be aware of this, but I am Brennan Selby, and the only BS I take is my initials."

You are the *lowest* of the *low*!

A fucking *pebble* in my *boot*—noone likes a *pebble* in their *boot*!"

He roars as he snaps his arm like a spring—the muscles ripple and flex, pushing the vessels to distinct visibility for a moment. All seven of the whip's strands catch the captive on his face and side. A strike strong enough to split skin, shred muscle tissue, and leave the right eye a mess, oozing what could only be ocular fluids. I relish watching it slowly collapse and fall out of the socket.

Brennan coils the scourge and fastens it through a belt loop in such a manner that, if necessary to release it, all he had to do was pull. Storming over to his bound prisoner, Brennan draws in his knee, stopping once it hits his chest, then, with full force, he plants his foot firmly against the man's hip. The prisoner screams—his cries marinated in the agony his body is undergoing.

His hand flies like a saucer to meet its target, while the screams transcend from a piercing pitch to a scratchy gargling tone. Bending over, he whispers, "Don't you ever think your life is worth something to me." He spits on the man's face, "My life prior was spent teaching lessons of death. From the delicate crime of passion to the visually deprived, premeditative slaughter."

Brennan then stands tall—taller than I've ever seen, like he was growing by the second. "I'll ask. One. Last. Time. Did you put out the mark on my head?" Entangling his fingers in his victim's hair, he yanks his head back, "OR do I need to continue my entertainment?"

The man began to sob, and his broken words fell out in sputters. "I-It was m-m-my uncle." The man slumps over, still breathing but unresponsive.

He fainted, seriously?

"That's a good boy, get your rest, I have much more in store for you," Brennan whispers as he releases the captives' hands—then ties them behind his back, as he attaches them to his belt. When done, he stands up, and parades over to the curio cabinet—my focus is back on the Downey low life.

A distinct sound of a crystal decanter clinks, followed by the sharp staccato of ice dropping into a glass. Heavenly ticks and cracks sound off as warm liquid caresses the ice—filling the glass. The light baritone pulse of the bourbon rushing through the aperture of the glass bottle, reminding me of... Auld Lang Syne... as a drink is poured.

Aw, I miss the smell of an old-fashioned with Honey, not to mention the taste.

My eyes wander to the grandfather clock, then back to the body at the foot of the fireplace.

I should have time to meet Emory and get back before he comes to.

Leaving Brennan to his thoughts, I make my way out of the West Wing, but by the time I make it to the bottom of the staircase, a gust of wind dashes past me. As I recover from my momentary discombobulation, I am startled as the front doors slam. I turn back to the hallway to see Brennan—his anger dyes his skin beet red as he stalks out the doors.

Following, I see Niven standing just outside the bookstore. I make my way over to her. I throw my hands up in preparation for what I have predicted would come next. "What in the name of the gods happened in there?" she questions. Moments pass as I fill Niven in on the atrocities that took place in the west wing, and before I know it, Emory is running at me—fear plastered to her rain-kissed face. I looked to Niven for help on what to do next, but she had already gone back inside and was standing behind the counter as we walked through.

My hand firmly around Emory's wrist, quickly, we writhe between the towering bookshelves. Emory says something to me breathlessly, but I don't quite hear, so I respond with a simple two-word response, "Not here." Seeing how that seems to work, I lead her to the nook. Turning to face her, I can see she has a lot to tell me.

Her fear cannot be present when she speaks, for I know the conversation would be easier if she were calm. Using my fingers, I brush her rain-soaked hair from her face. Looking into her eyes, I lock my lips with hers. This was the first time I would kiss her pain away, and I knew it wouldn't be the last.

NOTES

"Healing begins when we allow ourselves to be seen, scars and all."

CHAPTER 18

Emory

His lips… hot against my cold face, a split-second of passion. Pulling away, he clears his throat, "We should get you out of these cold clothes. You'll catch your death if you stay in them."

"Really," I chuckle, "That's all you got?"

"Maybe." He shrugs his shoulders. "Is it working?"

"Oliver," I close my eyes, sighing before I proceed, "As much as I want and need this, there are things I need to talk about first."

Wrapping his arms around my waist, he leans back. "And I will listen." A half-smile peeks from the corner of my mouth.

"Wonderful. First question: Why is Peter here? Did he show up with my mom?" I know I said one question, but the words just got away from me—apparently, this affected me more than I thought it had. I begin spouting off more questions, "Are they looking for Evelyn also? If so, where is my mom?"

"Peter?" His face twists. "Your mom's boy toy?"

"Yes, I thought I saw him in the garden. Something... or someone... was chasing after him. I barely recognized him. He didn't look well. He was covered in injuries, and the other... thing... didn't seem to have it in its thought process to lighten up." Oliver's features harden. His hand rises before me—an indication that he needs me to pause. "I'm done with this conversation."

Pulling away from his embrace, "What-" I bark back. "What do you mean by that?"

"Done, Emory. Finished. No longer entertaining the topic of discussion." My anger simmers over like a pot left on the stove too long.

I slam my fist into his chest. "What are you not telling me? I came out here to find my sister. I've gotten nowhere in the search for Evelyn." I want to cry, but my anger has my face so hot the tears turn to steam before they get the chance to fall. "There has been no word from my father. If you don't start telling me what is going on, I am leaving."

Why is he looking at me like that?

I can't take it.

*Is he... **really**... sad?*

Turning away from me, he disappears behind a display of old books. My curiosity getting the best of me, I follow. Dust is caked thick in a line behind the shelving unit, as a trap door leading somewhere secret is revealed to us. Yanking the warped, wooden, squared-off barricade open, we step into the darkness of the unknown—a massive room unfolds.

A soft light adds a significant amount of coverage, bathing the chambers in a warm saffron glow. To my utter astonishment, apparatuses occupy every corner—each with its own respective space.

"What?" My curiosity and I are out of our comfort zone. "Is this place?"

"None of this belongs to me, aside from the bed." Looking around, I don't see a bed, but that changes when he draws back one of the obsidian curtains.

Displayed before me is a Gothic, unhinged, dark romance girl's fantasy come true. The four-poster bed is made of ebony. Black lace drapery encloses the king-size mattress, dressed in an onyx shade of silk. Shackles reflect the candlelight as they hang from the headboard, while three holes were cut out of the footboard—one hole was slightly larger than the other two. Four silver hooks stand erect on either end with no signs of the chains they harbor.

"Don't worry, dove," he snickers, "You're going to be in control this time."

"I said-" A sigh leaves me as I cross my arms and huff. "I needed to talk first." He slides his suspenders from his shoulders, and flashbacks to our time in the cellar invade my mind.

"You want to talk—I want release." His low, sultry voice breaks my thought, "Now, how good are you at tying knots?"

The words leave my mouth before I can stop them. "I'm better at untying them," I say under my breath, "Shit."

He raises an eyebrow. "Is that so, little bird? That's fine, the cuffs will suffice." He starts to inspect them, lifting them with harsh movements—purposefully forcing them to make the spine-chilling clatter.

According to his reaction, I am making a face because he feels the need to reassure me. "Not for you, for me... remember. Don't get too excited."

I can't help but think—I'm still going to be the one in the cuffs. That thought quickly disappears when he fastens one onto his wrist, and my mouth drops open.

"Didn't you have something you wanted to talk about?" Asking as he positions himself on the bed. Bewilderment, like stucco on my face—an overlay for my excitement. It still isn't enough to take my mind off my troubles.

"Are you going to help?" His voice pulls me from my thoughts, and I look at him as he continues, "I'm beginning to think you are a watcher—if that is the case, this is going to be more difficult than I thought." He breaks out into a fit of laughter.

As he lies there on the bed, his many shades of gray adding an appetizing allure, I find myself panting like a bitch in heat. "I'm serious, Oliver." My voice cracks as he lifts his left hand, placing it strategically over his cock. Flexing it—just enough, so his veins do that... vein thing that makes all the romance chicks go feral. "Fine, I'll play your game then."

I fucking broke.

"No, you want answers… remember? How do you go from *'I'm being serious'*, to *'Fine, I'll play your game'*?"

Fuck he is even stunning when he tries to mimic my voice.

Throwing my hands up, "How?" I say a little snippy. "When the one who has the answers won't have it any other way." My answer even comes out snide as I snap my eyes shut, pretending I didn't see him shift his pelvis.

"Damn right, dove. You don't play—you don't get answers." His snicker makes me want to punch him, and it doesn't get better as more words leave his mouth, "Also, if you play the right way, I will give you more than answers in return. Do we have a deal?"

"Fine," my eyes roll to the back of my head. "Whatever you say." The word rolls off my tongue with annoyance.

"Good, now start by restricting me to this bed. In the process, you can ask your first question." My anger is at its boiling point, and his carefree attitude isn't helping. So, I decided that I may have more fun with this than I had planned. I put the other cuff around his left wrist, the sound triggering an unfamiliar sensation in my body. It felt electric and exhilarating. I may have also slapped them on, harder than he wanted—*my full intention.*

"Oh, dove, are we going to play rough? Did I piss you off that much?" The devilish look in his eyes offers no aid in satiating the hunger stirring within me. He continues, "It only takes five steps, so you only get five questions—make them count. Step one: The cuffs"

"Okay." What I chose to start with catches him off guard, "Are you a junior, or a third, however those things go."

Clamping his knees together, he uses his upper body strength to hoist himself a little higher. "Are you against sitting?" I look at all

the space around him as I nibble at the inside of my cheek. My gaze meets his again, and I shake my head in response. With a stiff wave of his right hand, he motions for me to sit. Being as short as I am, lifting myself to get on this bed is a challenge—an open opportunity for him to crack jokes.

You got this lil'bit.

Don't fall, half-pint.

I won't be able to catch you.

Once I'd managed to procure myself on the bed alongside him, I nearly crumbled with how sinfully comfortable it is.

Settling myself before his crossed legs, the bed shifts beneath his weight as he wraps his legs around me. "Reach in my pants."

Rage breaks to the surface as I react. "What!" The sarcasm drips over every word that leaves my lips. "We're just jumping right to it, then, where is the fun in that?"

"For my knife." He cocks an eyebrow at me, "It's in my right pocket."

"Oh, right," My eyes begin to widen with embarrassment. "What do you need that for?"

He groans, "Ugh. Five questions and you've already wasted two." His head hits the backboard. "I can count them, or you can do what you're told and save your questions for what you want to know."

So, this is the game he wants to play? Well, I'll play, but my patience is wearing thin—if that happens, we will be playing my way.

A brilliant image gyrates across my mind, and slowly I grab his ankles, stretching his legs till they are flush with the mattress.

Leisurely frisking up his leg, I make it appear as though I am crawling to him, seductively swaying my hips—never breaking eye contact. Once I had hold of the knife handle, I yanked it from the sheath clipped to his pants and slashed at his chest. He broke out in this thunderous laughter. "Why are you laughing?"

"So, you want to know about the photo?" He is deliberately asking the wrong question. "That's a good question, little bird."

"All right, you want to play it that way, we can play it that way." I examine the spot where the blade struck. His gray button-up shirt was slowly starting to turn black, as beads of red formed at its pores. The pooling caught me off guard--it didn't follow in line with the cut. *It went against it.*

I move past that thought, going back to when he edged me in the alley. I had the brightest idea to start cutting off his buttons one by one. Still, he laughs, "Oh no, this shirt was expensive." The sarcasm oozes from his mouth, like sap from a tree in the summer.

"You are still laughing," I speak through gritted teeth. "It won't last."

His eyes widen, before rolling to the back of his head, as he responds, "Still with the questions, when will you-" I press the point of the blade to his heart, cutting him off before he can finish.

"When will I what? Learn?" I bite at the air as I pressure him to answer, "That was a statement, not a question." Satisfaction and confidence seep into me as my lip curls on one side. "Now, answer my question, and I'll reward your response if I deem fit." An indentation forms where the point of the blade meets his body. "Whose name is under the roses?"

"Little bird?" Oliver sways his hips, a hungry look growing in his eyes. "If you don't move that blade from my heart, there will be consequences."

Tossing my hands out to the side, "Here, I thought this was what you wanted." Once my confused face transfigured to a more nonchalant expression, I barked back. "Guess, you're chickening out."

He leans in my direction, rolling one shoulder at a time. "Don't think for one second that I can't break out of these cuffs." Pulling at the restraints, I can hear the wood moan and creak, the corners of his mouth peek out over the cloth that masks it.

He is fucking smiling—enjoying every second.

"I would never underestimate a monster who hides in the dark." He says, looking down his nose at me, 'You should, however, fear one who isn't afraid to step out into the light.''

"Is that a threat?" I hold myself tall as I speak, forcing him to look up at me. "Because I don't take lightly to being threatened."

What is this rushing feeling? I feel inferior, powerful, and in charge

This new sensation is empowering as it devours me, and he sees it too. I must remember I'm not without my flaws—he just makes it so damn easy to forget. With my life, it was difficult to look past my imperfections. The difference between my sister and me is that I took heed when our father told us about the dreadful things in the world, making me paranoid and hyperaware of my actions.

"No one will ever do the things you want to do in life better than you, yourself."

"Everyone is out to get theirs—so, give only when you can afford it."

"You are the hero in your story."

All these quotes that I have lived my life by have been the same quotes I used to pull my sister through some rough times. I remember in school, she endured so much bullying. Her beauty never stopped the snobby girls from making her feel less than.

I would always hear the popular jockeys spouting obscenities about her and how each of them was going to get her in bed with them. My breaking point was when I overheard them discussing prom and their idea to jump her. Slapping hands once they decided the order in which they were going to take, when defiling her body after she was drugged.

On the approach that night, I spent every waking moment beforehand mastering my plan of action. I stayed up the whole time, plotting how I was going to stop them—prom went on without a hitch. My sister was having fun—all was good. I almost believed that they had changed their mind, until she didn't come back from the restroom.

When I found them and realized that three of them had already gone, my rage took over, and my plan hit the fan. As years passed, the three who took it upon themselves to deflower my sister all met their end. Karma came to them, and with her she brought a Demon of Vengeance. Their passing was not slow, nor painless—It was justice enacted by the gods.

As I fade back into the present time, I had an awakening. "It was you."

His hunger morphs to starvation. "What was 'me', dove?" My breathing is shallow as he rests his head against the backboard. "Are we doing this again?" Still facing the ceiling, his eyes shut as he speaks. "What would you do if I said it was mine?"

My exterior unwavering, while my emotions swirl. "What-" I am not sure where this conversation is going. "Do you mean?"

"What if I told you," His chest expands as he lets loose a frustrated sigh, "it was mine?"

"Did you ever-? Wait, did you say-?" Then, it hit me he wasn't asking '*What if it was me?*' He said '*mine*'. He was talking about the headstone under the rose bush.

It can't be, he is lying.

Why would he lie to me?

He can't be dead because I can see him—I can feel him. I think

back to every unexplained event in my life... was it him? Was he

the demon of Vengeance?

No, he has said it already—He is the Shadow. My Shadow.

Between the time I spent arguing with myself over the memory of my sister, a fog formed in my head. "Was it you? The night with my sister—at prom?"

He drops his head back to look at me. "Are we counting this as a question?" The moment he gave me his piss-poor response, it triggers me, and I seem to have plunged the Ka bar deep in his chest. "Way to cut my heart out, little bird." He lies back against the headboard once more, the knife still protruding from his body, as I sit there in shock and frozen to the spot.

"How long have you been stalking me?" The question slips out like a dollop of butter on a hot frying pan. "I'm sorry."

"Is this-" His eyes move to look at me, but his head stays still.

"Yes!" a little more aggressive than I intended, but I've needed this answer since the alley. "Yes, Oliver, I need to know."

"I-" He clears his throat. "I have never stalked you."

"Bullshit!" I shout at him as I slam my fist on the bed.

"I have *never* stalked you. That would be an invasion of privacy." I don't know what to say. "I have *haunted* you... since you took your first breath." Considering the information, I now know, I am still at a loss for words.

"Watch you undress?" He interrupts my thought, "No, dove. That *would* be stalking. On another note, I feel the need to make this fact noticeably clear... I didn't fall in love with you till after the first man I *killed* in your name, on your twenty-third birthday."

"You've... *killed*... for me? How many times?" Realizing that I had asked two questions, I pause. "Sorry."

I didn't care about his game anymore. I needed answers.

"Don't answer that." I bite my tongue and continue. "Next quest-"

"No, Emory, I owe you those answers." I am shocked by his response. "I am ok to pause our game, for now. The questions that

you ask, from here out, can only pertain to the subjects at hand: My being dead, the haunting you, and the things I have done to protect you —*deal?*"

Slowly, my chin touches my clavicle, then lifts again. "Good, I will make this quick." Rocking his hips, he shifts to a more comfortable position. "Yes, I am dead, I died a long time ago."

I don't know where this is going, and I am both terrified and on the edge of my seat.

"I have followed your family since my passing." He looks at his lap, "The night you turned twenty-three was the first time I had ever taken a man's life in the pursuit of keeping you safe."

I am taken back to that night at the bar—I don't remember anything past the first half of the night. Then, I remember waking up the next morning to the news of the guy who was talking to me, and that he had passed.

"I've killed for your sister also—the screwed-up thoughts in my mind told me it still led to your happiness."

It was him. He was the one who avenged my sister.

"However," he shifts his hips again, "When it comes to you, I dare not give the complete count."

A gentle pressure pushes against the small of my back as I swivel my top half to see what it could be. He was using his heels to force me towards him. "Any more questions on that matter? May we continue our game?"

Pausing for a moment, there was one more question I had. "I have one. In the cellar, and even just now... if you are dead... why do you still bleed?"

"Right." He scoffs. "Remove my clothes."

"Seriously?" I throw up my hands. "Why do you do that?"

"Do what?"

"Demand things with no context."

"Because I love watching your reactions, you have a filthy mind, little bird." The air shifts, and his demeanor changes. "I will answer this last question, mostly because it will make our game more intriguing."

He glances down at the dagger. I reach over, removing it from his chest. Then, working my way to the second button, my heart is pounding like a base drum. I tuck the blade under the little, round piece of plastic and stop. "No, I want the mask off first?"

"You've already seen my face-"

"Yes." Cutting him off, "And lovely as it is, I am curious to see all your scars at once." His eyes widen.

Once I release the knot in the mask, I finish with the rest of the buttons on his shirt, running my finger down its seam. Separating the hems. I draw the fabric back, revealing his bare chest riddled with scars. My fingers trail the lines, like a leaf floating with the ripples on a lake after a stone has been thrown in. Some of them are light pink with a white hue, showing their age. Others appear like dried-up wounds that could have happened a day ago. I caress them using a swipe of my finger, ending one to start another, with a sense of dedication and understanding.

"Now," The words come out soft, caressing my lips with a gentle breeze, "Tell me why you still bleed."

The crow's feet deepen in the corner of his eyes. "It's the Gods' cruel way of punishing me for choosing to stay and protect, rather than crossing over to live happily in the memories of my past." My head falls to one side, puzzled. I scoot closer—a toddler to their favorite storybook.

He notices this and continues, "When it's one's time to leave this plane, for what most humans believe to be a 'better one', the reality of it all is you are only stepping into a looped existence— reliving what good memories you made in a life you already had."

"How do you know that if you chose to stay?"

"A faceless—nameless deity, draped in all white, finds you lost in darkness. The echo of past mistakes... of chances not taken... beating you down harder than when you endure them in life." Sorrow presents itself briefly in his eyes. "The emotions of those moments are unbearably loud. For instance, all goes silent, and the messenger speaks:

Brave soul—one who has overcome hardships most would find insufferable. Before you... lies a difficult decision indeed. You can stay and keep the promise of protection you have made, or you can step into the realm of your raison d'être."

"He continued by saying:

Human souls have only two choices: they can stay and suffer the failures of their life, while spending eternity completing their 'unfinished business'. Or they can move to the Great Beyond.

I chose to stay." Rolling his head from side to side, "Little did I know the pain I volunteered for. I waited for those I loved to die as the loneliness of being forever alone, stuck rotting in a constant state of dread, slowly disintegrated my soul.

Waiting for the same time I was murdered—doomed to relive my grotesque death all over again, like a residual torture session."

Pausing for a moment, he turns his head, refusing to make eye contact, "Left with hope that eventually one would be reincarnated to live a better life to achieve that *raison d'être*." Practically sitting in his lap now, I rest my palm on his cheek—the hope that this gesture of '*understanding*' will calm him. I release the tie from around his neck, and as the knot loosens, I let it fall through my fingers. The cloth no longer secured around his face falls and billows behind him.

"What, is the *raison d'être*?" I inquire, "Did this '*mystical being*' tell you?"

"It's the Elysian Fields for most. The celestial spirit went more in-depth with that as well. But like I said," He pulls his feet up to meet his ass, causing me to fall forward a little. "Though it's just a loop of the memories made in one's life that they live through, a continuous cycle, and they don't even know that it's happening."

"Ok, so let me get this straight." I prop myself up on my elbows, his chest firm beneath them, "You choose to stay and suffer rather than pass and be happy?" He nods. "So, wait, that still doesn't explain why you bleed."

Sitting back, I suck my teeth, awaiting his response. "Right, I can only bleed from the spots I was cut when I died. It's one of the sick, twisted jokes that come with choosing to stay. It's the only way... I can feel." He gives me a sly glance. "After my duty, my promise was fulfilled. With that said, before your great-grandmother passed, she made me promise to remain here... for Charlie—your grandfather."

He inhales sharply through his nose, before the story goes on, "Weathering away, and desperate, I took a blade to my body. I don't know what I was thinking. Perhaps I hoped that the being would find me once again, or that things would get less… lonely—that maybe I had the power to end it all. I felt lost, that was until Niven came along and could see me."

"So, in the cellar," I trace the palm of his hand, as it hangs, locked in the metal jaws of the cuffs. The very hand he cut open, before he shoved it in my face—the taste of his blood still potent on my tongue. I carry on with my question, "Did you do that yourself?"

"The cellar? No, that is different." He shakes his head slowly, "When I died, it took a while for death to claim me. So, my residual passing in this state of existence is from the point of attack to the last breath—let me remind you, I didn't die instantly. My last breath wasn't *until dawn*." His eyes gloss over for a moment as he is brought back to that day. I climb onto his lap, taking his face in my hands, guiding him to look at me—trying to break his focus on the past, when a realization hits me:

I am falling in love with him—a ghost.

I am falling in love with my shadow

"*In the hush between heartbeats, love is the gentle promise that even in life's fiercest storms, two souls can find shelter in each other's arms.*"

CHAPTER 19

Oliver

All is fuzzy, *"Oliver!"* Her screams are blaring over the sounds of all the other souls coming to the Americas. Ellis Island, though not beautiful to the locals, is a shooting star in the pitch-black skies that consumed the lives of immigrants. Germany's threats of invasion brought to light an ultimatum I had to face and fast. Do I keep them here, where my protection over them can be broken with a simple piece of paper? Or do I act now and save them by giving up on the hunt for the very monster that slaughtered my best friend? My answer came in the act of putting them on a boat to the free world.

The condition of the boats from England to Ellis Island is crowded, unsanitary, and foul-smelling. The journey is long—I can't tell you how many days have passed. Some poor wretches have a *tough time holding in what little food they have consumed, as the ship tosses on the rough sea.*

With the cost of passage secured, our next step on this wild, split-second journey is getting to the port of departure. As we step off the boat, we take a deep breath, the air feels cleaner here—it's less... dense than back home.

"He would have been so proud." She looks around, and Charlie is playing with her silky brunette hair. Turning to look at him, she kisses his cheek—a faint lipstick stamp staining his skin. "Your daddy would have been so amazed." The light from the afternoon sun glints off a tear forming in the crease of her eye, but she doesn't allow it to fall. Looking up at me, "I don't know what we would have done without you, Ollie." The tear, defying her, submitting to the pull of gravity, plummets down her rose-kissed face.

"Charlie and you are family, love. Really, you're the only family I've got." I wrap my arm around her shoulder and tap Charlie on his nose with the pad of my forefinger—his giggle lingers as the memory fades into blackness.

The darkness persists—a reliquiae of memories that haunt and torment me. Charlie's laughter bled into her screams, "Oliver, no. Hang in there. Please don't leave us!"

It's been so long since that night happened. Mere flashes are all I remember. The fall air was crisp—the scent of pine chasing its skirt-tails, the anniversary of my best friend's death—right around the corner. For three years, I searched for the answers and investigated the evidence I gathered. I finally found out who did it, but I was too late— they got me, too. I would have never thought they would follow us, but that was my mistake... I let my guard down.

*I held on, pushed through the pain that blurred my vision. I had to get them out of that crowd—I had to get **him** out.*

Coming out of my daydream, my little bird is sitting on my lap, knife resting at my side. Her eyes are clouded with sadness. I can't stand seeing her like this, all downcast while the thought of saying the wrong thing has her paralyzed. Moving my hand without thinking, I am stopped by the metal around my wrists, locking me in place. *Damn it.*

See-sawing my hips, with one jolt, I shift her, and she falls forward. Catching herself with her hands, I watch the sudden fear melt the moment her eyes meet mine. Slowly, I lick my lips, watching as her gaze follows the path of my tongue, "Don't you have three more questions, dove?" I try to distract her mind and bring her back.

"Huh," She wiggles. "What was that?"

"Your next question?" I fight to keep my arousal at bay. "Let's hear it."

"Where is my father? I thought he invited me here to help me find my sister?" Caught unaware by her sudden shift in topic, I stop to think—I must choose my answers carefully. It was one thing to tell her about the spiritual existence of the *'being'*. However, I am not overly sure that now is the best time to address the situation with her father. If she even gets the slightest clue, then she will leave me, and I will be doomed to walk eternity alone.

"He isn't here. He… wanted those letters to be sent out, but he wasn't expecting an answer so quickly."

Her face twists. "Letters?" Tilting her head, she crosses her arms, eager for my response.

Shit, think, what do I say? The truth? No, then she will run. Half the truth? I may be able to manage that.

"Yes." I start. 'He wrote two… but I couldn't find your sister, so I delivered yours." I knew where her sister was. I visited the rehab center, and that's when I overheard Evelyn's puppy mentioning the plan he had for their escape. I was under the impression that I could save her, but I was quickly proven wrong. After hearing him, I washed my hands of the responsibility, giving him the room to be *'provider'*. I thought it best to go a different route—given my situation of being dead. So, I strategically planted the letter in her room for him to find.

Emory was already safe with Niven the night he had planned for the 'prison break'—according to statistics, that center's doctor-to-patient care was the lowest in the state. The kid pulled it off—he saved her. Not going to lie. I was. I am massively impressed with his execution of the whole plan.

Now, I know where she is and that she is safe, for now. The only thing left to work on is my character in front of Emory. When the time comes, I need her to choose me. She must choose me.

"Next question?" I inhale deep, resetting my train of thought, "Also, while you are asking and since you have meticulously removed half my clothing, can you finish the job?"

"Maybe," Remembering my mask is off, I smolder, "You can run that blade over my scars, like a good girl?"

She is fighting the enjoyment that *'being in control'* is giving her. I can tell when a bite from the blade pressing between my bottom ribs makes me wince.

Ok, little dove… I'll play.

"I told you before, my dove. I need release. This is the only way I can feel the remanence of the life I used to have. Oh, please… please… please," I begged, watching her twitch with sexual frustration, "don't be afraid to cut me." I suck air in through my teeth, "it's how I feel."

The corner of her mouth twitches into a smile. "So, if I don't like your answer-" Her pause is promising, I hang on to her words with an intense form of expectancy, "I can cut you?"

"If that-" I try to answer through my chuckling, "Is what you wish."

Oh, fuck. What did I just say? The words flowed from my mouth, coerced by her seduction like acid in my mind—all rational cells dissolving to its touch.

Yes, my little bird set me free.

She adjusts, then continues, "Why is Peter here?" My muscles tighten as my lips pull into a thin line.

Killjoy.

I can sense my eyes darkening, a black hole opening in space, swallowing all that dares to enter. I think she catches on because I can feel the point of the blade in my abdomen. "Skip, Next quest-" My words stop, as they are replaced with a grunt, and then a howl. She struck my chest, and a pool of blood oozed from my skin.

"Answer," she readies the blade again, "Now!"

Inhaling deep—I do just that. "Peter," I spat out his name, "Is a worthless human."

"Nice to know." This time, she sinks the blade into my inner thigh close to my groin, shearing a hole straight through my slacks. "That doesn't answer my question. Why is he here?"

"He is paying a long, drawn-out debt to your family." She pushes the piece of metal deeper, twisting it upward with one sharp movement. A new side of her is sprawled out before me—A glorious display of power.

Oh, my dove. Just when I thought you had outshone all the beauty in every realm, you proved to me that you can shine even brighter.

"Not good enough." Her words came out in a snarl. If she only knew the horrendous things this man and his family were capable of— she would have different thoughts. He was only with her mother to find her Father. Her voice rises an octave. "Why is he here?"

I canter closer. "You're going to have to do better than that, little bird. Do you even have it in you to torture? Because if not..." I pause and lower my tone, looking her square in the eyes. "I will just keep giving you bull shit answers. You are pretending to be a 'hawk', but your actions are screaming 'pidgin.' HA! Maybe I should change your 'pet' name. What do you think... pidgin?" Just then, I watch something click.

Removing the blade, she turns it, placing the finely honed edge under the band of my pants. Then, with surgical precision, she slices at the material, cutting it away like she is hedging a bush. With skilled accuracy, she guides the knife. The slick fabric of my slacks parted like the Red Sea did for Moses. Wide-eyed, she gawks at me.

The clothing, leaving its place on my body, joins the slightly tussled sheets beneath me. She straightens her back, pulls her shoulders together as her chest pushes forward. I find myself distracted by her tits, not noticing the point of my blade as it enters one of the scars just below my waist.

"Whoa, dove. Cutting it a little close, don't you think?" The searing pain radiates throughout my naked body, tissue dividing under the cold steel. Her eyes are full of astonishment. She follows the flow of the garnet river on its short journey to meet the burgundy sea forming on the mattress beneath me.

Her voice startles me from my daze when she speaks. "Maybe you should be a good boy and tell me what I want to know." She slides off my lap to rest between my legs, prying them open with her knees, continuing her thought once she has settled, "Why is Peter here, and what was the 'mist' that took him away out in the garden?"

"Took him away? A *'mist'*, what do you mean?" The atmosphere changes as fear creeps over her face. "Emory, I need you to free me... now. The game is over, no more questions." It was then that I felt her hand tighten around the corpus of my dick. "That, my dear, will not get you any answers."

Her grip tightens. "Last I checked, it was you cuffed to the bed. I just felt the need to give you more restrictions." She leans forward, and after that, I am gone. Her lips crash into mine, and we melt together.

Breaking away, she yanks the shemagh from off my shoulders... blindfolding me with it. An intense sensation works its way into my throat as I feel her hot breath brush against my skin. The way my other senses heighten the moment one of them is disabled... is riveting. "Let's see how long you last before you are ready to give me answers." Following the predicted path of fiery breath down my torso, I inhale sharply as she licks my shaft from its base, on a *'warpath'* to my *'warhead'*.

A pace that is equally pleasurable as it was nerve-racking. Suddenly, ambushed by this feeling, I'm caught off guard by the tingling that coats my body as her tongue collides with the nerve center located just below my tip.

So sensitive, so delicate, ah, gods. What is she doing to me?
My body is twitching in apprehension.

She lingers at this spot for a little while. Kissing and lapping up whatever pre-cum escapes, I feel her latch onto the head and begin sucking—the force behind it is like a vacuum that even NASA would pay extreme money for. Instinctively, my body resorts to flailing and jerking till… agonizingly… the sensation comes to an abrupt halt.

"Did you get these scars that night as well?" All my 'scars' were from that night. I nod with a simplistic response. The lack of words and longing she has me experiencing right now is conjuring a feeling of guilt that it wasn't enough. I can't even prepare myself—I sense the tip of the blade, the sting like angry bees on defense, she nicked my cock, drawing forth, what I can only imagine was a small trickle of blood.

I feel the warmth as I slide deeper down her throat. The soft touch of her lips while they hover, then a centralized heat rolling over me—I envision the little red stream vanishing with a swipe of her tongue.

Shivers dance up and down my spine, forcing my toes to, involuntarily, flex and curl. Her moaning penetrates my ears, a siren dragging me. Willing. To my end. Her lips barely leave my dick as she grumbles, the rasp in her voice weakening me even more, "Do you realize how wonderful you taste?" She skates the metal over me, and I feel the opening of a few more old wounds. "Let's see how much you can take." Whispering against my erection, I can feel her menacing smile hidden behind the words she speaks. The cool breeze spiraling and clashing, her groans vibrating, intensifying the sensation. Warm. Wet. Silken.

This feeling alone, "Oh, my gods." The words spring from my mouth before I'm able to bite my arm, an action that may have prevented me from sounding foolish. Like a feather, her hair sweeps over my stomach.

With a firm grip, her hand grasps my sack. The other one guides the tapered metal. The image my brain paints as it is trying to follow her movements is that of the knife becoming her medium of choice, doodling with it like an iron quill pen—my blood being its ink. Drifting it over my thighs, she hits all the responsive bits, a direct connection to my soul.

Gratification rises. The proximity closes. I am completely and utterly at this goddess's mercy, as her beauty tries to force it all to happen too quickly, so I try to distract myself. Convincing my mind to focus on irrelevant things: Sifting through the Rolodex of knowledge I had on knives. Reciting their names, qualities, and uses till my brain jumbles them up, "Little dove... you need to... slow... down." She swallows me, her nose presses to my lower stomach, the head of my cock slamming the back of her throat. "D-d-dove e-easy." I stammer through deep breaths.

An incredibly audible pop startles me, tearing me away from my ineffective attempt at being distracted. "You okay there-" My ability to hear her is muffled by the euphoria. A ringing from the sheer pleasure I can no longer keep at bay.

The Frigid draft. Lustful popping. All mingled together. Topped off with the prickle of awakening that followed the dismount of her swollen lips—it was too much—I couldn't fight it. A rush of my senses disables me further as I explode. "Well, I'll never say you're a bad shot ever again." She laughs heartily while haphazardly removing my blindfold.

I burst out laughing... I had shot her directly between the eyes, covering her pretty little face like those glazed doughnuts she used to love.
What was that saying, "You are what you eat?"

I laughed a little more due to the joke in my head. I offer an apologetic smile as she cuts away the rest of my shirt and uses it to clean up. We lay there in silence. Sweat from both of us mixing and forming swirls of the most intoxicating aroma.

To no one's surprise, the moment ends as elevated voices bounce off the stone walls. Crashes and bangs follow shortly after, interrupting what could have been my paradise. I recognize the deeper voice—Brennan. I knew then I had to get her out of here. Not because he might see her. No, I can't allow her to see him.

"*Intimacy is not just of the body, but of the soul—dare to be seen.*"

CHAPTER 20

Emory

It's been pure torture that I haven't been able to, truly, touch him till now. It was only recently that I held his hand, and now this and whatever '*this*' is… is intoxicating.

The control.

The intensity.

A strong, intimate connection, like a string tethering our souls to one another. I've never enjoyed causing someone pain—I've always been the peacemaker, fixing problems I was never originally a part of. I never had it in me to hurt another human or otherwise, but he wasn't human, was he? No, he wasn't. His body died a long time

ago, and while his soul ages like top-shelf whiskey, his appearance prevails, unfazed by time.

With every wound of his I open, I feel one of mine close. A fleeting moment in time, and this man has made a mark on my heart. Not a smudge, which can be smeared over time. A deep laceration that would leave behind an ugly scar—one that would heal but would always remain. Slowly, he became the only real thing while everything else dematerialized and faded into the background. The world revolves around him and me in this moment. The way he feels in my mouth, his taste, the subtle sounds that escape him, all mesmerizing.

All this power should be illegal. The reactions this man has... are magnetic. When I suck, he moans. Rhapsodies of praise and elation radiate from deep within his core. Breaking away from him, I allot the right amount of suction to provide that satisfying pop on release.

Not even seconds after the sound echoes off the stone, I feel a sticky, hot, mucus-like substance hit my face. "Well, I'll never say you're a bad shot ever again." My laughter is a difficult obstacle to talk through as he bursts into a giggling fit. I lean over, relieving him of the scraps that once formed his shirt, and use it to clean up the mess we made.

My mind drifts to his words about the 'being'. His voice becomes muffled as my mind is bombarded with thoughts, images, and more questions. I couldn't get his story out of my head.

What could it have been that had such a hold on him that he would choose to exist in misery? Did he love my Great-Grandmother? Or was it my Great-Grandfather? What was the promise he made?

Then my thoughts shifted to the words on the headstone he said belonged to him:

"Eternally shall I be a thorn upon the stem of thy Rose"

Voices interrupt our recently obtained joy, and I see the look in Oliver's eyes--his pupils were consuming their irises. As a compilation of emotions oozing from their sockets, telling a story of pure ecstasy interjected by fear.

He kicks at me, trying to get my attention. "The keys. Get the keys." He demands in a hushed tone. "They're in the nightstand."

I yank open the first drawer—I almost send it flying across the room. There, in the front right corner, sat a vintage set of keys. I grab them. Noticing the clothes they rested on, I make a mental note that they are there, knowing my clothes are still soaked.

As my fingers shake, I insert the key into the olden day cuffs, turning it and allowing the lock to release so the metal vise can spring open. Once free, Oliver scrambles to his feet, grabbing clothes from within the stand on the opposite side. Quickly stripping the wet material from me, I pull a thin white button-up from the drawer, and I begin to fasten it over my body. A rush of air brushes across my face, and I am swept off the bed and into the darkness of yet another hidden passage.

Beating on Oliver's back, bartering with him to put me down. "I have legs, damn it." It was only with the vanishing light that the corridor came to life. The sconces on the walls flickered on, dimly lighting the old stone catacombs.

"Oliver, at least tell me what is going on?" I holler, "Who were the people yelling? Where are you taking me?" No words, just the silence and the wind as it hastens past my ears.

Occasionally, he would glance behind him, before a loud thud interposed the quiet as we broke through a door, bringing us into the cellar. Here is where he finally puts me down

"Emory, I do not have the time right now. Please take my hand, and I will escort you to your room." He drops his hand in front of me, palm up. "Once all is said and done, I will come back, and we *will* talk."

I refused his hand, smacking it away from me. In moments, I am soaring through the air again, thrown over his shoulder like a sack of potatoes. Before I can get a word in, edgewise, I am thrown on the familiar champaign sheets as the door slams behind me.

The distinctive sound of the lock causes me to go into full panic. Slipping from the bed, taking the sheets with me, I charge the door once my feet hit the ground—I try to turn the handle. A loud howl emanates from my core when the knob doesn't turn.

"OLIVER!!" I scream before I rush to the balcony. I fling open the French doors as a clash of lightning strikes—bathing me in an electric blue. I stand there looking up at the sky as the clouds close in, adding to the already eerie events of the night.

"What a gloomy way to bring in the new year," I yell to the heavens, a smokescreen plea to whatever God is listening. "I haven't even found my sister."

It was this moment that the flicker of candlelight dancing in a far window of the library caught my attention. Something is swaying on the other side, periodically blocking out the light. At first, I thought it was Oliver.

The shadow begins to shrink in size as whatever is there moves further away from the light source and closer to the window.

Two people? Oliver and Niven, then. Oh no, I hope she is okay.

Staring for a while, I wait for the silhouettes to materialize into beings. My heart skips a beat, and the world slows around me when the figures finally come into focus. "Evelyn!" Her name erupts from my mouth with more intensity than lava emerging from a long-sense docile volcano—its cap finally bursting after several years.

I have finally found her—she is finally here... within reach.

"Thank you," I mutter to the being on high, as I glance up at the sky, overcast and sorrowful. All at once, visions take over—each emotion, digging up its own story to match. The obvious emotion is—

Relief: relief that she is here. She is safe. Stronger than the relief I felt with the five-car pile-up incident, and gaining the knowledge that she wasn't hurt.

Rushing up behind it came—

Depression: The depression I have been sulking in when the nights get lonely, and I didn't know where she was or what had happened to her. Depression, like the kind that consumed all parts of my heart when I heard my mother cry after that phone call that initiated this journey in the first place.

All at once, those emotions get tossed into the wood-chipper known as—

Anger: Anger that flows like hot magma through my veins. The questions in my head are only fueling the betrayal that feeds it.

How long has she been here? Why didn't Oliver tell me? What could he be hiding?

Standing here with these emotions, crumbling like earthquakes, rocking me clear to my center. The air around me is

closing in—suffocating me as though I were wrapped in visqueen. The bedroom door is within reach in a matter of seconds. I know it's locked, but that doesn't stop me. My hand is on the handle, and I start to pull down—with each denial, I respond in kind with another yank.

Frustration arises with every click against the lock. My rage grows stronger with every click of the metal, preventing me from going further. "Damn you, Oliver!" My screams pierce the air around me at a frequency barely audible to my ears. I begin throwing myself, trashing, and gyrating like an angry toddler mid-tantrum. I ram the door, using my entire body to add more momentum—much like the ginormous logs that were used in the medieval era to bombard castle gates. When that fails to produce, I revert to throwing anything and everything I can at it.

After what could have been hours, I rest my back against the wall, dazed from the excitement—my energy drained and wasted in the attempt to break free. I am fuming and confused, as my head spins, wondering why Oliver has locked me in here.

I am replaying the events of the evening, trying to figure out if there was something I missed. Now that I know my sister is here, my brain is no longer 'clouded' but 'crowded'—no longer a fog but a full-on obstacle to hurl over.

Is she healthy? Did Oliver go out and find her for me, to keep me protected?

I feel sick, my body movements feel distant, a ghost of my former self. I turn on my heels… my gaze locked on the open French doors to the balcony—all falls still around me. My heartbeat breaks the silence, faint and slow—but steady.

Lifting my foot from the wood floor, I feel my heel slam back into it as I start sprinting. Running. The wind molding around my body as my velocity increases, only to be cut short—almost careening over the banister as I skid to a stop.

I scream her name over the roaring thunder… my arm outstretched toward her sleeping face, bobbing in the window. "EVELYN!!" My tears are now one with the rain. I watch helplessly as a man I have never seen before holds her in his arms. He was a Ginger, and he looked an awful lot like Peter, with facial features to match. The only difference was that he was much younger and even taller than Peter. His muscles were prominent beneath her weight.

I take a step back, the rain still masking my tears as it joins the streams already present. Surveying my surroundings, I see the railing is a facsimile of myself—rivulets of despair intermixing with the tears from the heavens. To the left is a trellis decorated in vines, which appears sturdy as it clings to the side of the manor. I follow it with my eyes, noticing how it just barely touches the ground. I gauge the distance and decide that it is enough for me to hang from—falling a foot instead of a whole story. Impulsively, I grab the rail, straddling it… making sure my placement is perfect.

I can do this.

I repeat in my head.

Fuck. I looked down.

*Why did I look
down?*

Blinded by my panic, I am startled by a crash of lightning… and I slip.

Quotes Most Desired

"Little dove. When I catch you. I will devour you. If you make it easy, then you will be punished."-Oliver, Ch. 11

MCKENNA

"*Letting go is sometimes the bravest thing you can do for those you love.*"

CHAPTER 21

Oliver

My stomach turns with the lock, knowing that when she realizes what I have just done… she may never forgive me. The ache in my heart expands as what I planned would be my last resort has grown and bloomed before me—a carnivorous plant of doom, hungry and ready to consume all Happy Endings.

I place my hand on the door, "Please forgive me, little bird. The time for me to tell you everything… will be upon us soon." I swallow hard, "I only need you to hold on." My fingers drag over the oak door, disembarking one after the other till they all meet at my hip.

In the time it took me to walk through the manor, I was able to reflect on all my choices. To set aside a few, well-needed seconds to form a game plan on how things were going to play out.

How was I going to tell Emory?

What is her choice going to be?

Did I do enough...

on my part to convince her to stay with me?

Did I even deserve that...

after all my lies and betrayals?

I stop for a moment beneath the portrait that looms over the grand staircase. Removing my Scally, as my thick black locks fall to one side—I place the cap over my heart. "Ger, I could really use your wisdom in a time like this." Sniffling as I straighten my back. "In all my existence, Love has never been an option. You, on the other hand, were so good at it."

"I miss you," a single, woeful tear falls down my cheek, "Old friend." Placing my hat back on my head, I tip it before continuing my path back to Brennan.

On my way back through the cellar, I am stopped in my tracks by an unforeseen obstacle. Peter! He falls face down at my feet. His eyes blackened as bruises began to form—A kaleidoscope of grotesque-beautiful swirls, and a resemblance to the modern-day science experiment (where you put milk on a plate, drop color dye in sporadic places, then, with a Q-tip dipped in dish soap, you place it in the milk and watch as the colors twist together like magic).

Dry, crusted blood coats his pathetic face as he whimpers. Pleading. Reaching his hand out, feeling my presence, while every morsel of my soul begins to roister harshly, watching his hands as they grasp at my ankles, only to find himself grabbing air. The laughter that's projecting itself from my core may have enough power behind it for him to hear, especially in the state he's in, being as close to death as he is.

The walls begin to echo with a well-known sound, "I've seen the best and worst of humanity." Brennan's voice creeps down the hall, clinging to the rock like tar with every harsh tone—It's full purpose to torture his prey. "The thing is, there is nothing different. *'Will'* disguised as intentions—the weak following the strong."

Even without the knowledge of this man's past, I would still tremble at his voice. "I led a small team, then. Performed undesirable things to worse people." The timbre in his voice churns like curdled milk, blending with his footsteps as they inch ever closer.

"I reveled in the screams I brought forth under the staccato of the machine guns, the thrumming bass of the artillery. During that time, learning I had a penchant for information... well, the extraction thereof —I could make any imprisoned *'soldier'* sing as if he were one of the greats:

Luciano Pavarotti, Andrea Bocelli, Celine Dion."

Peter swivels, leaning in with his good ear, searching for the direction of Brennan's voice—no doubt trying to gauge the time he had to get away. "Command took notice of my instinctual ability to get *'proper'* intel." A screech erupts, metal to cobblestone, piercing even my ears. The way this man could manipulate sound and strike fear with just the knowledge of knowing what tool it was coming from, had me petrified—and I'm dead.

His voice booms again, "I began to hone my skills. I became a seeker of the voids between lies, where the truth hides." A crack breaks the sound barrier—an ear-bleeding sound in such a confined space.

"You see here, it came from the most basic desire in all humans... to *inflict*." The cat-o'-nine tails sounds once more as Brennan emerges from the shadows, coiling it around his waist. He crouches in front of Peter, stroking his jaw. Smearing the blood that has mostly hardened now, all over his face before removing his hand, bringing his palm back to kiss Peter's cheek. He flinches, releasing a small whimper as Brennan draws his fingers together, pinching Peter's face, causing his lips to pucker.

Laughing, he cracks his neck, rolling it from one side to the other, "Your screams are my masterpiece..." he raises the opposite hand, his fingers like a basket in the air, as though an invisible piece of art resides there. "Your blood is my bourbon." His saliva-clad tongue, shining in the dim light, as it lubricates his dehydrated lips. "My pleasure is watching your body seethe in pain."

Squeezing his fingers even tighter, causing cuts to form in Peter's mouth as the flesh slips between his canines... leaving lacerations in its wake. "I have been known to rival the greats, Rachmaninoff, Bach, and Shostakovich. I promise you, I will dream of your deformed, and blood-drenched body for years to come with an utterly delicious satisfaction."

A metallic rustling maneuvers its way through the air as he detaches the whip, allowing it to twist and sprawl out like the makings of a mushroom cloud—much like my good little romance readers have done to these pages, making it this far... you are such a good girl.

He snapped the whip, lightning quick, accompanied by a crack once it reached its apex. A visible shiver dances over his body in anticipation of the opening chorus of pain he is about to receive from his victim.

Excitement charges through my veins—I have never been so eager to witness someone join me on this side of the veil, more than I am in this moment. Wet and uncontrollably, my mouth starts to salivate. My soul is famished, craving such violence as this. Brennan begins to oscillate his arm, making the whip cavort, a serpent of deliverance—you may know her as Karma.

"Now you will tell me *everything*!" The length of Brennan's arm brought the tips to a blinding, flaying speed, just before the whips strike Peter across the chest. Layers peel away, liquifying the skin so perfectly that I can see the multitude of flesh coats that structure his chest. I watch, imagining it pooling at his knees, giving the portrayal of a Dali painting.

The cut reveals the deep crimson of his pectoral muscles, a masterpiece of revenge for all the pain and hurt he and his family have inflicted on others. Brennan then kneels in front of Peter, taking one of the nine tails and wrapping the end around the eye that dangles from its socket. Jerking both ends, he uses the whip like a garrote and severs it, "Now let me show you who you truly are." He picks the eye up from the ground, turning it on Peter. Brennan releases a thunderous laugh before dropping the appendage and smashing it beneath his boot.

The lashings proceeded, one after the other—his screams only audible in the catacombs of this labyrinth where only the dead can hear him now. Wiping the sweat and blood from his brow, Brennan stretches and rolls his shoulders—a boxer warming up before a fight. As his eyes shut momentarily, Peter sees this as an opportunity and takes off as fast as his damaged limbs could carry him. He weaves and dodges down darkened corridors, tripping over pebbles, completely unaware of me and my abilities. The candles spring to life—centerline lighting on a runway for Brennan to follow.

This parasite will never harm another loved one of ours again.

He breaks through the cellar door and out into the open air. Brennan is on his heels, but that doesn't stop Peter as he turns the corner, heading to the front of the estate. Rain is still falling, forming puddles, providing the water that kicks up around his shoes. He is slipping and sliding all over the gravel with the appearance of a newborn deer. The fact that he thinks he can escape Brennan is hilarious… in itself.

Setting back on my heels, I watch as Brennan stalks after him. Terror exudes from Peter's eye as he pauses to look behind him.

It must be difficult with the swelling.

The delight and jubilation delivered by the trauma this man is enduring has me bathing in joy... that is, until I am interrupted by a small whimper—breaking my concentration on him. My eyes follow the sound, and that is when I see her. She is clinging to the banister, her legs swaying like a flag, as it waves in the breeze.

What is this feeling, this warmth?

It doesn't last long when I realize she is slipping—no, quickly it is replaced with a sense of urgency. With no thought for my actions, I jump into Peter. His broken body and pleading thoughts make it taxing to take control of. I also haven't possessed anyone for decades— nevertheless, someone this close to the other side.

Unfortunately for him, I don't care about his well-being. My only concern is that he harbors enough energy to manifest my own.

Struggling.

Fighting.

Punching.

Using his fists against his legs, popping bones back in place, resetting them—I can't feel his pain, nor do I want to, I only need him to move. *"Please save me!"*

I roll his eye in response to his own thoughts. "You are a fraud to your core," I answer to his unspoken cries. "I am not here to help you. I am here to…" His left foot moves forward. "Save…" Then, the right, as I struggle to maneuver his dead weight, and before I know it, Peter is running. "Her!" I yell in Peter's voice.

Reaching his arms out, I catch her just in time. Her heart is racing, and her eyes are wide with fear. "Peter, what-"

I shake Peter's head, "I already told *life* you were mine." I respond to her, "I will be damned if *death* takes you away from me."

The recognition hits her. "Oliver!" Nodding, I look back as Brennan continues to stalk Peter.

"There is no need to run, little snake." His voice is dampened by the rain and rolling claps of thunder, but that doesn't make a difference in his deliverance. "You have entered my garden and meddled in things you cannot… come back from."

Using the limited vision Peter has, I scour the terrain looking for somewhere safe to drop her off. "Your family has taken *everything* away from me. So, I'm going to return the favor." With my destination in mind, Brennan calls out his next threat. "I am going to smash your brains in, then **fuck** the hole it leaves behind so I can be the last thing on your pitiful *fucking* mind."

I dart into the garden, kissing Emory on the forehead as I set her down on the bench—managing an apologetic expression before disappearing beyond the brush.

Fuck I must redirect him.

Then, it clicks. I am going to attempt to have a conversation with Peter's conscience. He is screaming, "I know this isn't me! My own body is betraying me!" I make a noise, equivalent to clearing my throat, but he continues. "I would have never saved that Selby bitch."

His screaming was too loud, and he has more than angered me with his last statement. So, I try again to get him to calm down for a moment. "Wait, maybe I'm not crazy. Is someone else there?" The fear in his tone was the sweetest form of justice, but I had to keep my eye on the prize: *getting him away from Emory.*

"Yes, Peter." The relief in his voice was disgusting. I had to keep telling myself, 'He will be getting his'. "I am your conscience."

"Ok, Peter. I need you to listen closely." Focus, Oliver. "That man will be waiting for you at the entrance. We must think of our point of attack."

I feel the body stiffen as he fights me. "Attack! I am not 'attacking' anything in the state that I am in." My patience is running thin, and his whining is not helping.

I think: *Does he have enough energy to charge him?*

I try lifting his arms to his face, only making it to about chest level.

Hm, not as much as I'd hoped.

I try to picture the garden maze, but since I have only taken the light away from Peter, and his mind is still readily available, the image is diluted.

I know there is another exit.

Think.

Think.

Think.

That's it, through Niven's Secret Garden.

"What am I seeing right now?" Peter voice, rakes through the hollow halls of his mind. "I don't recognize what is in this vision."

"Look," Now it's time to put my manipulation to work. "Do you want out of this?"

"Yes, please."

"Then you will relinquish all your energy to me."

I can hear the stutter before he continues, "You promise you'll get me out of this fucking maze?" I give him my word to get him out... of the *Garden.*

The path gets a little more vivid, and then I am booking it through the tall hedges bursting from the hidden entrance mere feet from where Brennan stands. His head turns at just the right moment. Looking in our direction before he disappears, to reappear even angrier and back on track.

"Now, it is all you." I tell Peter. "Run!"

A banshee-like jeer breaks from his mouth as he sprints through the driveway of the manor, and just before his fingertips touch

the wrought iron gates, I leap from his body. "I hope you suffer!" were the only words I left him with before he was rewarded with a 'pretty silver necklace'. Peter goes flying, his gurgling and gasping, frantic as his back slams into the ground. Standing there, I watch as his flailing steadily weakens with his surrender.

"*Grief is the price of love, but memory is its reward.*"

CHAPTER 22

Emory

Clutching on to the banister, I am doing my best with what little strength I have. My feet are kicking with desperation, a sense of longing to be on solid ground swelling by the second. Gravity serenades my body, as the pit of my stomach is bathing in fear.

I can't fall.

I won't be able to walk away from this if I fall.

I must find… a way.

My arms shake as I try to pull myself up and fail. I look around, and the trellis isn't too far, so I swing my legs, using my toes, as I try

to grab hold of it. I miss the first time, so I try again. Determined to make it, I struggle for another five times, until on the last go, my grip slips—what I didn't want to happen... happened, and now I am falling:

I finally find my sister, but before she can see me, before I can tell

her that I don't blame her for anything, I fall to my death.

I won't get to know why she is here.

How did she even get here?

Did the guy bring her here?

Who was he anyway?

If he was the one who brought her here, then why?

I have too many questions that need answers.

I can't die.

Not now, I just-

The fall feels like forever, like falling through space and time itself. My body is cold as the wind cocoons around me—I don't detect that I am falling. I start to wonder if I am dreaming, but that thought is short-lived—pulling me from my thoughts is the abrupt stop I make. I am startled when it wasn't followed by pain splintering through my body from the contact it would have made with the concrete. No, instead it was like falling into bed sheets on a soft bed after a long day of working. You know, the feeling where the mattress swallows you as the comforter wraps you in a soft... warm burrito.

I open my eyes to a face forming before me—it is familiar but disfigured, swollen, and red. I observe a little longer before it clicks. "Peter, what-" I watch as the look in his eye changes, and a stare that I have become accustomed to… makes its presence known. I witness his emerald eye shift to a striking baby blue.

"I already told *life* you were mine." The sorrow conjoined with anger was his specialty. "I will be damned if ***death*** takes you away from me."

I was right. "Oliver?" Peter is lost to me—there is no indication that he still occupies space in his body. The only thing I can see, and feel, is Oliver—nodding in response. His emotions convey care and worry as my relocation of him surfaces. My eyes glare at him with a grip like super glue.

His worry turns to panic as he peers over his shoulder, and I am pulled to take a gander, just past the arm, my face is buried in— trying to make sense of it all. A man is walking towards him—well, it is more of a flounce. His features match those of my father's, but not how I remember him. No, he is more like a younger version—It is as if he jumped out of the photo I found upstairs in the west wing. His modern-day clothes fit him snugly, while an exceptionally well-kept beard obscured his young face. It is the Citrine in his eyes that has me captivated, and the only feature that convinces me that he wasn't some figment my mind conjured.

When he speaks, it makes my mind race. A thousand thoughts and questions collide at once, but none of them are clear enough to grasp. His voice is cavernous, reminding me of the lake and the accident—It left me drowning in my thoughts, with every word from his mouth dragging me deeper into the sea of panic. Threats pouring past his lips, filling my cup of queries.

A. B. Owings

Who is this man?

What did Peter do to make him so hostile?

Could it be he is after Oliver?

If so, why?

My brain is on the edge of exploding as Oliver tightens his grip around me. Peter's face is so messed up that I am positive it was challenging to form any expression. Oliver manages to manipulate it effortlessly, simpering at me as a sign of reassurance.

I snuggle into his chest, soaking in this safe feeling, before it's gone, as Oliver sits me on the bench in the Garden. A warm and comforting kiss befalls my forehead, then I open my eyes to realize that he has abandoned me here. No answers, just stale wet air from the storm, causing my damp hair to mat to my face. Taking the time to look around, I study the moon-rays as they dance in the sporadic puddles on the ground. Standing, I walk back over to the bush of Juliet roses and peek down at the headstones.

Instantaneously, I remember the garden chase. Then, I rush my way back over to the bench, the one that displays the stunning etching of the bird sprawled across the back. A closer look, and the engravings start to become a little clearer. The rain must have washed away a bit of nature that once grew there. Dirt is still caked in most of it, but the black of the dirt enhances the etching, providing a bold outline as it allows every detail to bask in the glory it deserves.

Someone put a lot of time and work into this piece.

Once I finish admiring the craftsmanship, I could barely make them out, but I see there are words—an indication that this, too, is a memorial:

263

Looking at my hands, my nails are average length, and I try to scrape the clumps out of the divots in the wood. I manage to smear it instead, as the rain still lightly falls, adding to the moisture.

Only a few letters are revealed: *M*I*N*E*. That was all I was able to get to before there was a thud and a splash as something fell in one of the various puddles around me. I turn slowly as terror clamps my limbs, holding them together like they're in a Vise Grip, hindering my movement. I fight back the feeling, forcing my body into action as I turn around. There, a few feet in front of me, I see Peter—again. This time, he doesn't move, he only… lies there. His breathing is shallow as he lies on his back in the small pool of rainwater.

A flashback of when my mother met him blinks into focus like a static TV.

Mom took us out for smoothies—she wanted to help us feel better, it was the first weekend we didn't receive a letter from our dad. It had been a year—they were always so prompt, every Saturday morning a package showed up on the doorstep for each of us... even mom.

When we stepped out onto the porch to find the delivery box was empty, Evelyn and I were crushed.

***Evelyn**: (scoffing) Ugh, whatever.*

She threw her hands up and stormed inside, shouldering mom on her way past, and once the door slammed closed, turned her gaze to me.

***Mom:** (sighing as she brushes her hair behind her ear) I really am sorry. I will message and try to see if maybe it was a delivery thing. She smiles wearily.)*

Mom walked over to the porch swing and sat down, putting her head in her hands—I joined her, resting my hands on her shoulder. I didn't know what to do, I wasn't even a teenager yet, but that didn't stop me from trickling my fingers down her back to comfort her—I learned that technique from the best... her.

***Me:** Mom, (I say with a worried tone) can we go get some frozen yogurt?*

Her sniffles fade to chuckles as she lifts her head to reveal the ruby color forming in her sorrowful eyes. She wipes her face dry before taking me in her loving arms.

Mom: (She nuzzled her nose to mine) Of course, pookie.

I jumped from the swing with joy, bolting through the house to tell Evelyn the most amazing news.

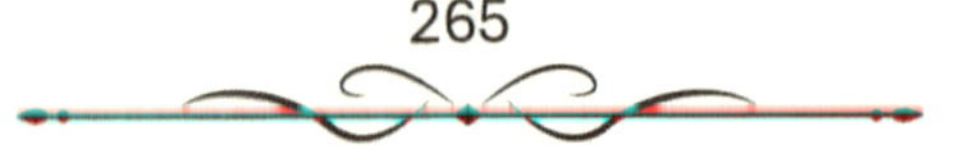

__Me:__ (Shouting like the kid I still was) Evelyn! You won't believe what I got mom to agree to.

I rushed through the house, throwing open every door. I found Evelyn in the garage, cross-armed at dad's old work bench—her face buried in her elbows, while her body shook with misery.

__Me:__ (My voice comes out softer than silk) Evelyn? (There is no response) Evelyn? Guess where Mom is taking us?

__Evelyn:__ (The tone of her voice muffled from speaking into her arm) Where?

Feeling like I cracked her armor a little, I permit myself to unleash the pure excitement that has built up in my little body, in the short span of standing there in her melancholy moment.

__Me:__ (Yelling in raw, uncut ecstasy) Frozen Yogurt!

I witness her head shift as a sparkling sapphire orb peeks from beneath her lashes, like castle guards on night watch over the kingdom.

The air turns colder, and I am pulled from my memory. Flower petals are swirling like a tornado around me, as the voices of my mother and sister echo off the stone in the garden. Specks of light begin to form amidst the swirls as the memory breaks up into pieces in front of me. I reach out to touch what would have been the next segment, and I am pulled into it like a vacuum.

We are now in the car, and hits from the 2000s are playing on the radio. Mom and Evelyn have their arms outstretched before them, their hands clapping 'bye' to an imaginary being. It doesn't take long before the all too recognizable building dominates the view from the windshield as mom pulls into a parking spot.

*   **Me:** (In a guttural gremlin voice) Smoothie Giant! (I shriek like a starving pterodactyl)*

*   Mom laughs as Evelyn joins the yogurt chant. We climb out of the car and form a line to march in tune with our victory cries. At the register, my sister and I had added almost every topping you could-- our cups were overflowing with sticky-sweet goodness. Mom reached into her purse to grab her wallet, and a man from out of nowhere shoved her into the glass display case of sweets made in-house.*

*   **The Man:** (Brandishing his firearm and pointing it at the cashier, his identity completely concealed) Empty it into the bag! (He slams a burlap sack on the counter with his free hand) Now! All of it!*

*   **Cashier:** (A college boy, unfazed by the pistol mere inches from his face) Take whatever you want, you won't get far.*

*   Not even minutes after the words left the cashier's mouth, a swarm of officers barreled through the store's entrance. S. W. A. T. plastered across their breast plates.*

*   **Officer #1:** (Cuffing the criminal) We all knew it was only a matter of time before you would try to attack another college student. Evidence led us to this one (She looks at the cashier and nods). Thank you for your cooperation.*

*   She began tapping the perpetrator's calves with her shoes, telling him he was allowed to walk and that this is the direction I need you to go. They clear the threshold before another cop approaches my mom.*

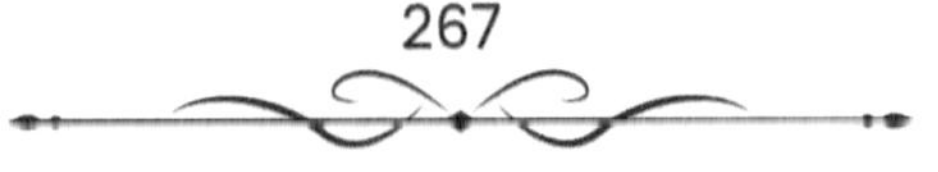

My concentration is broken again as a booming voice erupts from the shadows, "You can try and run, but you will never be able to hide. I will always find you." It echoes through the small alcove of shrubbery—the thickness of the floral tornado thinning.

"Once I get my hands on you," The voice cries, fueled by anger and a longing for vengeance. "I will ensure that you die slowly, little snake."

A small clearing formed in the petals allows me to watch as Peter inhales deep, then shouts, "Suck my dick, y-you Selby fuck!"

Selby?

Was this thing that was after him once...

a Selby?

All in this moment, the misted figure appears again, placing its hand on Peter's shoulder and violently jerking him to where he is now in a partially seated position.

Blood flies from Peter's mouth as an invisible force cold cocks him across the face. He gurgles and chokes, trying to clear it from his throat. The mist solidifies into a man as he licks the crimson dots within reach of his tongue. Inhaling through his nose, his eyes rolling to the back of his head as he releases a sigh of pure bliss. At the end of his exhale, he allows an animalistic grumble to escape.

Then, with euphoria on his tongue, he speaks, "Good thing Niven was a great nurse in her prime, or I wouldn't have known whether you were diseased or not." He swipes a spectral thumb over Peter's busted lip. "Funny enough, you weren't," Putting it in his

mouth, he sucks it clean, then continues, "But I always knew your family was filth—I can *taste* it in your blood."

The word '*taste*' activates the memory once more, only this time, instead of the vivid image awash in bright pigmentation, its depiction is more akin to that of a scene from "*Pleasantville*", devoid of color and indulging in the many shades of gray with hues and undertones of black and white. Peter's screams act as an overlay, causing the moments in this memory to appear broken up into pieces, like fast-forwarding a VHS tape, stopping to play it here and again, to see where in the show you are.

The officer is speaking to my mom. Then, a whirling of images, assisted by sped-up sounds, rushes past me, and we are broken down on the side of the road heading back home from our frozen yogurt excursion.

Peter's howls replace the screeching of the car, as the memory continues.

The front passenger side tire blew out, and Mom swerved as the remaining tires screamed for relief. We came to a stop—Evelyn and I both frantically threw ourselves from the vehicle and kissed the ground, happy to not be moving anymore.

Evelyn: *(Almost in full hysterics) Solid ground! (loud smacks emanate from her direction as she physically kisses the asphalt)*

Mom: *(hollering over traffic) Girls! Girls, is everyone ok?*

Now that I am thinking back on it, I don't know why we wouldn't have been 'okay', it wasn't like we crashed. As I got older, I learned adrenaline mixed with fear was the reason we were all afraid after the fact. Another spout of fast-moving images, and we are all in Peter's squad car on our way back home. Then the darkness consumes me, and the sound of reality pierces my ears.

"I hope you've done your *fucking* **penitence**!" The man pulls something from his waist, spitting as he says the word *penitence*. "You'll be meeting your maker soon enough, little snake."

A glint of metal, then, quick as the bolt that lights up the night sky, he jams a knife into Peter's abdomen—slamming it upward, maneuvering it under the heart's protective cage... and piercing it. With another strike of lightning, scarlet spews from Peter's mouth and gushes from his wound, bathing the man of mist in a crimson shower.

"Y-you will p-pay... S-Selby dirt!" Peter spits, the mist only chuckling at Peter's last words before pushing him face-first into the puddle beneath him. His screams, muffled by the water and exhausted by his many injuries, were hopeless below the strength applied. Petrified by the events playing out before me, all I can do is stand here and watch as his body convulses and gyrates, the air leaves his lungs, and water takes its place... my vision tunnels—my breathing becomes restricted and depthless.

A stabbing in my head and the feeling of water filling my lungs have me falling to my knees in the mud within seconds. My vision is going in and out as I gasp for air. It's like I am drowning all over again—like I am drowning *with* him. The mist forms before me, the golden glimmer in his eye eluding an amount of sadness that should have been too much for one person to have to experience alone.

"Is that you, Oliver?" His eyes are searching, as if he doesn't see me. "If it is, please let Niven know that '*things*' have been '*handled*'." He looks over his shoulder at Peter, "I must clean up fast or this could get ugly." Then the man of wisps was gone, as though carried on a strong wind—Peter was gone too.

What.

The hell.

Just happened?

I try to stand, as the wind begins to pick up around me, a whirlwind of dust and dirt swirls where Peter once lay. Strands of smoke start to lash out, defying the gravitational pull of the dirt devil, and an ear-splitting howl roars above the whooshing from the spiraling air. Then they charge at me, and an uproar of cackling breaks forth from a disembodied voice... filling my head, enhancing the agonizing pain that is still present. "He can't save you." The ghostly anomaly wailed.

"P-" before I can finish his name, eyes appear mere feet in front of mine. These are not the same eyes as before. No, these were like a swamp green—where the gilding eyes of the previous Phantasm portrayed sadness, these were filled to the brim with sheer hate and envy.

I knew this aura—it was Peter, and as if he were looking into my soul, he spoke again, *"At least I was able to rid the world of a few* **disgusting. Selby. Peasants***."* In a trice, he launches into hysterics. Then, I am knocked back. Hitting my head as the fog shoots through my body, vanishing as the world starts spinning, and I am thrown into the void of darkness once more.

My mind is a labyrinth of memories—each one a moment in time that Peter helped Evelyn or me. A vision of the garden looms

before me—I look around and see that I am alone. Not fully understanding, I take a step forward, and a path begins dimly shining beneath my feet. The memories rise into the endless sky and separate a few feet away from each other. I look back at the lit runway before me and descend into the ominous hedges.

Deeper into the abyss. The shrubbery is moving—breathing as if it is alive. I can still see the images. The first one gets closer as I advance further, and I start thinking of it, trying to remember it. This was just after the car accident.

__Peter:__ Hey champ, can you stare at me for a bit? I need to check your eyes using my flashlight for a sec. To make sure they are dilating. (Bending at the waist before me, he shines the light in my eyes. I am blinded, as my vision turns into a dancing phantasmagoria of colors.) One more question, (His voice is disembodied.) Where is your father?

The colors grow brighter, then flash white, and I am standing amidst the hedges in the garden again—a new path forming to the right of me. The hedges appear gray-scaled as thick branches sway sporadically throughout them.

Without looking back, I bolt to the mouth of the towering, colorless shrubbery. The light from the last memory fades the further away I get. As I pass through the thin, leafy entrance, it collapses behind me—the light snuffed out with it, except for the dim gleam from the moon. I scan my surroundings, not much really to see, the soft silvery glow from the sky offers very little assistance.

Taking a deep breath, I walk forward, and as I plant my first step firmly in front of me, the bigger branches begin to shake. My heart starts to race as the feeling of terror consumes me, and not giving myself any more time to stand there in fear, I book it—kicking up the soft dirt as I run. The walls appear to be closing in, causing my adrenaline to spike and make the hairs on the back of my neck stand on end.

Then I make the worst mistake of my life—I look back, as I do, and something grabs me. Screaming, I search to find the culprit, slapping my body like I am covered in ants. Finally, I can pull far enough away from the hedge to see that it is one of the bulky branches. To my surprise, it isn't a branch at all—it is an arm, complete from shoulder to fingertips, and it's got me locked in its creepy grasp.

Punching.

Clawing.

Pulling.

*None of this does any justice or brings me any closer to escaping this thing's death grip, so I do the unthinkable—I give in enough to ease the tension, then, lifting my arm to my face, I clamp down on the meatiest part of the hand just below the thumb until it releases me. Stumbling backward, I do my best to stay mindful that there is a possibility that **all** of them are like this. I don't have time to think, so I let my instincts guide me. I squeeze my eyes shut and shout to the sky.*

"I know you are out there, and the pagan Gods have never listened to me, so-" I am overtaken by a strong wave of surrender and sorrow, as tears propel from my eyes. "Please, God, if you can hear me... Help me!"

A crash of lightning responds to me, and rain begins to fall. I stare up in awe, allowing the two liquids to mix: the rain and my tears. A moment passes, and a sound interrupts my prayer of thanks, one so subtle but distinct like a snake slithering in the grass, as I open my eyes again, I see the hedges separating and moving further apart, making a clear line to the end.

Still crawling, I rush to be free from this section of the labyrinth, and once at the clearing, my body crumbles to the ground with exhaustion. My rest is cut short when a familiar sobbing erupts somewhere within the clearing. Turning to my belly, I find the second memory has descended--it was Evelyn the night of prom, sitting in the ambulance. I had called Peter because I didn't know what else to do at the time.

Peter: *(sitting next to Evelyn in the back of the ambulance as they check her vitals before they move her to the hospital for testing.) Are you okay? (Evelyn doesn't speak. She pulls the blanket the EMTs gave her a little tighter and nods, avoiding eye contact.) I just don't understand. (He continues, I lean closer, not remembering this part, I was shaken up just as much that night.) Where is your father? (Evelyn shrugs) What kind of father would allow this to happen to his daughter? (She finally looks at him, an obvious look of disgust on her face.)*

Suddenly, she opens her mouth to speak, but no sound joins it, then another flash, and back to the garden. I pound the ground with my fist. "I don't understand." I yell toward the stars afresh, "What does all this mean?"

I am answered by the sound of a large stone being rolled away, and I am greeted with the opening of a new path. This one, however, seems straightforward. It is a short one, and the clearing is one I have become very accustomed to—in the clearing is the stunning rose bush and the intricate bench. Stepping through, I notice a small glow emanating from the carnation bush behind the bench, drawing my immediate attention.

As I walk over to it, the shadows that once silhouetted it were diminishing, and the gorgeously detailed bird came into view... as did the wording that was once caked with dirt and debris. As I lean in to read the words, there are no more obstructions—the bench is clear, but the message is not. I am thrown into a moment of Deja Vu, and the night's events with Peter and the misted man replay themselves. Another flash of light, then darkness as the burn and lack of oxygen return, Peter's words ring crisp and clear in my head.

"He can't save you. At least I was able to rid the world of a few **disgusting. Selby. Peasants.***"*

Opening my eyes, I see the familiar Canopy curtains that drape down the four-poster bed, the same rose-gold embellishments—I sit up.

How did I get back to my room ?

Did I dream that?

I hear the roaring of water come to life in the bathroom, and I lean over trying to get my eyes to see around the corners. Waiting to see who emerges, I crawl to the edge of the bed, unable to take the suspense any longer. I make it to the end as Oliver strides through the doorway with his shirt unbuttoned all the way. I can feel the heat rising, boiling beneath my skin.

Oh, for fucks sake, he is so hot!

My want for him is molding into the strongest need I've ever had in my life. "Oliver?" The words finally slip from my mouth.

"Yes, dove?"

Ah, fuck why is he so...

He giggles—not like a girly giggle, or even the typical guy giggle, this giggle is seductive, low, purposeful. I find myself staring at his mask, imagining his face beneath it, wishing he would leave it off, wanting him to feel comfortable around me so that he didn't have to hide.

"What is it, little bird?" I shake my head. "You are biting your lip… again. Do you see something you like?"

Focus, Emory, this is important.

If it was a dream, then cool, we can embrace this moment.

What if it wasn't, though?

"No?" I am pulled from my thoughts by his words, their tone laced with dejection, "Do you not like what you see?"

Snapping out of whatever dream state I had drifted to, "What, oh, um, no that's not what-" I quickly look away from him, "Oliver, when you dropped me off at the garden… I saw something happen."

His head tilts to the side. "Go on," I tell him about the misted beings. I elaborate even further in explaining how one of them, I was sure, had to be Peter. The whole scene played out before me once more as I went into every detail—into the things I saw 'the mist' do to Peter.

"He…. he killed him, Ollie." The confusion in his eyes did little to help me believe that what I saw wasn't a dream. "Then there was the stabbing." I grab my head in memory, and the pain returns with a vengeance as it haunts my mind, "The pain radiated throughout my skull."

It wasn't until I clasped my head to my forehead while mentioning the jabbing pain that his expression finally changed.

"Suddenly, the awful sensation of swallowing water took hold of me." One hand messaging my temples, my other now clutching at my throat, I continue, "It was a massive amount, to the point I felt like I was drowning."

He stood straight once I informed him of the 'drowning feeling'. I could see the anger fume from him as I continued, "But I must have been dreaming because Peter's spirit spoke to me." I tried to reiterate what the Peter-like mist had said to me. I even thought about mentioning the maze, but his reaction to what I told him already is telling me now is not the time.

His fingers ball up, just before his hand meets the wall—he applies such force that I was surprised it didn't leave behind a gaping hole.

"Not yet." He said through gritted teeth, "I need more time. It's too soon." Punching the wall again, he shouts, "I'm not ready." Then, he glares back at me, fear and despair leaking from his eyes, and whispers, "She isn't ready."

"The scars we bear are proof of survival, not shame."

CHAPTER 23

Oliver

"Ahh!" Brennan's cries echo across the courtyard. Peter had managed to bite him, as he was unwrapping the cat-o'-nine that corkscrewed around his throat. Crawling at first, Peter claws at the dirt for traction, allowing him to pull himself to his feet—but barely. It didn't take Brennan long to recover, grunting as he shook the pain away.

"Hmm, you know my mom always told me not to play with my food." He rolls his shoulder, producing a succession of rolling cracks from his neck to his upper back, presenting a subdued sound as if thunder surged through a dense forest, "I can't help it, though it's too damn *fun*!"

I watch as they both disappear into the garden. My heart leaps from my chest once the realization sinks in. "Emory!" Racing to the archway, I get there just as Brennan is dragging Peter's lifeless body out… by the collar of his shirt.

I speed past him in Emory's direction, slamming my shoulder into him—hitting him hard enough that he must back-step. When I make it to her, she is lying on the garden floor, drenched from the water as it seeps into her clothes from the puddle she fell in.

Scooping her into my arms, I stare at her for a moment. Her porcelain doll face is shimmering with the rain that clings to it. Droplets bead on her lashes, so still they look like crystals.

"I am so sorry, little bird," I mutter, kissing her forehead. "I should have never left, but I had to get him away from you."

Pressing my forehead to hers, my Newsy lifts slightly as I close the gap between us. "I wish there were more I could do." The water glistening on the bench from the rain catches my attention, and I feel my heart skip a beat. "So, little time." Then I turn, lifting her with ease as I rise to my feet—then carry her away.

As I kick back the door, I hurry to lay her down on the bed. Brushing strands of hair from her face, then to my surprise, I see that a spot near her temple is matted. She must have hit her head—I check her breathing, it's regular, but she doesn't budge as I peel my soaking wet button-up from her body. I meander over to the wardrobe that displays an array of outfits in her size. I settle on a silk black nighty and a white sheer robe.

"You will be waking up soon, dove." The color of her skin is a pearlescent blue as it absorbs the light of the moon. "So, I will get things ready."

Again, I find myself running her a bath, only this time it will be different—this time I will know for sure. Steam forms on the mirrors as the temperature rises, and I unbutton my shirt to avoid overheating. I hear the bed creak slightly as she shifts, and I make my way to the door to see her bent over on her hands and knees—crawling to me. It didn't matter if that was her intention—the imagery was already there.

The intrusive thoughts stir up... yet again. I drift into a daydream, and I am sitting in my office with her chained to my desk. The candlelight mixes with the shadows, casting an ombre of black and gold over her glistening skin. The shimmering sweat coruscates on her from our previous tussle in the sheets, as I lean forward—my elbows digging into my knees. With a whisper, I give her the next command. "Crawl to me, my dove." The sound of the metal sliding across the hardwood... possesses my hands... I squeeze them closed. The popping sound of my knuckles reverberated off the walls.

Slowly, she drops her head, then looks up through her lashes. The glittering silver collar shifts as her shoulders drop with her forward motion. Watching... closely, I notice her tongue swipe over her swollen lips before biting down on it. Deliberately, she takes her sweet ass time releasing it—the slow, soft pull as flesh slips through the clutch of the adamantine enamel clamps. Following her lead, I settle back into my chair right at the same moment she reaches me... kneeling at my feet.

"Now," Sitting back, she rests her ass on her heels. "How may I please you, my shadow?"

Her naked body, the ultimate distraction. "I-" My eyes scan her form, "Little bird, I want-" Swallowing hard, I take a deep breath—releasing it as I speak, "I want to watch you... pleasure yourself."

A devilish smirk forms on her face as the look in her eyes lusts for more commands, "Anything else?" She asks when I don't catch her hint.

"Yes, call out my name." She is fighting to keep her smile from giving her away and showing how much she genuinely enjoys our little game, "Tell me how good it feels." She lies back on her elbow... rotating her legs to rest in front of her—spreading them. Her opposite hand begins doing the things mine were *itching* to do.

Then, her voice as sweet as her arousal, fills the air. "Oliver." She moans. "Oh, Oliver."

"Louder, princess." My hand shifts to my slacks.

"Oliver!"

By the gods, little bird, you are... so...

"Oliver?" Her words came out sterner this time, snapping me back—I shake my head, rolling my eyes to clear the euphoric blur caused by my wet daydream. She has lowered herself down... Knees bent, legs splayed out to the side, with her hands resting in her lap.

"Yes, Dove?" I watch as she battles with her libido, practically biting a hole in her lip. I chuckle, purposefully adding a seductive tone to it—doing little to help with her struggles.

Nice to know I'm not the only one hot and bothered.

"What is it, little bird. You are biting your lip... again." Vigorously, she shakes her head, like a puppy with a new chew toy. "Do you see something you like?" Her face contorts as a roller coaster of emotions fights to take control.

"No," Hoping to redirect her thoughts, I ask, "You don't like what you see?"

That did the trick.

She pauses, then responds, "What, oh, um, no, that's not what-" I can see the battle she is fighting with herself, as she looks away from me. "Oliver, when you dropped me off at the garden-" Shuffling slightly, I shift from one foot to the other as she continues. "I saw something happen-"

I allow my head to canter until my ear kisses my shoulder. "Go on." Listening, she explains in heavy detail what she saw '*the mist*' do to Peter.

She must be talking about Brennan.

If she is seeing him as a 'mist' then it won't be long.

"He-" The mix of fear and sadness in her voice solidifies the fact that she isn't ready. "He killed him, Ollie."

She puts her hands to her head, "Then there was a stabbing that radiated throughout my skull." My heart leapt into my throat, and in that moment, all my attention was on what she said next. "Suddenly, the awful sensation of swallowing water took hold of me. It was a massive amount, to the point I felt like I was drowning." I stand straight, hanging on to every word she said. "But I must have been dreaming because Peter's spirit spoke to me." Eyes wide, doing all I can to bite my tongue, so as not to interrupt her.

"What do you mean it spoke to you?" I swallow hard. "What did it say?"

Her face twists with confusion, but she still answers.

"He won't be able to save you. At least I was able to rid the world of a few disgusting Selby peasants."

That family will never learn—even in death, they are distrustful and lowly.

My nails are stamping crescent-shaped indentations in my palm, as I squeeze even harder. In the fraction of a second, my knuckles became one with the drywall—holding back so as not to leave a hole. "Not yet." I plead with the universe and all the powerful beings that reside in it. "I need more time. It's too soon." Repeatedly, I press my fist to the wall, "I am not ready. She isn't ready." I look back at her —her expression is dubious and unsure.

"Oliver," her voice was soft with worry. "Are you ok?"

Blinking, I look up at her. "Yes, my dove." I lie, but it doesn't stop there. "It all sounds like a bad dream."

"Well, then," her head lowers as her eyes scan the blanket and the clothes she is wearing. "What happened to my clothes?"

It only takes me a moment to produce a reasonable response for her, "I found you in the garden." The lump is getting bigger, harder to swallow as the lies pile up. "You must have passed out, so I carried you back here... and with the rain—well, that I believe is self-explanatory."

She looks down, in thought, then back at me. "What about Evelyn?" At first, hearing her ask this question confuses me. Then, I remember her dangling from the banister, and the confusion answers itself.

She.

Saw.

Evelyn!

"What about her?" I realize now she had to have seen her, or else she wouldn't be asking. "I don't think I am on the same page. Will you fill me in?"

"Was she just part of the dream, too?" I scratch my head through my cap, shifting it slightly, under the extreme discomfort that my lying has put me in. "Well, I don't know what you think you may have seen. So, I am unsure how to answer."

How do I tell her?

"Look," Knowing I will regret it later, I play into the lie. "I don't know what it is you think you saw or dreamt, for that matter. All I know is you are stressed." The churning in my stomach, from my perfidious behavior, is sickly. I try to change the subject. "I drew you a bath, maybe it will help... would you... like me to join you... this time?" She begins to open and close her mouth like a fish on a hook.

By the gods, I love watching her flounder.

I slide my shirt slowly off my shoulders, watching and waiting. It ripples and bunches as I pull the cuffs over my hands—one by one. Relinquishing my hold of the fabric, permitting it to fall, my hands are quick to the button of my slacks, as I stalk toward her.

"Ollie-" She stammers, resting back on the palms of her hands. A few more steps towards her, she falls silent again—a slight quiver of her elbows as her body defies her.

"Emory... I will never be able to take your pain away," She brings her legs around, as she leisurely crab crawls away from me. "But... I can show you how you can be in control of it."

Her body visibly melts before me—her shoulders collapse inward as I maneuver to the side of the bed. "Allow me to be your Olive branch, for you are my dove." Grabbing her wrists, I pull her to her knees, placing her hands on my chest. "Whatever pain you feel, let me be your cutting board." I put my blade in her hand before letting my pants fall to the ground. My erection springs forward, and her eyes deviate towards it. "Would my dove like a branch to sit on?" I look down at her, giving her a sly smirk.

"What... about-" her voice is airy and lustful. "My sister?"

"We will cross that bridge when we get to it. For now, take your... frustrations... out on me." I tilt her head back, forcing her gaze on me. Slowly reaching up, I grab the tie holding the cloth to my face and pull. I admire the adoration in her eyes as she searches for a hint to my next move, and I decide she has had enough time, so I end it by crashing my lips into hers, like the Titanic hitting the iceberg—her response is to give in while skating the knife over my skin. My breathing hitches, for her teasing is inebriating. Using the tapered end, she stipples it across my scars, stopping on the one just over my heart —she sinks the metal into me. Vermillion oozes from the cut, but she doesn't stop there.

"You once told me you knew where my sister was... was that just a power move?" she pushes further, until the guard is flush with my skin. "Or was it the truth?" Searing, delicious pain awakens my body and courses through my veins.

"Yes." My grunt mixes with laughter, and I answer her in a huff. "The answer is... yes."

She drives the blade deeper as she twists her wrist 90 degrees to her right. "That... answers nothing, Oliver." I take her hand in mine, twisting the dagger even more, demonstrating to her that this is… exactly… what I want.

"You give me something," The words leave my mouth like poisonous venom, its only goal being to disintegrate her plan. "I'll give you something. Quid pro quo."

"Oh really?" She cocks an eyebrow. "What do you want?"

A smirk stretches over my face as I lift her, wrapping her legs around my waist, interlocking my lips to hers, as she yanks the knife out.

This is the best fucking foreplay I've ever had.

I continue giving her half ass answers, and with each one, the blade enters various parts of my body. An Herbal scent fills the air as I blindly search for the handle to turn the water off. Once all falls quiet, I pull her away from me and stare into her eyes with a newly awakened hunger. "My turn."

Notes

"Power is not in control, but in the trust you give and receive."

CHAPTER 24

Emory

Our bodies are entangled before I can even catch my breath from his kiss. My legs wrapped around his naked body as he backtracks to the bathroom. I feel one of his hands leave me, then a silence that clings to the walls, joins the condensation as the temperature and tension rise. Pulling me away, he forces our eyes to meet, and growls, "My turn."

In a moment, I am clinging to him as his hands leave my body, gripping my ass firmly. He swirls the head of his cock between the lips of my vagina until they spread willingly for him. Wide-eyed, I look at him.

"It's ok, my dove." He reassures me. "I am sure you are ready, now."

My face twists, and a feeling of 'I could have taken him a long time ago' crossed my mind.

*What did he mean by telling me he was sure I was 'ready'? Ready for what, **him**?*

"HA!" I involuntarily laugh aloud, but before I can rebut, he slams into me. Every Inch of him nestles tightly inside me. He stands there holding me close to him, till his breathing stabilizes. He methodically bounces his hips, manipulating gravity to work in his favor. "Ollie-" I try to speak. I try to keep my mind focused on the questions, the questions about my sister, about the garden...

Why does he make me feel so alive?

I feel like a soul lost in the cosmos, and he is my lifeline. My nails dig into his back as I make my marks, adding them alongside those he already possesses. His massive hands are all over me, exploring every inch of me, like a homicide detective at a crime scene —treading lightly so as not to tamper with any evidence, but diligently searching, all the same.

"Oliver, please don't-" I breathe, "Don't think this gets you out of anything."

He pauses for a moment. "What did you say, little bird?" Lifting his face while giving me the side eye, he continues, "Don't, what?"

Then, he slams me against the wall of mirrors. I don't even give it a second thought when I answer, "Don't ... stop." I plea, as he looks at me, his face free of the cloth he used to hide it, and glares at me in all his glory. "Please don't stop."

"Don't stop what, my Dove?" His scars call to me, an unspoken hint to the story of his past… a past I know extraordinarily little about. His voice rings in my brain again, "I haven't done anything yet."

Still throbbing inside me, his purposeful pulsations act as a countdown.

One.

"Do you-" I try to play the game, "Do you know where my sister is?" My voice is shaky as I ask my first question.

"Yes."

Two.

"Why-" I try to keep my mind clear, and questions straight forward—the fuzz from my inevitable climax creeping up on me. "Why would I have d-dreamt that?"

"Your body and mind have been through a lot." He sighs into my neck, "It could have been stress."

Three.

"What happened to Peter?" He yanks his cock out of me, grappling me by my nape. "Ah!"

"You want answers, Emory?" He speaks through gritted teeth. "You really want to ruin this moment with his filthy name." He isn't angry. He is frustrated, sexually frustrated.

It has never crossed my mind before, but it must have been years since he had felt a woman.

Then the real questions start rolling through my brain-housing group.

Wait, he is dead... How can he feel me? Are we tethered in some way

that allows our bodies to intertwine the
way they are?

Fated—no destined?

Was I always meant to find him?

*If so... **why?***

My feet hit the ground, and he begins to drag me by my hair to the bath he made for me. The scents were calming and aromatic—the opposite of the dynamic environment.

Lavender and chamomile, again—are these the only scents he has?

Aside from his morally grey attitude, seeing how much he cares, warms my soul—until my face gets plunged beneath the water. I am bent over the claw-foot tub, as terror hits me and flashes of the accident cross my mind in a cinematic reel displayed in high definition. Panic takes control of my body, as my arms begin to flail, and my legs kick out in all directions. Smacking my knee into the side of the tub as I fight to get free, and in doing so, I open my mouth as a response to the pain. My hands finally grasp the side of the basin—water goes over the edges due to my thrashing, and I slip, only to be slammed back into the water.

The moment of horror lasts a lifetime in my mind. I continue in my pursuit to get free from his grip, and my mouth bursts open again. All the air is released when Oliver rams into me from behind, and I inhale a great deal of water this time. At this point, my lungs become a water-skin for the botanically infused liquid. I don't notice right away, with the unexpected distraction, that I am not drowning and that the feeling of fear has been replaced with exuberance.

The sensation of his cock in me, mixed with the horror and PTSD from the accident, forms a dangerously delicious cocktail. They are like two diverse forms of adrenaline competing for control. It isn't long before the intoxication, from the pounding I am receiving, has me on cruise control. No longer did being submerged in the water scare me. *No, I welcomed it.*

Once he finally pulls me from the water, he holds me in his arms, shaking me violently. "My dove, please. Please wake up, my dove." My lashes flutter as my eyes open, and his beautifully broken face is looking down on me. "Oh my gosh, I thought I lost you." A single tear falls from his eye, like a lone diamond sifted through the sediment of a riverbed after being eroded from its point of origin and washed away, and lands on my lip.

"Did... Did you finish?" I muster.

A small laugh is his response. "That is what you are concerned with right now?" He shakes his head, lowering it slightly before he continues, "No, little bird, but that is ok."

"Come, let me bathe you." Cradling me in his arms, he lifts me over the side of the tub, resting my ass on the edge for a moment. The water is nice and warm, inviting even—I didn't notice that the first time, having formerly been mortified from my initial introduction to it. Before placing me in the water, he strips me of my already wet clothing and tosses them in the sink.

"You will still join me, yes?" I drop my head in an erroneous display of sadness, while keeping my eyes on him as I wait for his response.

"Of course, my dove." Slipping out of his slacks and into the water, he does something that he hasn't done since the moment I've laid eyes on him—he removes his Scally cap. Locks of hair, as black as a raven's wings, fall from the chasm of darkness that has kept it hidden this whole time—pieces of various lengths sway just above his eyebrows. I feel his index finger push up on my chin, commandeering my mouth to shut. "Catching flies, little bird?" Embarrassed, I release an awkward chuckle. As I move through the water, positioning myself between his legs. "Oliver-"

"Yes, dove?" He brushes my hair from my face. My eyes scan every millimeter of the surreal site before me. The trickling of water adds an appropriate soundtrack. From my periphery, I see him raise a rag to my forehead. I wince at the initial touch but embrace the pressure as he cleans a wound, assuming I got in the garden. The alabaster bubbles that float atop the water disappear, as rose-colored suds fall from the cloth to take their place.

Glancing down, I catch the tip of his dick bobbing just above the water, like a turtle's head on a lake. I look up, and before he can protest, my lips are around his cock—my face beneath the water afresh. Taking him into my mouth, I press my nose to his stomach. There was something about not being able to breathe that added a sense of thrill to the experience. I slide my lips up and down his length.

He is so fucking incredible.

Little pulses hum under his skin, skating over my tongue—like raw energy through exposed wires, little shocks riding the current to the head of his dick. I pause, swirling my tongue around the tip, running it over the slit, collecting all the pre-come before I drop to the sensitive spot just below the mushroom top, a collection of delicate nerves. I work at it till I feel him jerking beneath me... his grip tightens in my hair... a pounding, drums under the water from him slamming his fist against the porcelain. Then, there is an explosion—I feel it as it slides down my throat. Hot. Thick.

Fucking delicious.

I feel his body collapse, his back briefly suction-cupping to the curve of the tub. The tension that once held his muscles captive has now relinquished its grasp, and his breathing—although it is interrupted on occasion by a small hitch is pacified.

"What… was that?" His voice comes out breathy, "Where… where did that come from?".

The exhaustion hits me as I look up at him… my eyelids are at half-mast, as I snuggle into his chest. Tracing his scars with my fingertips, I soak in the moment, embracing the feeling of belonging. I could stay in this moment for a lifetime, but reality snaps back, "So you said you knew where my sister was?" My head bounces on his chest as I hear a 'tsk' emanate from over my head.

Lifting my weight to where I am sitting, he exits the tub, never looking back as he disappears into the next room. Exiting the tub, I grab hold of a robe hanging on the wall to the left of the doorway. As I peer into the bedroom, I see he has laid a change of clothes out for me on the bed. In a few strides, I am at the bedside, running my fingers over the silken material before I allow the towel to drop to my feet. I lift the stunning grey gown, slipping my hands between its seams, letting the cloth drop, feeling the fabric cascade over the curves of my body—his eyes are on me, as I glance over my shoulder at him.

He is all covered again, but my eyes have seen the truth, and now I can't unsee it. Frantic knocking on the door draws our attention from each other. Oliver walks to the door, opening it to find Niven hyperventilating on the other side.

"I had no other choice, sir." Her hand flies to her chest, an attempt to steady her breathing, "My remedies couldn't save her."

"Dove," He is facing me in seconds. "I need you to listen to me."

"Wait," Confusion numbs my face. "It never clicked before." His hands land hard on my shoulders. "How can she see you?"

"She is a medium, Emory. This is serious." His hands move from my shoulder to my face, "I need you to listen-"

He plants a soft kiss on the center of my forehead, and I watch as he tries to back away from me, his hands up, palms facing me to keep me calm, "It's Evelyn." Trepidation and fear flash in my eyes as the walls are set ablaze with a scintillating deep red light.

An ambulance?

"She is here... you lied!!" Pushing past him, I run down the stairs. My eyes are blurring as tears begin to pool, and my vision gets all distorted, causing me to slip on the stairs. My eyes clear, as the liquid falls from my eyes, permitting me to find the front door and throw it open. I am standing on the front steps. The world freezes, as I do when the cold air hits me. Everything is moving in slow motion, and I watch as a dove soars above the yard. My eyes follow it, my vision flowing smoothly with the flight of the bird of peace. It's as though it is guiding my gaze, and it is.

I finally see her, my mom, with Evelyn's arm draped over her shoulder, assisting her to the emergency vehicle. "Mom!" I scream at the top of my lungs, but she doesn't hear me. As I am about to yell again, my voice is overshadowed by a roll of thunder, yet another winter storm rolling in.

Damn winterstorms.

"Mom!" I continue, "Mom!"

Since I am getting nowhere shouting at my mother, I try a different approach. "Evelyn!" And like those moments in old movies—the time slows, the storm muffles, and all that's left in this world is *my sister* and *me*.

Watching for some sign that she heard me, I wait—tears on pause until it happens.

She looks up.

Our eyes meet.

My chest constricts

We both start crying as she breaks away from our mother—we run for each other, her hand outstretched towards mine. I reach my hand out to her. We are so close. She is right there. Then, like the same end of magnets meeting, we are repelled away from one another—Oliver has me by the waist, and she is stopped in midair—hands flailing, feet kicking, with a mist coiling around her torso. We do our best to feel each other, touch one another. To embrace each other's warmth, so we pull against our restraints.

Suddenly, Oliver loosens his hold a little, and a surge of relief rushes through me. I see my hand is hovering over hers, and I give in to gravity… but my perception betrays me. My hand sinks straight through hers like she is a projection—a hologram. I watch in horror as the mist devours her—inch by inch. I am hauled backward, back into the dark halls of the manor. The door slams shut, and I drop to my knees after Oliver releases me.

What is happening to me? Was that even real? Am I—

even real?

Notes

"*Forgiveness is a gift you allow yourself to give, even when others don't deserve it.*"

CHAPTER 25

Christian

"What don't you understand, child?" Her voice is like razor blades to my ears. "I can't help! My tonics aren't working!"

My mind is reeling, and I am doing everything in my power not to bash this witch's face in. I yank the folded envelope from my hoodie pocket. "Then why was she sent this letter?" I shove the parchment into her wrinkled hands. I run my tongue over my teeth as she tears back the paper, and I'm confused even more when the expression on her face shows disbelief at what she has just been handed.

"Where-" She stops reading to look up at me, and tears start to pool in her eyes. "Where did you get this?"

"Lady, did you not hear me?" I scoff. Pointing up to the little room at the end of the hall, gesturing towards Evelyn. "I found it in her nightstand at the rehab center, and I'm glad I took it before that ginger-headed crackpot of a doctor started dosin' her."

I watch as her eyes morph from sadness to relief, then full-on anger. "Red hair, you say?" Her voice changes, and I can't place her accent anymore, but she kinda rolls her 'R's. If I had to guess, I would say German, but it was only in this moment. When I first met her, I swore she was from Jersey—I listened as she proceeded. "Pine green eyes and vacant expression?" She finishes asking her question, although it sounded more like a statement.

Cocking my head at how spot on her description of that dirtbag is, I am almost certain she knew him. "How did you know that, and why does it matter to you?" She sighed, and the words that left her mouth next... have me backtracking on my disrespectful attitude toward her in a heartbeat.

"Because he killed my husband... and my son..." Tears roll down her face. If one is educated enough in micro-expressions, they would know that her lackadaisical approach to the situation at hand may not be because she doesn't care. No, from what she has just told me, she was hurt too much in an abbreviated length of time, in ways it appears she will never be able to overcome.

Her voice shakes a little as she speaks. "And I will be the devil's daughter if I allow him to take the lives of my grandchildren." All her Jersey was subdued, overtaken by her angry German side at this point.

Spinning away from me, she heads over to the register counter. The phone is in her hand, and to her ear in a matter of seconds. "I need an ambulance to my address immediately." Her German accent is gone again, as she finishes the conversation and hangs up. A heaviness falls on my shoulders as I watch her stare at the receiver. Her hands are shaking, her breathing unsteady… she swallows hard, then picks it up and dials another number.

Leaving her to take the phone call, I saunter up the stairs to check on Evelyn, who has been going in and out of consciousness. I kneel at her bedside, placing the back of my hand to her forehead—no fever, but she is clammy to the touch, and sweat is beading on her skin like she was sprayed with a layer of Rain-X.

"She called for help, sugar." I trace her hair line as I speak, "You're going to be ok, hang in there, baby."

I brush her cheek with my forefinger as footsteps approach me from behind. I try not to be startled—five years overseas makes you skittish.

"You've been here a bit," The woman's voice is soft. "Yet I don't know your name."

"Christian. Ma'am." Still looking at Evelyn, I stand, slowly. "My name is Christian."

"Very well, Christian. I am Niven. I have called for emergency transportation. Also, I… have also," she clears her throat, "I have also called her mother." Her hands clasp together as she straightens her back. "Now, if you will pardon me a moment, I must get work done before everyone gets here."

Screams erupt outside, pulling both mine and Niven's attention in its direction. Looking back at Evelyn, I tell her, "I will be right back, baby." The wind combs through my hair as I dash to the door. Niven is already outside, her hands clasped over her mouth in shock—following her line of sight, a clear picture of what has her frightened comes into view.

It's that piece of shit.

Without a second to lose, I charge past Niven. The film of red that forms over my eyes almost prevents me from feeling the grip of her frail hand.

"Please don't, she needs you." I hate that she is right. I don't know who the other man is, but I am grateful. I am also a little judgmental—although I admire his weapon of choice, I am also against such a shiny silver necklace decorating that doctor's worthless throat.

I look around, and Niven is nowhere in sight. I hear her calling from the library, just as the man hollers. I glance back one last time— the man and the doctor are gone. Rushing back inside the building, I find Evelyn is seizing on the floor. Niven is holding her, "Sugar!" I only pause a moment before I slide across the hardwood floor, quickly getting within range, to help Niven keep Evelyn on her side—so she doesn't asphyxiate on her tongue or fluids that may form. This was a useful trick I learned in the field.

"I thought I figured out the drug." Niven is no longer fighting back her emotions. "I am sorry, I am all out of ideas. It's like there are multiple contributors to her condition."

She is no longer trying to appear unbreakable. Watching this old woman's walls collapse and witnessing the mix of emotions that must be spiraling within her, let me know I am not alone. Then, the realization hits me. "It was a *fucking cocktail*!" I scream in anger as Niven's eyes shoot up to meet mine. The fear of not knowing what would happen next causes consternation among both of us. It doesn't take too long until she comes out of it, but it felt like forever.:

"No wonder my tonics aren't working," I look to Niven as she speaks, "We've been trying to treat one at a time."

"Well, no matter now." I interject, "There is no time left, and help is on the way."

Once all has settled, Niven places her hand on my shoulder. "Bring her to the room to rest. Her mother and the ambulance will be here in due time." Bowing my head to her, I give her my thanks, then head upstairs. Opening the door to the little bedroom using my shoulder after fighting with the handle for a moment, I lay her limp body on the bed. lean down to kiss her cold lips, and I whisper. "I want to take care of you for as long as we both shall live, sugar. Please hold on for me."

Evelyn

The Nausea comes and goes like the rising of salt water to the ocean's shore.

Darkness again

Was my self-torment not enough

Here we go, I get to relive the last time I let my sister down—

fortheumpteenth time.

As the water ascends around me, so does my doubt that I will ever outlive my guilt of always letting her down. My whole life, I fought for our father's love —blaming her when he left. I was always making the wrong choices, falling in with the wrong crowd of people on my egotistic road to self-worth.

Around every corner, through every single downfall, my sister was the one who was there for me —Always. When I crashed in that five-car pile-up, who was the one who convinced Mom that something wasn't right?

She was.

Around every corner, through every single downfall, my sister was the one who was there for me —Always. When I crashed in that five-car pile-up, who was the one who convinced Mom that something wasn't right?

All the euphoric elevations from the ecstasy, the many different rewards from the multiple divergent 'highs'—only fed the narcissistic side of me, while the rest drifted into the shadows. As time passed, I faded further away, till I no longer recognized myself in the mirror. The only thing I saw there was: a gaunt, malnourished husk of who I once was and the ghostly whisper of potential that I could have possessed.

My wallowing is interrupted by a deep, soft voice that echoes and leaves behind a residual sense of happiness. In the state that I am in, time is but a construct at this point, and gravity is nonexistent—I am floating. Then, like the eye of a hurricane has passed over me, it all comes to a full stop. The calm before the storm, I feel my body being propped up against something firm—the soft scent of cinnamon and pine fills my nostrils.

I am overtaken by an extremely sharp but quick pain that prickles through my body as it starts to wake up. My eyes begin to flutter and fight against the bright light as I strain to open them. A blurry figure is standing over me, and I try to reach up, but my body is heavy with fatigue.

"Christy?" My voice is gentle, as I push back the urge to vomit—I am confident I placed the voice.

"Yes, sugar," his voice is sweet and gentle, "I am here."

He takes my hand, his warmth being a welcome reminder that—what is in front of me—is real. For so long, I was stuck in a void, lost inside my own head, drowning in my failures.

"We got help coming, baby." I feel his hand slide across my back, "Are you ok to walk?"

Sliding my foot straight in front of me, I jokingly wiggle my toes. "No? That's ok, I have you now." I give him a tired half-smile. He slides his arm further around me, draping mine over his broad shoulders—then we make our way downstairs. My mother is here speaking with an elderly woman. I hobble over to stand next to them, the hope of being introduced to the woman who took us in, presses to the forefront of my mind.

Christian stops short, keeping us a few feet away—though not out of earshot. I try leaning forward to overhear their conversation and nearly fall flat on my face. "Oh, Niven, you look stunning. It's been so long-" My mother stops mid-conversation as I approach, almost kissing the ground one more time before I get to them. "Oh, Evelyn, honey."

"Evelyn," Her hug is tight—the love that exists within her embrace seeps to my core. "This is your grandmother... Niven."

My gaze falls on her gorgeous heterochromatic eyes. "Hello." We don't get much conversation in before the walls start changing colors, triggering a drug-enhanced episode. I fall into my mother's arms as Niven runs out the door. I feel my body being maneuvered like a sack of potatoes as my arm is draped over my mother's shoulder so she can guide me to the ambulance.

Halfway there, a voice on the wind reaches my ears: familiar, soft, and scared. Looking up, I scan the horizon—my gaze falling on... Emory? Her figure is trailing and blurred, so I blink many times trying to clear my vision, blaming my elevated state. Finally, she comes into view, and she is running at me, her hands outstretched—screaming my name.

I peer down and notice, subconsciously, my body is reacting to this image. I am compelled to start shoving, jabbing, and trying to break free from my mother's hold. Once she can no longer hold me back, I run to Emory and do not look back. Hands outstretched—screaming *her* name.

Am I hallucinating?

Is she really here?

I don't care.

I must find out.

Our hands nearly touch when a massive, muscular arm yanks me away.

"No!" I shout, kicking and screaming, "It is her. Emory is right there. Please let me go."

"Evelyn, stop! You are sick." He carries me with ease. No matter how much I throw myself, nothing throws him off kilter. "Let me get you to the hospital, and I'll make sure you have a bed right next to her?"

Is he serious?

Did he not see or hear her?

So much was coursing through my brain. Still full of doubt, I try to make sense of what he said, "What are you talking about?" I wrestle with him, trying to pull away, but in my debilitated state, I am no match for a man of his stature.

"We must go now, baby." The urgency in his tone fades, "Please!" I pass out from overexertion.

Christian

Upon arriving at the hospital, the doctors advise me that it would be faster if I stay back while she is examined. I comply when I see the state her mother is in—there is no way I am going to leave her worrying by herself. While the suspense of waiting for the results is torture, the boredom has it beat.

"So," Her mother finally breaks the silence. "We were unable to get acquainted."

"My name is Christian, ma'am."

"Oh, manners," Raising an eyebrow, as a small smirk crept across her face, "How did you meet my daughter, Christian?"

"In the most unlikely of places," I chuckle. "Rehab." The smile fades from her face.

"Oh." I break the awkward moment by snorting as I fail to hold in my laughter. She starts with a small giggle that gradually grows into a deep belly laugh—now I know where Evelyn gets it from. An awkward silence follows the laughter, but before the conversation can get out of hand, the hospital erupts in an endless stream of shouting.

A loud boom caused by the crashing of a crowd of medical workers bombarding the emergency entrance, attracts everyone's attention. One of the doctors runs over and grabs a clipboard from an EMT. "What do we have?"

"Another T40, Jane Doe." He calls out over all the other noise, "I swear that's the fifth victim this week to fentanyl."

The doctor nods his head, then looks to the female EMT performing chest compressions. "Can you tell me anything else?"

"Estimated mid—30s. One, two, three." She tries to continue CPR. "Found unresponsive in a motel room. *One, two, three.*" She was speaking so fast, but not too fast for me to understand with my prior combat knowledge. "CPR was initiated upon arrival—alongside two doses of naloxone, they were administered with no response. *One, two, three.*"

As they rush to get to a room, I try to catch a glimpse of the person's face. They said she was a Jane Doe, but that all changes once they make a sharp turn and the patient's hand slips. There, bouncing slightly to every pump was a shimmering silver bracelet, with a singular charm. My heart is ramming against my chest as I try to slow my breathing from the sorrow swelling up like an old sponge in dirty dish water.

"Mrs. Selby-" I try to sound unfazed, "I must go check on something, I shouldn't be too long, OK."

She waves to me from her seat in the waiting room, as I place my hands together in prayer and mouth, 'thank you'. I make it to the room and watch through the small window as the doctor's muffled voice seeps through the cracks and spaces surrounding the door.

"Patient is unresponsive, still not receiving a pulse." His voice is calm but assertive, "Get the crash cart!"

"Crash cart on the way." A slightly shorter nurse responds, "Oxygen mask ready."

The doctor crosses his hands, one over the other, then, picking up where the EMT left off, he starts his compressions. *"One, two, three, four-"* His breathing is sharp, forcing their escape with every pump. "Come on, breathe."

Plastic crinkles as the nurse tears open the sterile packaging and clicks pieces together, just before stretching elastic around the patient's head, "Still no response. Oxygen mask in place. Bagging now." She twists the medical bag to the mask, which clung to the patient's face like a face hugger from the *"Alien"* movies.

"Next dose of naloxone—push it," the doctor hollers amidst the commotion, calling out orders at the apex of each pump, then he takes a step back while the nurse pushes a clear fluid through an IV. A clear view opens as everyone steps to the side in preparation for the next step, and that is when my fear becomes reality.

There, lifeless on the hospital bed, is a ghost of my past, her bracelet glinting on a counter behind the doctor—a reminder of a life I left behind. The doctor then flicks a few switches on a nearby machine, "Charging the defib-" Buzzing fills the air as he rubs the paddles together, spreading the gel that one of the assistant nurses had previously applied, "Clear!"

A high-pitched pinging sound as the machine sends the charge to the pads, followed by a leaden thud as they met with her exposed chest—The shock causing her body to jolt. All is quiet for a moment, waiting for the monitor to change, but it remains flat. Then the doctor's voice breaks the silence, "Resuming compressions-" clasping his hands back together, he is back at it, "We're running out of time!"

Bursting through the door, no longer in control of my own actions, "Please save her!" Two nurses are at my side in seconds, their hands on my chest.

"Please, sir," They start pushing me back, guiding me out of the room. "We need you to leave."

"Last round of naloxone." The nurse who has been helping the doctor calls out, "Still no pulse. Rhythm's systole."

Before the door closes on me and the two nurses, the doctor makes eye contact with me, a sadness, like a parasite consuming all emotion—he glances at the monitor, then looks around at the rest of his team. "Time of death-"

"Adelaide!" I scream, "No. Try again, Doc, please." The world slows to a crawl around me. "Adelaide!" My chest is heaving as my body heats up with rage.

I know she is gone—they tried everything.

"Please let me say goodbye." I look to the doctor with a plea in my eyes. "At least give me that."

The nurses look to the doctor, who nods in response, "You know our patient?"

"Yes, her name is Adelaide Smith. She was 32 and had the whole world ahead of her." Tears blur my vision, "I wish I could have saved her. At one point in time I tried, but I couldn't even save myself... I. Should have tried. Harder."

The doctor places a hand on my shoulder, then looks to his staff, "Let's give him five." He swirls his finger in the air like he is

summoning some kind of magic lasso, and they all start to file out of the room, looking back at me, he says, "I am sorry for your loss, and... thank you... for helping us identify her, now we can contact her family."

With one last pat, he leaves the room. I stare at her, then take in a deep breath and walk to the side of the bed. "Oh, Adelaide..." A single tear falls, landing on her hand. Her skin is pale, and a purplish hue presents itself like a faint blush. She looks peaceful, as though sleeping, "The universe has lost a very unique light." I speak directly to her, knowing that everything I am about to say will literally fall on deaf ears, but for some reason, I still feel like her spirit is here, and I hope she is listening. "Your laughter was contagious, like that of an infant when they belly laugh for the first time."

I place my hand on her wet, slicked back hair, "You faced countless struggles and fought demons that even I was unaware of." I run my hand over her hair, from her forehead to the bed, as I continue, "My wish is that you are at peace now amongst the Angels in the heavens..." I press my lips to her cold forehead and whisper, "Say hi to my mom—she always had a soft spot for you."

I grab her hand for the last time, plant a firm farewell kiss, and remember the jewelry that caused the tan line now visible in its absence. I turn to face it, shimmering on the counter behind me, the singular charm of two hands locked in a pinky promise, delivers a symbolic punch to my gut as our promise echoes in my psyche:

Let's promise no matter the cost, no matter the stakes, we will always do what's right by each other.

Whatever it takes.

Putting the cold steel to my lips, I whisper, "Whatever it takes."

As I leave the room, I see the doctor who gave all his efforts to save her, leaning on the counter with a hospital phone to his ear. He looks up momentarily, and when our eyes met, he nods—I respond in kind.

In making my way to the waiting room, I see Evelyn's mom stand and stagger to a doctor's side, as she fights the exhaustion that is trying to conquer her body. I sit down next to the seat she was previously occupying and indolently watch. Their body language is minimal so I resort to reading what little I can of their lips.

As I fidget with Adelaide's jewelry, my actions sit idle in a 'no man's zone', trapped amidst a heated battle between my heart and mind. The news channels chattered. A toddler cries. My senses are over-stimulated and sensitive—on edge for the other shoe to drop. I catch in the periphery, Mrs. Selby's knees buckle, and I am fast to her side, catching her before they completely give.

"Thank you, doc. I'll take it from here." I sit her down in the nearest chair and ask, "What did they say?"

"There... is nothing... they can do." Her weeping made it difficult to understand, but I managed.

Once it registers, I take her face in my hands, "What do you mean? Do about what?" When I get no response from her after that, I run to Evelyn's room, the sound of the steady beep of the machine bleeping louder the closer I get. In making it to the room, I witness both girls lying there, eyes closed, a nurse at both of their sides.

Evelyn's nurse is detaching tubes and turning off her machines—the beeping goes quiet.

Throwing myself at Evelyn's bed, I place my head in her lap. "No!" My screams reverberate throughout the hospital bay, "Sugar, you can't leave me." My tears fall on the thick, warm blankets the nurses have provided for her, leaving damp spots in their wake as they seep through the fabric. "I am not whole without you. Please stay," My screams become more of a loud blubber, as I grip the material with all my strength. "Please, Evelyn, hold on. Let. Me. Love. You." I gently pound my fist on her shin out of sync with my words, my face sodden with salty tears.

"You are the gold that holds together my broken pieces." My blubber now a soft plea, "The demons hide when you are with me... If you leave... I am afraid... they may... consume me." I feel a mental switch flip as I look up and see her face. Instantly, I am filled with rage, "I can't lose you too! Please, sugar. Baby. Don't... don't... *don't leave me*!" I slam my head face down back into her lap as my body violently shakes while anger and sadness fight for control. Time escapes me as I hold on to her and sob. Pressure makes itself known on top of my head as her fingers curl in my hair. "*Sugar!*"

I look up, and the nurse is still standing there staring at me, liquid pooling in her eyes. "That... was so sweet." Peering over at the monitor, which had previously been turned off, it is now on and sounding normal.

"I thought-" I begin, "I thought you were calling it?"

The nurse's face twists as confusion mixed with her empathy for the situation. "Called what? I was only here to replace her machine," she gestures toward the hospital equipment. "We haven't got our new machines in yet, and no one wants to step up and mark the bad equipment, so it's a guessing game." She places her hand over her heart, "I am so sorry I scared you. Ms. Evelyn is just fine. Her body has been through a lot, and she will need a lot of rest, but she will be just fine."

My gaze falls back to her as the nurse leaves the room. "I thought I lost you, Sugar."

Quotes Most Desired

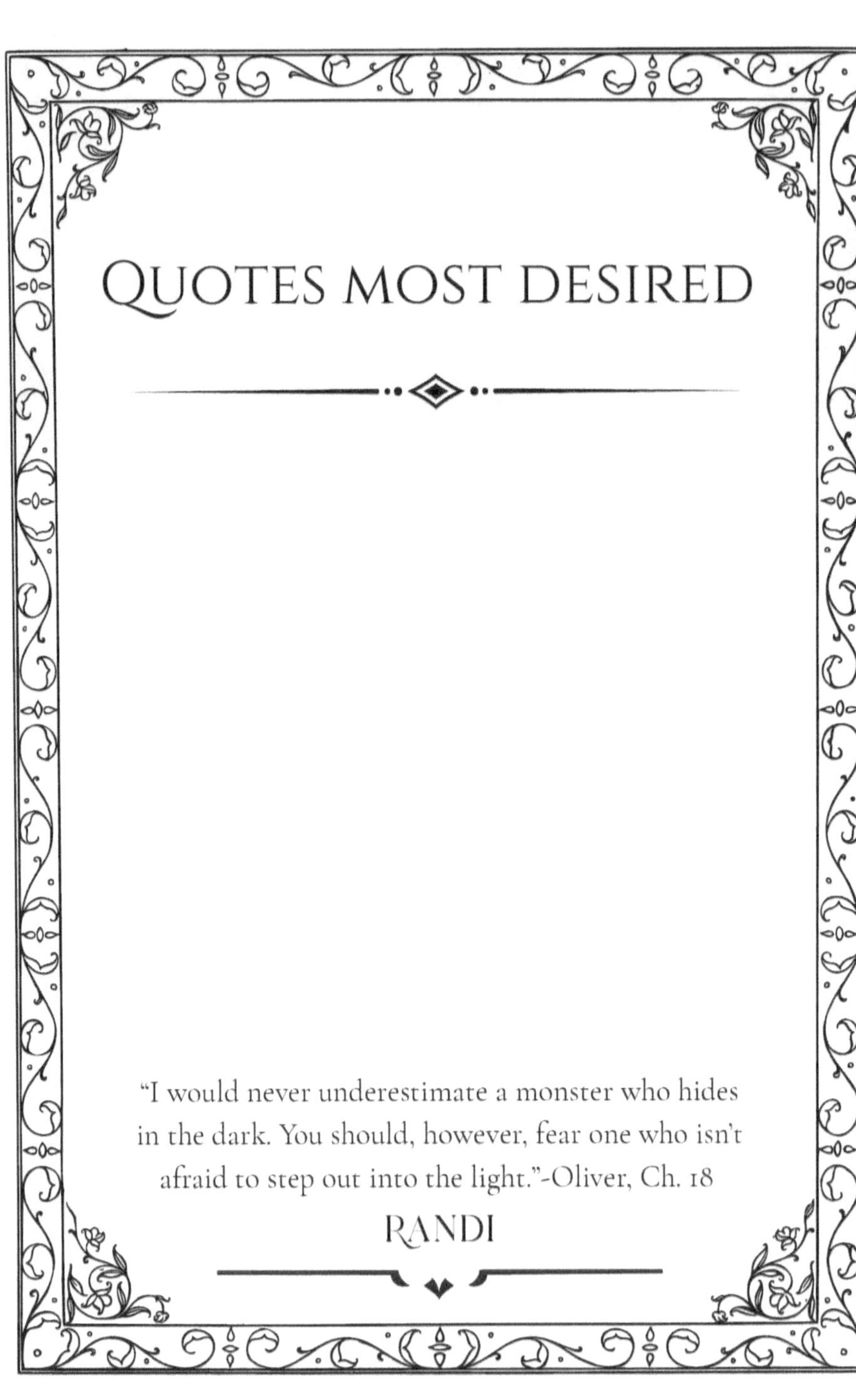

"I would never underestimate a monster who hides in the dark. You should, however, fear one who isn't afraid to step out into the light."-Oliver, Ch. 18

RANDI

"The truth, once revealed, can either break us or set us free."

CHAPTER 26

Oliver

Flashback a few hours

"Why didn't you tell me?" Niven stops me before I can chase after Emory, shouting at me. "I didn't know Evelyn was still alive—you never mentioned her, Oliver." I know now that was a bad idea, but I had my reasons. I listen as she continues. "And then, you send her here... with this!" She flings the letter at me—the one her son wrote years ago.

Her anger with me is valid. I knew there was a better way to do this, but I just didn't have the time. Bending down, I pick up the paper that is now draped over my shoe. "If I had told you, would you have been able to care for her properly?" I walk toward her, as she just stands there, mulling over the thoughts I have activated in her brain.

her brain. She knows that if she had been aware that her granddaughter was going to be brought to her door, she would have panicked.

It's been years since her son passed, and he was her only child, not to mention she never got to meet the twins. He did everything in his power to keep them away from the cursed family history that haunted their bloodline. They were never in danger so long as they stayed away —they never cared about the women. Girls were lineage killers.

I make it outside just as Emory takes off in pursuit of her sister. *Now is the time.* I wait, allowing her to get a little closer, and just before they could touch, I am at her side. My arms wrap around her, and I rest my head against her back, as she kicks and thrashes. She places her heels on my thigh, digging them in deep as she tries to push off and propel herself forward.

Fine little bird, you want to hurt?

So be it.

I loosen my hold slightly, only enough so that her hand can float over Evelyn's, and just as I predicted, she lets it fall. I watch as it passes through her sisters, then I pull her in tight and start my backward descent to the mansion. The pain in her voice as she shouts after her sister is… a form of pain I never want her to feel after today.

"No, Oliver, what is happening to me? Where did she go?" The doors slam behind me as I settle her on the ground. She delivers a swift slap across my face, and I have never been more thankful for the cloth I am forced to wear.

"Oh my," she clasps her hands over her face, in shock at her actions, "I am so sorry."

I shake my head in response, "No, my dove. You have nothing to be sorry for." I reach up to comb her hair back, but she backs away from me. "It is I who should be sorry." The change from a 'sad' hurt to a 'betrayed' hurt in her expression cuts deeper than any cut I've ever endured.

"What do you mean, Oliver?" Gravity takes hold of her hands as they fall to her side. "Why would you need to be sorry?"

"Emory, I am going to need you to listen to me." My hands jump out in front of me, as I watch her eyes—an intimidation tactic, used when helping to get the party on edge to calm down.

"Why should I listen if you have been-" Tears well in her eyes. "If you have been lying and hiding stuff from me?" She straightens her back and pushes her chest out—confidently and composed. She speaks firmly, "Why. Are. You. Sorry?"

"May we at least find a place to sit?" I cross my hands in front of me, one over the other, in response to her body language. "We don't have much time."

She nods, and we make our way to the nook, passing Niven in the library cafe along the way. She looks at me, her eyes red and misty. Emory and I take opposite seats in the nook, while flashes of our moments here try to distract me from the situation at hand—I shake them off. "Ok, here we go."

You have been in limbo, and the reason your nightmares have been getting more vivid is that… you are dying.

Her face contorts in disbelief, "What do you mean, I am dying? I am right here." She waves her hand in my face as though I can't see her.

The reason you can stand here the way you are is because your soul is in limbo, your body is in the hospital, and you have been in a coma for the better part of two weeks.

Your soul has unfinished business, and the night you headed on this journey was the night your mother received that call—it was about you, not your sister.

The hospital called to tell her that you were brain-dead, and there was nothing they could do, and since you felt your sister was in trouble, your soul left your body to save her. When that happened, it caused the machines to spike, giving the doctors a sense of false hope.

"Then," She leans back against her chair, looking around, uncertain of what she is hearing, "How is it that I just saw her?"

Remember in the dungeon, during our game, when you asked questions?

She nods.

I wasn't telling the full truth. Your sister was in danger from Peter. You both still are. I hoped that by telling you all of this... that it would help both of you. Peter went to your sister's rehab center the day after your mother got that call. He was tasked to 'rid' the world of everyone who possessed the last name Selby.

"The accident?" she looks at me, "I remember now, I knew the other car looked familiar... it was Peter's. He was trying to kill us?" I bob my head in response. "But... why?"

Unfortunately, I don't have time to go into that story. The longer you stay away, the harder it will be for you to go back to your body.

"Go back to my body, I am so confused, Oliver. You just told me I was dead?"

I. Can't. Lose. You! I knew before the call what it was about. I spent EVERY DAY by your bedside. Listening and watching as they tried everything to save you. I thought I had lost you for good, until it happened—your soul rose from your body: Teal, bright, and magical. Finally. I had. Hope.

"Then why didn't you tell me that I could have gone back sooner? I could have saved both of us." The tears she was holding back break free and cascade down her face.

"No, Emory. It doesn't work like that. You are brain-dead, and there is no coming back. You are either going to live the remainder of your life attached to those machines and your sister will OD on her quilt, or you can give her one last 'see you there' and spend your afterlife with me."

She lowers her head as her gaze falls on everything but me. "Would I have time-" she looks at her hands, "To speak to her, then fight for my life?"

I can't lie to her anymore. "Yes," the weight on my chest gets heavier, "But there is no guarantee you will make it off the machines."

"What about you?" Her eyes finally meet mine, but her gaze is flat and emotionless.

"What about me, Emory?" I haven't cried in a long time, I almost thought it was impossible until now.

"What will happen to you?"

My voice is shaky as I respond, "You will never see me again." A tear falls, and my heart is in my throat. I watch as the dream of having her by my side in misery fades before me.

"I'm ready." I open my mouth to speak, then snap it back closed. "One last question," I nod for her to proceed, "What of my father, was he ever going to show up?"

I swallow hard, then answer, "No, your father died when you were young." The anger that seeped from her irises strikes me like a thousand daggers.

"And my grandmother... my grandfather?"

My deceit continues to pile in front of me, but no more lies-- she is either going to stay or she isn't. "Peter killed your grandfather the night before he ran you girls off the bridge." I pause, knowing the next thing I say is going to be the nail in my coffin. I stand and walk over to a tiny office in the far corner of the nook, pulling a photo off the wall. Once I am back alongside Emory, I hand it to her, "And... Niven... is your grandmother."

The photo in her hands is of a thirty-year-old Niven sporting the stunning blue dress displayed in the Tailor shop. Her gorgeous dark hair is in loose curls on her shoulders, while her eyes gleam with pride, adding a sense of sophistication to the image. Emory doesn't say anything, she walks out and doesn't look back.

We arrive at the hospital in silence, and as I guide her to the room, she looks around, then finally breaks the silence, "Why does it look like everyone's body is lagging?"

Sighing, I answer. "At first, when your body is fighting, they can look normal, like they would any other day." I glance over at her, "As your body slowly starts to fade, so does your perception of those living around you. If they are in good health, they will appear to you as… mists."

Looking away, I can see her head lift in my periphery, and I feel her eyes staring holes into my profile. "So, the mist in the garden?"

"Is," I interrupt her. "Your brother."

"Wait, my brother?" She seems to soften her tone when asking. "I have a brother?"

"Yes, his name is Brennan, and he is your older brother." She stops walking and just stares at me.

"Is that why our father left us?" I look down at my feet as she continues, "And what about Peter?"

"Don't you cry for that scum." I stop when I hear her whimpering, "He isn't worth your tears." I take her face in my hands as they pour down. Once she gains composure, her eyes open and lock with mine, "It's not for him … is it?"

She shakes her head, "No, this whole time we thought our dad didn't love us anymore?" She sniffles, "And it turns out, we have a brother and our father died... I just don't know what to do with all this information."

I take her in my arms, embracing every moment I have left with her, because in the end, the choice will be hers. "We can figure that out later, right now my job is to get you to your sister."

Once in the room, I draw back the curtains, and she stands between the beds. Evelyn on one side, and her body on the other. "I'm scared, Oliver."

I hold my hand out to her, and she takes it, "No matter your decision, I will always be with you. *Not until death can we live.*" She takes in a deep breath, and as she is calming herself, I take my last shot, "Dove, I was wrong for keeping all of this from you. I just wanted to know what it was like to feel again." My chest begins to tighten.

"I've always protected you from the moment you took your first breath. I was tethered to your family since before you were born." I fight to keep my voice steady, "Not a moment in my afterlife did I ever believe that I could be there for you, or with the relationship we have built, after you took your last breath." Breathe in. Breathe out, "I'm not proud of the night I failed you, but I don't regret anything that came after. Please... stay with me."

The walls are closing in on me. "Please choose me. We can watch over her... protect her from beyond the grave. We can help try to keep her on the straight and narrow." I fall to my knees before her. I beg for nothing, but I am about to lose the only thing that makes me feel whole, "I would have never had a chance to woo you in life, and before I was ok with that."

Please look at me, why won't she look at me?

She is sitting there staring at her sister's sleeping body, "Please let me fight for you in death. Emory Evangeline Selby, will you please spend eternity with me?"

Still no answer, she hasn't even budged, then Evelyn cried out her name. That attention seeking—wait, no, I am being the attention seeker with my pathetic pleading.

For once, Evelyn was right—she must be the center of attention, and I need to respect that.

Then Emory speaks, her voice is soft and angelic.

Evelyn

 The lights are so bright that a headache from hell has my eyes glued shut. I know I heard her voice, though, and I would be ok with just her voice, "Emory?" I call out, praying for a response as I listen:

Evelyn,

My beautiful sister.

I love you so much. I need you to hear me. I need you to know—this was not your fault. Not even a little. I didn't get to say goodbye, and I know that silence haunts you. But I am at peace. I promise.

We had our moments, didn't we? Like when you told Mom I ate all the Halloween candy, knowing full well it was that stray cat you snuck into the house. Or when we used her gardening gloves to wash dishes

because the water burned our hands. We got in trouble, sure—but even then, we were laughing. We were always laughing.

The whirlpools. The secret tea parties. The way we made magic out of nothing. Those memories will find you when you least expect them. Let them. Let yourself cry. I'll be crying with you.

You'll feel it forever—that space where I used to be. Like something was torn from you. Because it was. You'll feel lost. Like the darkness never ends. And maybe it doesn't. But the light will start to flicker again. Slowly. Gently.

You'll want to scream. Curse the world. Curse me. Do it. I'll be right there beside you, screaming too. But don't forget this:

You are strong.

You are brave.

You are wanted.

You. Will. Survive.

There will come a time when you'll need to talk to me. And I'll be there. In the quiet. In the stillness. Whenever you see a dove—that's me. Just checking in. Just reminding you: I never left.

I want you to live. To love. To grow. To build a life so full it spills over. Have a family. Dance in the kitchen. Get old. Laugh until your ribs ache.

And when the time is right, I'll be waiting—Always.

The image of an intricate bench flashes before me and I focus on the etching:

MY DOVE,

NOT TILL DEATH CAN YOU BE MINE

EMORY EVANGELINE SELBY

1992-2021

My eyes spring open—my face is drenched, and her voice echoes one last time:

"Find me in the garden after winter"

Blooming after hardship.

As the thought runs through my head, I look down at Christian lying in my lap. I place my hand on his head, entangling my fingers in his luscious red locks. He lifts his face. The crimson in his cheeks and the white of his eyes is a stark contrast to Jade. "Why the long face?"

He sniffles, "Sugar, I thought I lost you."

I scoff. "I am too stubborn to die, remember."

His face only gets more serious. "Evelyn?"

"Yes, Christian?" I rebut.

"Will you marry me?"

WOW, that was unexpected. What do I say to that?

I say the first thing that comes to mind, "And what would my last name be?" I shake my head. What a stupid question, but it worked.

He laughs, "*Downey.*"

Oliver

I am still in awe of the words so elegantly spoken by my Dove to her sister. They were moving. Earth shifting. It wasn't the best thing I heard her say, though. No, the best thing was when she turned to me and said, "Yes.

My heart melted.

I don't even give her a second to rethink her answer before I grab her around the waist and spin her, kissing her as I tell her, "Hold tight, Dove." I know that her choice for what is coming isn't going to be pretty. "This is going to hurt—please know I have you."

She watches as her mother walks in, and they gather around her. Christian helps Evelyn sit, then they all nod simultaneously. Evelyn's monitor beeps... the doctor switches off the machine, and everyone waits. Tears flow as it flatlines. "Here it comes—are you ready?"

Emory looks at me with fear in her eyes, "Is it going to hurt?"

The world begins to move just a little too fast around us. "Yes, my Dove." She buries her face in my chest. I know what she is feeling, because I've been there:

It's like your body has become a battleground. Every nerve is a live wire, every breath a razor. It's not sharp like a knife or dull like a bruise—it's both, and more at the same time. It pulses, burns, and crushes.

Like molten metal poured into your bones, or a vice tightening around your spine, inch by inch, with no release. It hijacks your mind, causing your thoughts to scatter like leaves in a storm. You can't focus, nor speak. Crying feels like acid, falling from your eyes, burning your skin on contact. Time distorts—seconds stretch into eternities. You become hyper-aware of every heartbeat, every twitch, and tremor. Even the silence hurts.

Emotionally, it isolates you, makes you feel trapped in your own flesh, screaming inwardly while the world moves on. There's fear —of it never ending, and of losing control, and being reduced to nothing but suffering. It's not just pain. Its despair wrapped in fire.

I watch the doctors come and go as she falls limp in my arms. To you, the reader, it may feel like nothing, but her suffering is far from that. To take my mind off the pain I can't save her from, I allow my mind to wander.

Then the previous events come rushing back of Christian running into the room. Crying as he spouts his undying love for her, as I watch her wake up and place her hand on his head.

They exchange a few words, blah, blah, blah—then I hear it. That cursed name Downey.

Emory is having her spiritual awakening, as she painfully meets the being of the beyond. When I told her we could protect Evelyn, this is not what I had in mind. When I told her we could be here with her, to watch over and protect her, I wasn't expecting that would include—him.

I vow to do everything in my power to rid them of the Downey line and forever save them from this ancient curse. She isn't safe so long as he has his hooks of false love sunk deep into her, self-righteous heart.

So, for the time being, I will enjoy my gift from the universe. Allowing karma to whisper her poison and enact the punishment fit for his family's wrongdoings. As for me, I have been saved.

Dark, cold, weightless.... found in a stygian ethereal realm.

"*Every story leaves a shadow--it is up to us to decide whether we live in it, or step beyond.*"

EPILOGUE

Brennan

"Where do I fit in? Where do I see myself in this Story?" I call out to an empty room, as I sit by the fireplace, a glass of bourbon in one hand and a Havana Cuba-no cigar in the other. "I can feel you here watching me, speaking to me without sound."

The wind shifts in the room as I feel the presence come and sit across from me, only a flicker of response as it makes the flames dance. There is a slight shift in the pattern of the dust floating above the chair, so I raised my glass. "So, my phantom friend, who are you and what do you want? Is this the infamous 'Oliver' who has haunted my entire existence?"

A whisper rides a ghostly breeze, "Yes and no," it says. I take a deep draught from my glass, then lift the cigar, clipping its end, and nestling it into the snifter—letting it soak in the remnants of bourbon like a promise of decadence. In time, I'd chew and smoke it and savor every note of fire and spirit. In the meantime, I will slowly masticate my long-pork sausage bites.

"If you're a ghost from my past, I since buried you all around the same time I entombed myself—there was no choice. I arose in the ashes of a corpse and began anew."

The figure seemed to sit back and relax, as I watched the dust stir on the coffee table, a name appeared. *Christian Downey*. I retrieve my cigar once more and light it, taking a long pull, and relax when it hits just right. "I am going to assume this is Oliver. Why, *now*, do you make yourself known to me? Why the change of heart?"

A dart flies across the room, landing in the bloodstain left behind by my grandfather. The same name was etched out in the dry burgundy stain. Inhaling deeply, I settle back in my chair. "Allow me— if you will—to recant a story of love, death, and war."

The room goes silent as I speak to the chair across from me, and if to motion me to continue via a gentle caress of a hand, and a breeze that strokes my cheek, I watch as the wind kicks up dust and a shadow takes his place in the chair before me.

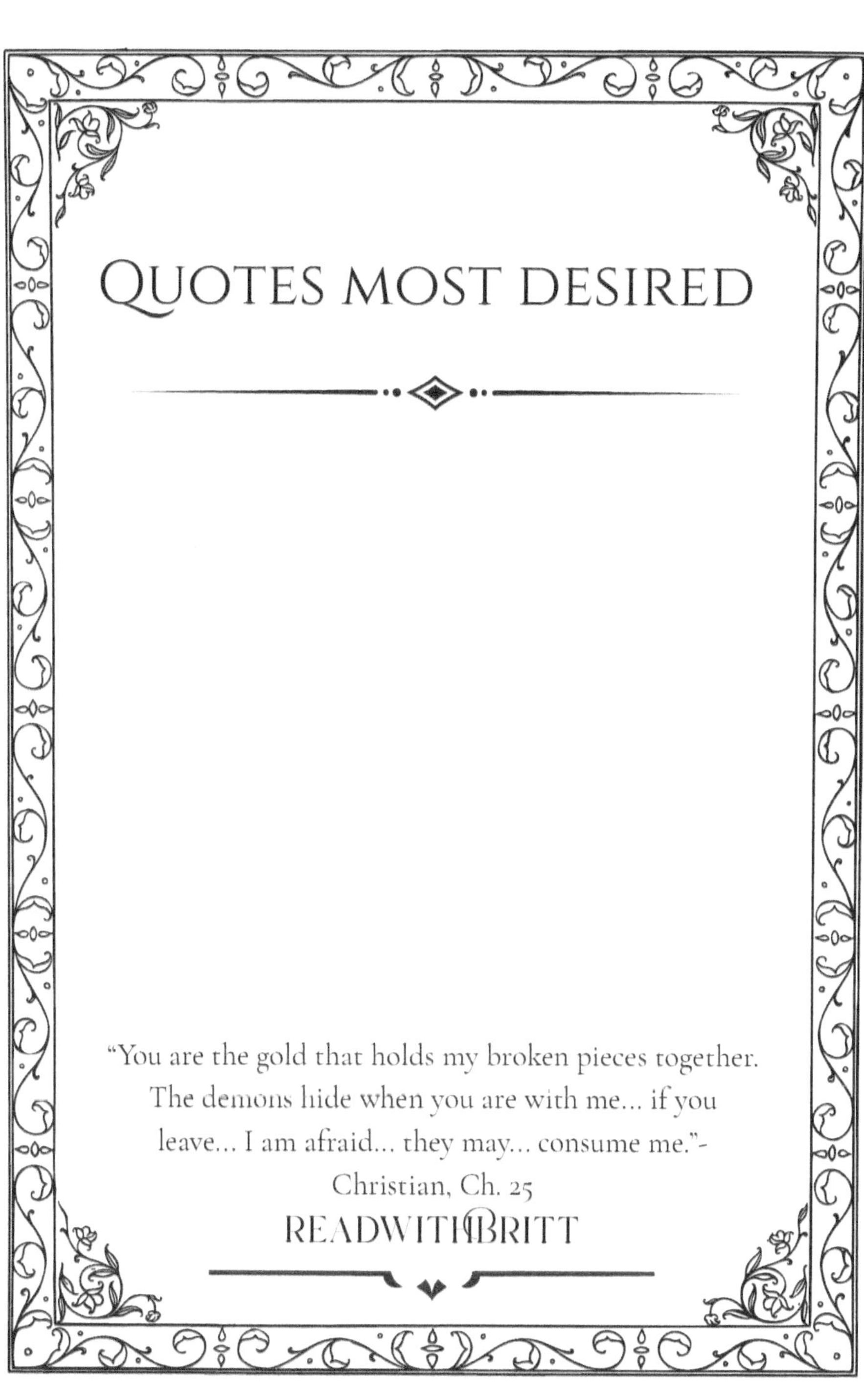

QUOTES MOST DESIRED

"You are the gold that holds my broken pieces together. The demons hide when you are with me... if you leave... I am afraid... they may... consume me."- Christian, Ch. 25

READWITHBRITT

"This may be the
first time you beg
me to stop,,, but
it wont be your
last." -Oliver ch. 2

ATHENA

In Memory Of
JACKLYN SMITH
1988 - 2021

Thank You

I want to thank everyone who believed in me. First and foremost, I would like to thank *everyone* who takes time out of their day to read my work—to all the eager readers who volunteered to be part of my journey. The Alphas, Betas, and ARCs, I am beyond blessed for all you have done. A huge thank you to *all* the authors who shared their knowledge and resources to help an aspiring author achieve their dream—you all are the true heroes, thank you. Now, this is only a brief thank you.

I will go into depth in the "Acknowledgements". Now, to the biggest supporters in my career journey to becoming an author, I want to thank God and my amazing husband. Both taught me that you should always follow your dreams, especially if they scare you, because if they didn't, then maybe the dream isn't for you.

Your unhinged author,

A. B. Owings

ACKNOWLEDGEMENTS

So, I would like to start with those who have had a direct hand in making this dream possible. To begin, I feel blessed to have the patience God has given me — without it, this wouldn't have worked--not to mention possessing the talent it takes as well.

Next, to my amazing husband. I know the long nights and even earlier mornings with our three devious angels were, trying to say the least, but you made it work and are the best support anyone could ever ask for. In the moments when things got emotional, you gave the best words of encouragement.

When I got stuck in parts that needed to be a bit *darker, and* the knowledge I obtained didn't *'make the cut'*, you came in clutch with yours, providing both an *'anger outlet'* (when work would try your patience) and a well-needed, well-deserved break for me. I can't wait to see/hear what people say about the parts you helped create.

To my sister, Jackie, who, without our memories, this story wouldn't be possible. I miss you and love you so much. When you left us, I can't tell you how many days I sat in sorrow, asking the heavens, "Why didn't I do more?" On April 9th, 2021, you earned your wings. I didn't know that four months prior to that day, on December 22nd (my 28th birthday), that it would be the last day I would ever speak to you again.

I told you that you were going to be an aunty, and you were so proud. Unbeknownst to me, you would take your last breath four months before he would take his first. I tell my littles every time they see your photo on the mantle that all they have to do is close their eyes and whisper your name. Then you will fly down from your mission in heaven and give them a little kiss. While their tiny eyes are shut and they whisper your name, I will lightly blow on their little cheeks. Our oldest would giggle and say, "I felt, TT gave me kisses." Then he will look to the sky and say, "Thank you, God. I love you, TT Jax."

Although you can't read it, I still send you messages on your birthday, and cry into a bucket of double strawberry twist ice cream while repeating your favorite line from "The Crow" as it plays somberly in the background... because *it can't rain all the time*. I still see a few little signs of you keeping your anonymity: Blue Jays, Kentucky rain by Elvis, and someone saying *Bubbly-gum*.

You are sorely missed by many, and your voice shall never fade. I hope this book can be your voice to help others heal, because that's all you wanted. I would have never thought that the release of this book would happen in the year I'd officially be older than you. I pray you are looking down on my family and me, and that we are making you proud.

I would love to thank my fellow author and Co-editor, Laura, who reinforced my confidence in my high school education (although not perfect). I was absolutely honored to have you on this journey. Not only did you assist me, but you were also working on book two in a series of your own {featured after the Acknowledgements}. You came into this friendship not just to edit/fix my mistakes but to teach me where I went wrong and why. I hope I made you proud. Your teaching was top-tier. Thank you so much.

To my Beta readers, though, you were few. I was so blessed to have had your input and your patience when the technology started acting up. We had some hiccups, and I hope that in this final copy, I have made you all proud as well.

Now, for my Alpha readers. With too many to mention all at once, I am so grateful for your time. I hope you enjoyed the honorable mentions of the favorite quotes you all gave me. I have scattered them throughout the book. If you can't find yours or don't remember if you gave me one or not, please don't fret, you are still just as important and valued. I can't wait to see who all signs for the next journey, *book 2*.

Finally, to Hanna, Lyha, Lione, JJ, Jess, Jocelyn, Steph, and *everyone* that believed in me and my willpower to get through this...

If you enjoyed this

Then you may love

The Enchanted Vines Series by Laura Schweizer

Book 1

A debut fantasy romance by Laura Marie Schweizer
When secrets ignite and past betrayals resurface, Quinn Corliss finds herself at the center of a brutal conspiracy where nothing is as it seems.
Quinn lived a quiet, carefully guarded life, until a mysterious threat shatters everything she thought she knew.
What begins with a strange woman and chilling warnings quickly spirals into a world of deadly secrets, forbidden magic, and dangerous alliances. As Quinn is pulled deeper into a criminal underworld she never knew existed, she must uncover the truth about her family, her gifts, and the dark forces closing in around her.
At her side is Raeban Avery, a man bound by duty and haunted by secrets. As their connection intensifies, so do the risks—because in this world, love is as dangerous as any weapon.
With ruthless enemies closing in and every whispered secret threatening to upend her reality, Quinn must decide who she is, and who she's willing to become to survive.

Book 2

Quinn Corliss thought losing everything once was enough.
Shattered by betrayal, she retreats to the academy that once felt like home, desperate to rebuild her life from the ashes. Her focus is survival—legalizing her tonics, finding peace, and forgetting the man who broke her heart.
But forgetting Raeban Avery is impossible. His guilt runs as deep as his love, and every step toward forgiveness feels like walking through fire.
Meanwhile, a darker force weaves his way into her life—Able Axelson, Dreylon's most feared crime lord and Quinn's own father. He'll stop at nothing to claim her, her work, and the power she holds.
Between love and loyalty, freedom and family, Quinn must navigate a world where every choice comes with blood on its roots—and some shadows refuse to fade.

About the Author

A. B. Owings writes dark, emotionally charged fiction that blurs the line between love and obsession. With a fascination for broken characters, twisted relationships, and haunting atmospheres, Owings crafts stories where romance and danger walk hand in hand.

When not writing, Owings can usually be found reading gothic literature, hunting down obscure horror films, or wandering old houses imagining their secrets. From Dusk is their debut novel—a slow-burn descent into madness, sisterhood, and the razor-thin edge of desire.

www.ingramcontent.com/pod-product-compliance
Lightning Source LLC
Chambersburg PA
CBHW031201310726
48969CB00001B/168